A Very Polyamory
Music Festival

Written by Allison Eden

A Words Are Swords Publishing Book

Published in the United States of America by Words Are Swords Publishing, Los Angeles, California.

www.WordsAreSwordsPublishing.com

This is a work of fiction. Any references to people or places are entirely coincidental.

A Very Polyamory Music Festival

Written by Allison Eden

Published by Words Are Swords Publishing

2025 Edition.

Table of Contents

Dedication

Many people helped make this book possible, and I appreciate the hard work and words of encouragement from the kind folks at Words Are Swords...

... But I want to dedicate this book entirely to my polyamory family, whom I would be lost without.

To Ryan AKA Wit, who is the most understanding, generous, kindest man I have ever had the pleasure of knowing. Thank you for putting up with my mischievous ways and for administering discipline when I need it most.

And to Bree, my first love who has been with me since the very beginning and I would follow to the end of the earth.

I have no regrets in life because every road I've taken in life has led me to the two of you. Every day I wake up and feel like I'm living every girl's fantasy.

I love you, I love you, I love you for always.

Poly Fam Forever.

— Allison Eden

Introduction

This book is the true love story of how my lifelong best friend became my lover and how my awesome relationship became even more awesome by adding a third person.

Note that in this series, my personal experiences are written from the perspective of the character Jess, but the character named Allison is actually based on Bree's real-life experiences, despite the character Allison having the same body type as I do in real life.

To put it simply, the things that happened to Jess actually happened to me, but she looks like my girlfriend. Meanwhile, the character named Allison actually looks a bit like me.

It's confusing by accident.

Enjoy.

Chapter 1: Welcome to Electric Love

Cars lined up in both directions as far as the eye could see. Traffic was literally at a standstill with none of the cars to her right or to her left budging forward even an inch.

Even in metropolitan hubs like Downtown Los Angeles or Manhattan, where gridlock is an expected daily occurrence, this was pandemonium.

Jess figured that they had been sitting there at least two hours if they were there a minute without moving forward.

Other people in the other cars, also stuck in traffic, were not honking, screaming obscenities at one another, or otherwise losing their shit. On the contrary, they had their windows down, were blaring music, and were all smiling, laughing, and having the time of their lives. Jess noted that everyone stuck here in traffic with her must be teeming with excitement because she herself was as excited as she could remember being in a very long time.

The first day of Electric Love, a 3-day music festival Jess had been looking forward to and planning for nearly a year now. This was the first year of the premium event that boasted massive interactive art installations, an all-star line-up of over 50 musical performances, and a number of activities

Hosted by an open-minded community that embraced the free-love and mindfulness lifestyle.

Jess loved music festivals. Jess and her boyfriend, Josh, tried to make it to at least four or five of the big ones throughout the year. But the problem with the big ones was that they were always over crowded, very expensive, and in recent years they seemed to be attracting a type of crowd that they just didn't vibe with.

So when the Electric Love Festival was announced, it looked like it offered all of the awesome stuff that they loved about the big name 3-day festivals, but just on a smaller scale. Jess found that it was these smaller, first year events that ended up being a lot more fun in the end.

Jess's best friend, Allison, did not agree with this sentiment.

While Jess and Allison had attended many festivals together ever since high school, Allison went through a hard break-up with her boyfriend, Richard, last summer, and to say she wasn't taking it well was putting it gently.

Jess had an exceptionally hard time getting Allison to leave the house in the following months after her break-up, and it took all of her negotiation prowess and all of her patience to convince Allison to join her and Josh at Electric Love Festival.

"Don't leave me hanging at another festival, Ally. I need my Festie Bestie with me," Jess recalled her desperate pleas to a teary-eyed Allison after she hadn't left her house for several weeks following the break-up with Richard.

"You have Josh. You don't need me." Allison cried in a tone of despair. "Besides, you'll probably just ditch me to go and fuck your boyfriend in a tent like you always do."

"Look, I'll promise to stay by your side no matter what. This will be nothing like that cluster fuck that happened at Electric Daisy Carnival. And besides, Josh is bringing one of his guy friends from work, so they'll probably be off doing whatever it is straight guys do at festivals when they're alone, together."

Jess put her hand on Allison's arm and forced a warm smile.

This made Allison laugh a little. "Are you serious? I'm telling you, girl, the level of trust you place in Josh is going to blow up in your face one of these days."

"Ally, just because Richard was a shitbag doesn't mean that all guys are. I told you I love and trust Josh completely."

"Well," Allison sniffled, considering this. "Is his work friend hot?"

Jess suppressed a frown and started looking around Allison's bedroom, as if searching for a distraction.

"Uh, actually, he's... Married."

Allison blanched, her eyes going wide as her mouth fell open. Jess could see tears starting to well up in her eyes again.

"Well, what the fuck!"

"Ally, Ally, Ally!" Jess cut her off before she could start crying again. "Girl, why would you want to bring a guy to the festival when we can find you some strange dick?"

Jess handed her a tissue. Allison took it and blew her nose.

"But there are so many hot sluts at festivals. Why would any cute guy want me?"

Jess had to fight back a laugh at the obvious attempt to fish for compliments.

At 5'4" and 111 lbs. (on a bad day), Allison's petite frame visibly enhanced the curves on tight, bubbly ass and perky 36C breasts. Naturally dirty blonde hair fell to the small of her back, although Allison was fond of trying out a variety of different and often breathtaking hair styles-particularly at music festivals. Her hazel colored eyes and naturally long eyelashes were famous for capturing the attention of boys.

All of this, coupled with her classic Californian-style tan on her sun-kissed skin made the men she would pass on the street refer to her as: "A straight dime piece."

But there are tens, and there are Los Angeles Tens. Allison was unmistakably a Los Angeles Ten.

But Jess refused to bite at what was an obvious compliment catfish.

"Ally. Even as ugly as you are, there is bound to be a guy out there willing to put up with you."

Ally responded with an explosive and throaty laugh.

"Okay..." Instantly, Jess's face was slapped with a beaming smile. "But you have to pick out my clothes and you have to be my wingman. And no ditching me!"

"Oh, girl, of course!" Jess tackled Allison, in a hug and they toppled over on the bed.

Back in the car entrance to the Festival, in Josh's Jeep Grand Cherokee, the five friends had the windows down and were all belting out lyrics to Griz's "Let the Good Times Roll."

Josh sat in the driver's seat, wearing his Oakley aviator sunglasses and tapping the outside of the Jeep door to the music. He was enjoying the cool breeze blowing into the sleeves of his light cotton t-shirt, under which some of his chest and arm tattoos were visible when the light hit it at just the right angle.

A young lady wearing an American flag bikini top and bottoms walked up to the driver's side and handed him a wild-flower she had obviously just picked from a flower bed where they grew not more than 30 feet away. She held about a dozen more in her other hand

She said nothing, and when Josh took it from her, she moved on to the car in front of them and did the same.

This made Jess, who sat in the passenger seat, smile a beautiful, toothy smile.

Jess was wearing a simple one-piece summer dress that stopped above her knee, mid-thigh. It was adorned with an intricate mandala pattern that one might find on a Persian Rug. She had on a completely different outfit underneath the sundress that she had painstakingly taken the time to put together for later on in the evening, as soon as it got dark out.

Allison sat directly behind the passenger seat and was wearing practically the same outfit as Jess, since it was she who went through the painstaking task of designing the clothing. Only the pattern on Allison's summer dress was completely different, as well as the color scheme of her nighttime festival outfit.

Despite this, the two girls' clothing styles complemented one another.

Next to Allison sat Jon, Josh's co-worker at a Graphic Design agency. His basic jeans and T-shirt look was practically a mirror image of what Josh was wearing, only Josh's muscular frame made him fill out his shirt a lot more.

Isabel, Jon's wife, sat beside him to the left, holding his hands in his lap. She wore a simple white crop top with a black bikini top visible underneath, and cut-off jean shorts with a black thong bikini bottom underneath with straps hugging her hips. She had simple, straight black hair that fell to the small of her back and ridiculously long fake mink eyelashes with eyeliner outlining her beautiful brown eyes.

The cleavage revealed by her tie-on black bikini top underneath her basically see-through white crop top made her fake 34D breasts very prominent.

On the ride into the festival, Isabel joked that, "When my mom came to America from the Philippines, the only family heirloom she brought with her was her small ass titties, which she graciously passed on to me. So, when Jon and I got married, I made him buy me these instead of a huge ring."

Isabel propped up both of her fake breasts with her two forearms.

Everyone in the car laughed, then Jon added, "Joking aside, that was the best investment I have ever made." And everyone laughed again.

Allison craned her neck, looking at them, she couldn't seem to look away, mesmerized.

"Well, they look great," she said a bit too covetously. "How big are they?"

Isabel smiled at having the attention of another female. She brushed her hair behind her back and puffed out her chest.

"Do you like them? I didn't want to go too big. I'm trying to keep it classy, you know? I told the Doctor I wanted 32D, but during the surgery, he bumped it up to 34D because he said it looked better."

"What did those extra two inches end up costing you, Jon?" Josh asked, trying to avert his gaze from Isabel's chest because he knew that if he did, he would have to face the ire of Jess later on.

"Actually, nothing. Honestly, I think he mixed up the size of the implants at the last second." Jon gave Isabel's left breast a hard squeeze, eliciting a big smile from her. "But you can't argue with the results!"

Isabel leaned forward, addressing Allison. "I'll show them to you as soon as we pitch the tents."

"I'm pitching a tent right now," Jon grabbed the easy lay-up, to a light chuckle.

Later on, when the five of them were still sitting in line at the car entrance, Isabel spotted two women sitting on the roof of a four-door sedan, lying back, sunbathing topless.

"Is that normal?" Isabel asked, the only one out of the five of them who had never been to a festival.

Jess and Allison were the only ones who laughed hard. "Yes," Jess said finally. "At least, it's Festival Normal."

Jess eyed the two topless sunbathers. Both of the women appeared to be her age, possibly a few years older. Their hair was clearly matted, frizzy, and in desperate need of a brush. Because neither of the two women showed any signs of tan lines, she figured that they were both frequent sunbathers and more than likely both identified themself as hippies.

One had breasts that looked like they never came into contact with a bra and flattened midway down her flat stomach. Jess would be surprised if the other woman's breasts exceeded an A-cup and very likely never needed a bra.

"See, Allison!" Jess said, turning around in the passenger seat to look her friend in the eye. "This is your competition."

Both of them cracked up at this inside joke.

After their laughter died off, for a few seconds, Isabel chimed in excitedly. "Then I guess it's okay if I show you my boob job now, Ally.

Everyone in the Jeep looked at Isabel, except for Josh, who looked at his friend Jon. Jon smiled, then gave Josh a small nod of approval, as if to say, "Hell yeah, you can look at my wife's tits!"

After the nod of confirmation from Jon, Josh looked to Jess for approval. She shrugged, which told Josh, "I guess you can look, I mean, if you really want to."

This was not the solid confirmation a man who was trying to avoid conflict was seeking.

Josh tilted his head down and narrowed his eyes at Jess, which clearly said to her, "Look, I need a firm yes or no from you, because I don't want this to come up later and be a problem."

Acknowledging his resolve, Jess retorted with a warm and genuine smile, then gave him a single nod in Isabel's direction. Josh grasped the obvious translation of this as, "Okay, I'm going to look, so we can both look together and then talk about it later when she's not around."

Josh's response was a small, half-smile that said to Jess, "Okay, but be nice."

In the back of the Jeep, Isabel made a show of revealing her fake boobs. First, she took off her seat belt, dragging the buckle over her tits for no apparent reason. Next, she leaned forward, reaching both hands behind her neck to grab her sheer white crop top and pulled it up and over her head. She threw it on the floor of Josh's Jeep.

Then she reached behind her back once more, pulling the tie strings of her bikini with the speed and showmanship of a burlesque dancer.

Jess gathered that she absolutely loved the attention of having all of the eyes in the car on her (and a few pairs of eyes belonging to men in the car next to them) and wanted to draw this out for as long as possible.

Well, Jess thought to herself, *it's not like we are going anywhere fast.*

Finally, the bikini top fell into her lap, revealing her huge, full fake breasts and quarter-sized nipples poking out the center of each.

Jess didn't know what she expected to see, having only ever seen fake boobs in porn videos, but she had to admit that they looked very nice. They actually did not look very different than her natural breasts, which were slightly larger than Isabel's implants, but she did look harder than hers and Allison's did.

Isabel implored them to all take turns playing with them, which they did. When Jess gave them a firm squeeze, it confirmed her suspicion that they were indeed much more hard than her natural boobs. She could feel the implants just below her muscle, though if Isabel had never told her she had breast implants, she never would have guessed while she was wearing her crop top.

Allison couldn't seem to keep her hands off of them, much to Jon's delight.

When Josh gave them only a cursory squeeze, Jon became incredulous.

"What the fuck was that, Josh? Here, this is how you do it."

Jon commenced to slap the ever-loving shit out of Isabel's tits.

He whacked them so hard that the audible smack of skin on skin got the attention of everyone at least three cars in either direction. Jon continued to slap his wife's boobs as hard as he possibly could until her entire breast was as red as her nipples. Isabel, meanwhile, was cackling away like she thought this was the height of comedy.

More than one man actually got out of their cars and started walking over to the Jeep with the purposeful walk of guys who thought they were "Captain Save a Hoe," but as soon as they saw Isabel laughing, they backed off.

"See?" Jon said when he was done, shaking his hands because of the obvious pain he caused himself. "You just can't break 'em!"

When he saw everyone in the Jeep, and several guys standing outside the car looking in, with a shocked, slack-jawed expression, Jon said, "Shit, that's nothing compared to what we do in the bedroom."

Isabel left her rosy-red tits hanging out for the remainder of the car ride into the festival.

"They need a little air after all that," she offered by way of explanation. On the way up to the ticket booth, Allison nudged Jess's arm. When she looked back, Allison silently nodded to Jon. When Jess looked over, it was clear that Isabel had her hand down Jon's pants and was giving him a tug job while she idly looked the other way out the window, a vacant expression on her face.

Meanwhile, Jon was beaming with joy and had both of his hands folded on the back of his head. It was all Jess could to stifle a laugh by covering her mouth with her hand.

Finally, Josh pulled up to the car ticket booth and handed the young man working the booth a bundle of tickets.

"There are five of us here. The parking pass is in the envelope, too."

The kid counted the five tickets inside the envelope Josh handed him, then peered into the windowless Jeep to count everyone.

"What do we have here? One, two, threeee..." His voice trailed off, then his eyes went wide when he saw Isabel topless in the back, with her hand clearly down the pants of her husband.

Isabel gave her biggest smile, waved at the kid, then blew him a kiss. The envelope of tickets fell from his hands as the kid just stared with the shocked expression of a boy who had never seen a pair of tits before, at least a pair as nice as hers.

All the while, she never took her hand out of Jon's pants. If anything, she increased the speed and ferocity of the hand job as soon as she noticed this kid was watching her.

The ticket taker's jaw hit the floor - he was paralyzed.

Then Isabel stood up and leaned as far as she possible could out the window, bending from her waist, so the kid could get a clear look at her. When she managed to get her tits only about six inches from the guy's face, her mouth formed an "O" and she slapped her cheek with fake concern.

"Oh, no. It looks like you dropped the tickets!"

The kid didn't move, but mumbled, "Uh... yeah."

Then Josh drove off with the entire Jeep in tears from laughing. Isabel continued to hang out the window, waving at the poor kid, then the envelope of tickets started to blow away, but he couldn't take his eyes off of Isabel's tits until they were far in the distance.

When Jess looked back to see Isabel still hanging out the window topless, she noticed that when Isabel stood up, she accidentally pulled Jon's dick all the way out of his pants.

Everyone was laughing so hard that no one seemed to notice but Jess, and as soon as she caught a glimpse of his fully erect penis, she felt like that little boy at the ticket booth who couldn't look away from Isabel's chest. Jon's dick was BIG. Possibly even bigger than Josh's, which was by far the biggest dick she had ever seen outside of porn.

Eventually, Jon noticed and tucked his dick back into his pants. Jess looked up to see Jon nodding to her approvingly, as if to say, "I know I've got the biggest horse cock you've ever seen."

Jess looked straight ahead, livid. She could feel her skin reddening in embarrassment. She just saw her boyfriend's best friend's dick, and he knew she saw it. How was she going to explain this to him?

She wouldn't, she decided. The most adult way to handle this situation was to pretend like it never happened and vehemently deny it if anyone should ever bring it up.

Chapter 2: Unicorn Paddles

Before long, they found a parking spot among a sea of cars.

They all got out to stretch their legs. But as Jess got out of the car, she came upon a short blonde woman a few years younger than her. She squatted in the grass next to where the Jeep was parked and the car next to them. She must have just squatted down, because Jess didn't see her there when they parked.

The only thing she was wearing was a sky-blue hoodie painted to look like a Unicorn, complete with a unicorn horn on the hood.

The poor woman looked trashed, judging by the look on her face, and was having a hard time keeping her balance as she squatted down to pee next to the car.

She looked Jess straight in the eye, smiled, and slurred something along the lines of, "I've just got to have a little tinkie."

She was barefoot and completely naked from the waist down. Sitting on her haunches, the Unicorn tried to correct her wobbling with one hand directly in the grass behind her, and her other hand fumbling for the side of the Jeep.

As soon as Jess noticed that she was peeing on her own hands and feet, Jess came to her rescue. "Oh, Honey, no!"

Jess grabbed a hold of the Unicorn's hand that was grasping the Jeep for stability and helped her balance until she stopped peeing. Then she helped her to her feet.

"Watch out. Don't step in that. You just peed there! Oh, no!"

Jess helped walk the Unicorn a safe distance from the puddle she created next to the Jeep.

"Where did your pants go, sweetie?" Jess asked with a concerned frown.

The intoxicated Unicorn looked down, nonplused by the fact that she wore nothing that could be considered either pants or shoes.

"Huh? I don't need pants." The Unicorn shrugged, then Jess let go of her hand, watching the Unicorn's bare behind as she stumbled away towards the music.

Jess looked back at the car to see everyone else cracking up.

"WOW! Did she have a landing strip?" Jon heckled the loudest. "I haven't seen one of those since, like, the 90's!" He elbowed Josh.

"She couldn't pop a squat to save her life, but she sure does know how to trim her pussy hair straight," Josh pointed out.

The guys carried most of their camp gear until they found a reasonable spot to set everything up.

For about an hour, they all drank beers and did shots while setting up their camp, which consisted of two large tents that were facing a common hang area they set up with a canopy, rug underneath, complete with a bar and various collapsible furniture.

Both Josh and Jess's tent, as well as Jon and Isabel's had a large self-inflating air mattress in them along with hanging cubbies for clothes, storage for food. Jess was adamant that their tent also have a vanity so that the girls could all get ready properly.

"You want us looking our absolute best, don't you?" was Jess's closing argument to get Josh to buy the expensive and bulky traveling vanity.

Allison's quarters were a bit more meager than everyone else's, since she decided to come last minute and had minimal time to plan or pack. Allison had a small, single-occupancy tent with a sleeping bag, and that was it.

As night began to fall, they all laid out a plan as to what performances they wanted to see. Jess was relieved that they all agreed, for the most part, on what music to go see.

"One more thing before we head out, guys," Josh said with a mischievous smile on his face.

He disappeared into their tent and emerged a minute later with something cupped in his hand.

"Rolls for the night!" he said by way of explanation as he handed out one capsule of white powder to each of his friends.

"To Electric Love!" He held up the capsule in one hand and a beer in the other.

They all repeated "To Electric Love!" and swallowed the MDMA pill with a beer chaser.

"Oh! One more thing before we head out," Jess said excitedly, anticipating the things to come.

"You mean lock up all the phones, money, and valuables, because we're about to get lit?" Jon said, and everyone chuckled.

"Well, that, too," continued Jess, "But Allison and I spent a long time working on our outfits tonight, and we wanted to do a proper reveal."

"Reveal?" Jon asked with one eyebrow raised, confused.

"Oh, fuck yeah, let's see 'em!" Isabel was as excited as she was drunk, still wearing her jean short cut offs and absolutely nothing else.

"Babe, is this one of the new outfits you designed at your job?" Josh asked.

"What job?" asked Jon, "Where do you work, Jess?"

Josh answered, proud of his girlfriend's work, "Jess works at a company called Festival Drip where she designs new outfits they sell at festivals."

Jess beamed, "Yep! And actually, babe, they are going to use both of our outfits - The one I'm wearing, and the one I made just for Ally!"

Allison smiled ear to ear, excited to give this new outfit its maiden voyage.

"That's incredible, Jess!" Josh picked Jess up off the ground and spun her around once before putting her back down, giving her a peck on the lips.

"Thanks!" She said, returning the kiss.

Then, to Allison, "Okay, Ally, on three." Both Jess and Allison grabbed the skirts of their summer dresses at either side. Jess felt genuine excitement at the thought of revealing the outfits at Electric Love. She felt even better that her boyfriend genuinely appreciated all of the hard work she put in.

"One, Two, Three!" Jess counted off, then both her and Allison peeled their dresses up and over their heads to massive applause from Josh, Jon, and Isabel.

"Oh my god!" Jon's jaw hit the floor. "Can you make one of those for my wife?"

Isabel playfully punched him on the shoulder.

They were wearing strappy garters with fishnet stockings and cupless harnesses underneath their bare breasts and over their shoulders.

Jess's had a high-neck collar, and Allison's had flowery embroidery above the garter. But what made them stand out the most was the fact that both rave outfits were glow-in-the-dark. Jess's strappy little outfit was glowing in all pink while Allison's was glowing in all neon green.

Jess had glowing pink heart pasties covering the nipples of her huge natural tits, while Allison wore glowing green stars in the center of her slightly smaller tits.

It was honestly one of the hottest and most revealing outfits that Jess had ever designed, and she was excited to see what kind of reactions she would get from it tonight.

The look on Josh's face told her everything she needed to know.

"Babe... You look... Oh my God... Is that my girlfriend?"

Jess sauntered up to him, slowly shaking her ass from side to side as she did. She stood on her tippy toes, closed his slack jaw, and kissed him on the cheek. Then, in her sexiest, most seductive voice, Jess said, "I'm all yours, baby."

In response, Josh reached down and grabbed Jess by the hips, lifting her into the air.

Jess let out a little squeal of surprise, then wrapped her legs around his waist and threw her arms around his neck. Jess let out small moans as they started making out, oblivious to everything going on around them until Allison cleared her throat very loudly.

Josh gently set Jess back on the ground.

"Um, you look lovely, too, Ally." Josh said, trying to push down his erection.

Allison stood there with her arms crossed impatiently under her boobs.

"Right. Can we please get going now?"

Chapter 3: I'm Peaking

The five of them walked to one of the nearby stages to see one of the headlining artists.

It wasn't long before they started to feel the effects of the pills. Jess figured this because not only did it seem like the night was becoming warmer and she stopped freezing her tits off, but their dancing was quickly becoming much dirtier. Especially the way she was dancing with Allison.

The two women glowing in neon moved fluidly to the four on the floor house beats.

Meanwhile, Jon and Isabel disappeared as soon as the group got on the dance floor, determined to go off and do their own thing.

Josh stood a few feet behind Jess, dancing and shuffling to the music, but mostly he was watching Jess and Allison. As a warm and tingling sensations spread throughout all of her extremities, Jess could feel the bass reverberating through her muscles. Her head felt warm, like she had a fever, but it was not an unpleasant feeling. Her sensitivity to tactile sensations had been thrown into overdrive, which is why when Jess saw Allison dancing next to her in her full neon green glow, she pulled her friend in front of her.

Lacing her fingers through Allison's lime green fishnet stockings on the back side of her upper thigh, just below her butt cheeks, Allison took half a dozen babysteps backwards, then only when she felt the soft warmth of Jess's natural breasts pushing up against her naked back, and the front of Jess's hips spooning her bare behind, only then did she look back to see who it was who started to grind against her from behind on the dance floor.

Allison smiled a pleasant, mollified smile, then bent at her hips, leaning forward just enough for her breasts with the glow-in-the-dark green stars glued on to her nipples to slant forward. From behind her best friend, where she gyrated to the music,

Jess saw her friend's tits from the side when she bent at her hips, and immediately, the image of Isabel's fake boobs came to mind, and Jess thought about how they strangely felt soft and hard at the same time.

The next thing she knew, Jess was cupping both of Allison's perky tits in either hand, as she pulled her friend's back close to her chest. The warmth of Allison's bare back against her felt amazing, and so did running her fingers over her tits.

Underneath the vinyl pasties, she could feel Allison's small nipples were hard as daggers. Allison let out a soft moan as she pushed her ass back against Jess's hips, doing a slow twerk, to the music.

In turn, Jess started moving her whole body like a belly dancer, grinding up against Jess's back by moving her entire body in a serpentine "S". The only other time Josh had seen her do that was in their private bedroom, and she was sitting on top of him at the time.

Meanwhile, Josh was taking a break from dancing, sitting in the grass with his back up against one of the support columns for the stage.

Josh was already starting to feel his roll. He was seeing tracers from where the lights were coming from and started sweating profusely, with a warm, almost feverish feeling spreading all through his body.

The thought popped into his head that if this is what just one pill was doing to him, he wondered just how Jess and Allison were managing, as small as they were, considering Josh weighed at least as much as the two of them combined.

As if she was able to hear his thoughts, Jess appeared standing directly in front of him, looking like a sexy pink angel in her hot pink fishnets, strappy harness, and heart-shaped pasties.

For a moment, Jess stood over her boyfriend, just appreciating what a splendid man he was and how lucky she was to have him in her life. As soon as Josh saw her, he beamed the brightest smile. Jess always appreciated how Josh's smile could make a fireworks show seem boring.

She wasn't sure when it happened, but at some point the house DJ's performance had ended, and a trance artist took his place.

Jess instantly recognized the song as belonging to Above and Beyond, a track that had always inspired sensual feelings in her when she heard it. Now, as she started to really feel the molly, the bass-filled peaks and valleys of Above and Beyond were getting her really horny.

She stood there, swaying her hips to the music, looking down on the chiseled, handsome features of her boyfriend. He was seated with his back against the stage support column with both his knees bent in front of him, feet firmly on the floor.

Jess took one stride forward so that the front of her pink thong underwear between her strappy pink garters was only two or three inches away from Josh's face.

Josh stared, transfixed by what she teased in front of him, like dangling a juicy carrot right in front of a horny ass rabbit.

He breathed in her intoxicating vanilla-scented lotion that Jess always wore. He came to associate this smell with the soft and supple curves of his girlfriend's body.

Jess plopped down in Josh's lap, almost knocking the wind out of him. She wrapped both her wrists around the back of his neck and the two started deeply into each other's eyes. Jess could feel his abdomen rise and fall with every breath. She was so close now she could feel his heart beat, and she was sure that he could feel hers.

As the music went on, everything else in the world faded from existence. It was just her and his eyes. Their heart beats in sync, matching the exact same pace, and she could physically feel the deep inner connection between the two of them.

This was love, Jess thought. This was the true and pure love of two souls that joyously shared everything in this life.

For an instant, Jess thought about how incredibly lucky she was to have this person in her life that she could share this experience with. The deep connection of that love filled her heart until it began to overflow.

Then she was aware of how brightly she was smiling. How happy she was to be here at this moment, with the man that she loved more than anything. They didn't need words to understand that they both felt the exact same way in this moment. It was a moment she wanted to freeze and live in for all eternity.

Jess leaned forward and kissed Josh, breasts dangling heavily in front of her. He parted her lips with his tongue, and she eagerly accepted it into her mouth, sending her tongue into his mouth to dance with his as their lips pressed together in a deep and wet kiss.

Josh playfully bit her lip. She sucked on his tongue. The two lovers were making out like it was their last night on earth, Jess suddenly realized that she was grinding her hips into his, rocking back and forth on his lap.

Josh broke their kiss only to plant several more on Jess's neck, causing her to moan loudly.

That's when Josh wrapped both of his big hands around her lower hips to steady her, bringing her grinding to an abrupt halt.

"Babe," he whispered in Jess's ear. "You're fucking turning me on. Do you feel how fucking hard I am right now? We can't do this here."

"I don't fucking care." She whispered breathily.

Jess's eyes fluttered, but remained half closed. She reached in between her legs where she found Josh's jeans and the warm, throbbing bulge underneath. With fast and needy hands, she quickly unzipped Josh's pants and pulled out his fully erect dick.

A hungry smile parted Jess's lips at the sight of her boyfriend's long and girthy cock. Quick as a thought, Jess sat up about 8 inches, pulled the pink thong panties covering her wet ass pussy to the right, quickly guided Josh's member into her wet hole, then sat back down on his lap before anyone around them realized what they were up to.

As soon as Jess took Josh's entire, hard cock into her, her eyes went wide.

Simultaneously, both her and her boyfriend breathlessly mouthed, "Oh, fuck!"

Jess was not used to taking all of Josh's entire cock all at once. It was by far the biggest dick that she ever had inside of her. And to avoid any discomfort, she typically liked to start slow, only taking about a quarter of his fully erect cock into her at first. Then a little bit more with every thrust.

Every boyfriend her entire life had told Jess that she had an abnormally tight pussy, and at times she wasn't sure if it was a blessing or a curse. Either way, in that moment, Jess was grateful that she happened to have an abnormally wet pussy, because the added natural lubrication helped her take a big dick that she otherwise wouldn't have been able to fit inside of her.

Whatever apprehensions Josh had before about them hooking up in public now seemed to dissipate into the electric air.

With his big hands still wrapped around the fluorescent pink fishnet tights covering Jess's ass, he helped her rock back and forth on his hard cock.

Jess tried bouncing up and down in Josh's lap, as she knew he loved watching her bounce on his dick, but the exaggerated motion, along with the loud slapping of her ass on his thighs was loud enough to warrant a few curious looks from the other festival goers around them.

Jess gave a little yelp every time his dick fully penetrated her, and it took an extraordinary amount of self-discipline not to moan and scream in ecstasy at the top of her lungs.

In the throes of passion, Jess was having a hard time keeping her hand off her clitoris. She knew how quick and easy it would be for her to cum if she were able to just play with her pussy for a little bit, but they were already getting strange looks from passerbys, and if she started flicking her clit it would have really blown their cover.

Besides, Jess didn't really want to rush an orgasm. She was enjoying this too much. Not just the sex on ecstasy, but part of her was really enjoying the clandestine aspect of this as well, and she wanted to keep it going for as long as she could.

She wrapped her lips around Josh's again, rolling her tongue playfully across his. Josh was pulling her ass forward and back again and again while she curved her hips up and down.

Jess hoped she would be able to rub her clit on Josh's dick but it only painfully rubbed against his denim jeans, and once on his zipper, which really caused her to lose focus for a few seconds.

The second time she caught her clit on Josh's zipper was even worse and Jess thought for a second she might even be bleeding. This caused her to totally throw caution into the wind, and with an internal, "Fuck It," she was going to fuck her boyfriend the way that she wanted to fuck him and no one was going to tell her otherwise.

Except for the little sober voice in the back of her head that screamed, "You're on drugs and this might not be a great idea!" But that part of her was always a party-pooper anyway.

She broke off the kiss and, instead of tongue-wrestling her boyfriend, she covered her three middle fingers with a generous amount of saliva, and with one arm still hooked around the back of Josh's neck, she pulled the front of her pink thong panties far to the right, where it was safely out of the way.

Then she started rubbing the front of her pussy. Hard. In big, exaggerated circles while she bounced up and down on practically the full length of Josh's cock. A few times, it even came all the way out of her pussy and, luckily, squeezed back in.

Jess was feeling good now, and there would be no holding back. Her soft and little moans turned into loud yelps of pleasure, which Josh called her "porn star noises.".

None of this went unnoticed, of course. Before long, bystanders were cheering the couple on, whooping, and a couple of people even pulled out their camera phones.

Jess's inner voice said, "Fuck it. Let them watch. This is what true love looks like."

Meanwhile, Josh sat mesmerized by Jess's huge tits bouncing directly in his face.

As the crowd around them quickly started getting bigger, so did the intensity of Jess's sensual satisfaction and the animalistic pleasure spreading through her body.

Jess wasn't sure if the two were directly correlated with one another, and she really didn't care. The only thing in the entire world that mattered right now was her and her lover.

But all of that disappeared in an instant when Jess felt a hard slap on the back of her shoulder.

"Oh my God, I fucking knew you would do this!" It was Allison standing behind her.

Chapter 4: The Human Ant Farm

Her arms were folded under her boobs, shaking them up as she tapped her foot haughtily. The look on her face broke Jess's heart. Allison was clearly trying to hold back the hurt, but her face betrayed her, just as Jess felt that she had betrayed her best friend by breaking a promise without even thinking about it.

Doing her best to choke back the tears, Allison's face contorted with the unmistakable sadness of disappointment.

Immediately and without forethought, Jess stood up so she could wrap her arms around Allison, instinctively wanting to embrace her in a hug to console her, but the moment Jess was on her feet, she was gone.

Allison shoved her way past the crowd of onlookers, disappearing into the sea of festival goers.

"Ally, wait!" Jess called behind her, but it was too late. She had no idea which direction her friend went.

"Shit!"

She ran after her anyway. Jess shouldered her way past Poi spinners busy giving lightshows, performers on stilts, small groups of ravers huddled together dipping little metal spoons into baggies of white powder, then holding it to their noses, dancers who most of been wearing at least 20 pounds of plastic Kandi bracelets, and countless others wearing an ear-to-ear smile of genuine happiness.

Jess was not one of these people, and although just moments ago she was feeling the happiness and tranquility of absolute love, she was now quite distraught.

When she made it into a clearing where the crowds of people dispersed, Jess spun around, canvassing her surroundings.

She was standing at the midpoint between two stages parallel to each other in the distance. The stages were lit up by elaborate production lighting and surrounded by different themed art installations.

On one side, everything was themed as something to do with Noah's Ark. She saw various performance artists walking around dressed as different animals, an art installation that looked like some sort of Tim Burton psychedelic petting zoo, and the stage itself was done up to look like a huge boat.

The other stage that Jess had just come from was in the theme of a carnival, complete with all of the typical carnival rides one would expect. Jess wasn't exactly sure because her eyes were fluttering uncontrollably, and every time she turned her head, she saw tracers coming from any source of light.

"Jess!" Josh called behind her.

Jess spun around, feeling grounded by his loving, masculine presence.

"Baby, I fucked up." She wrapped her arms around him, wiping her tears against his chest. "I promised her I wouldn't ignore her, but I... I..."

Josh wrapped his arms around her, pulling her close and stroking her head.

"It's okay. I understand." He whispered to her, and suddenly everything was right in the world.

Jess looked up at him with teary eyes and sniffled. "Help me find her? I need to make things right."

"There, I think I see her!" Josh yelled as he pointed to a green blur in the distance sitting atop what looked like a life-sized ant farm.

She grabbed Josh by the wrist and ran through the throngs of people toward a three-story structure, translucent on the side so you could see through the walls.

There was a ladder at the very bottom leading up to the first level. From there, people were crawling over small hills and mounds to get to one of the two ladders that led to the second story, and the same for the 3rd.

Most of the ladders leading up to the dark red top of the structure were only big enough for people to stick their heads through. It was, for all intents and purposes, really a life-sized, three-story-tall human ant farm.

Jess could see Allison with her head popped out on the roof, between the 3rd and 4th floor. Jess recognized her by the glowing green star-shaped pasties she wore. From the ground below, it also looked like she was standing on someone's shoulders, but she wasn't sure.

For a few minutes, both Jess and Josh tried calling out her name to get Allison's attention, but the music was so loud that they figured there was no possible way she could have heard them.

She would have to go in after her.

When Jess and Josh reached the entrance to the human ant farm, he saw how small the entrance was.

"Jess, I'm 6'2"." Said Josh. "There is no scenario in which I go inside that thing and don't get stuck."

Jess looked again at the tiny entrance and passageways. He was right.

"I'll go get her. Please be here when I get back." They kissed.

"Of course." He promised with a smile.

Jess mentally prepared herself for the ant crawl. She really did not like being confined to small spaces and had had panic attacks from similar situations in the past, but to save her friendship with her festie bestie, it was more than worth it.

When she was finally ready, Jess made her way to the ladder leading up to the first floor. A drunk chic was currently engaged in working her way up the ladder and having a difficult time of it. Jess grabbed her by the side of her ass and threw her out of the way, off the ladder.

"MOVE BITCH!" Jess shouted. "I've got a friendship to save!"

The drunk girl fell to the asphalt, not fully understanding how she got there. The Human ant farm maze was actually a lot more difficult to navigate once she was inside it. It reminded her of a play place for kids they have at fast food restaurants, only slightly larger and with more vomit.

Jess was flying through the passageways trying to get to the top as quickly as possible, both to get to her friend, but also because her fear of confined spaces continued to bother her, and she could feel an imminent panic attack on the horizon.

Finally, on the third floor, she could once again feel the cool night air blowing through openings at the top of the maze. Desperate for fresh air, Jess found the first ladder leading to the roof that she could find and bolted up top, throwing yet another drunk girl out of her way as she did.

From atop the three-story human ant farm, she could see much further than she thought she would be able to. She clearly saw both stages as well as every carnival ride in the distance. She saw masses of people as far as she looked in every direction, and then she saw Allison's beautiful face, tight next to hers.

"Allison!" Jess shouted to get her attention.

Allison craned her neck to look at Jess. She had a strange sort of smile on her face, like she was trying to hold back a laugh. But she did look genuinely happy to see Jess.

"Oh, Hey, Jess," Allison said simply.

"Look, I want to tell you how incredibly sorry I am. You're my best friend and I would never do anything to intentionally hurt you," Jess spoke from the heart.

"Oh, yeah, I know. Don't worry about it," Ally replied.

Jess had a perplexed look on her face. "So that's it? You're not mad?"

Allison giggled, "No, I'm not mad at ya, I love you Jess."

"And I love you, too, Ally."

Allison's face twisted and contorted as she made strange shapes with her mouth. Her eyes fluttered, then rolled into the back of her head as Allison made a sound that was somewhere between a laugh and a scream. Then her muscles all at once relaxed and she began to pant, trying to catch her breath.

That was when a black crop of hair popped up from the same opening where Allison was standing. It was a man with a mop of shaggy hair, smiling brown eyes, a bulbous nose and a soul patch on his chin.

"Hello hello," He said in a cockney accent, addressing Jess. "Name's Bobby."

Bobby wiped the little bit of dribble and who knows what else off his lips, then extended a hand over to Jess, only it was too far away to reach.

"Jess, this is Bobby." Allison said by way of explanation.

"I see." Jess immediately felt nothing but scorn for Bobby. "Ally, can we please talk with our feet on the ground? I want to hug you."

"Oh, yeah." Allison looked at Jess, then Bobby, then Jess again. "Bye, Bobby."

She gave him a peck on the cheek, then ducked back into the human ant farm.

Bobby, meanwhile, looked devastated.

Jess giggled to herself, then began the arduous process of climbing back down to ground level. She suddenly had much more empathy for ants after spending time in the farm.

Back on solid ground, Jess was finally able to embrace Allison in a warm hug that she wanted to give her before.

"Ally, will you ever forgive me?" Jess asked, not letting up in the bear hug.

"Of course, Jess. You're my best friend and I'm sorry I overreacted."

While so furious earlier in the evening, Allison now seemed so casual and nonchalant.

"Now let's get out of here before..."

A man fell out of the farm, dropping off of the ladder and landing on the ground with a painful thump. Seeing him, Jess and Allison recoiled-and the man on the ground-Josh ran over.

"Hey, Ally! Oh, man, are you alright?" Josh helped the fallen guy to his feet.

Bobby jumped up and brushed the dust off of him, then, to everyone's surprise, he stepped over to Allison and gave her a peck on the cheek.

Allison's face reddened, even in the dimly lit night.

"Hey, Als," Bobby said, then turned to Jess and Josh, "These must be your friends, I'm Bobby."

Then Allison opened her mouth, but before she could get any words out, Bobby said, "Can I buy your mates a couple drinks?"

Jess looked at Allison, Allison looked at Josh, Josh looked at Jess, and they instantly all came to the same realization at the same time-that this guy was a tool, but none of them were going to turn down an offer for free drinks.

"Yeah!" they all said at different times, putting on a fake smile for Bobby.

Each of them instantly in an unspoken agreement-they would get a round of drinks-then ditch this poser.

As one group, the dance-walked to the music in a line over to the bar, which was flooded with a sea of people three layers thick.

"What's your poison?" Bobby turned around to ask the group of three as they weaved there way through the throng of the bar.

"Vodka." They all said in unison.

"Right, then," Bobby said. "Three vodkas, one rum and coke."

As Bobby turned to push his way through the crowd of people, Jess and Josh both turned to Allison.

"What were you thinking?" Jess asked.

"Had to find the biggest tool you could, huh, Ally?" Josh chimed in.

Allison threw out her arms defensively. "I don't know! I was mad, and then he started going down on me, and..."

Allison was cut off by Jess and Josh's simultaneous reactions.

"I knew it!" Called Jess.

"Ugh, gross, Ally, no!" came Josh's disapproving glare.

"You mean that you came in the middle of our conversation on top of the farm?" Jess gestured to the three-story maze in the distance.

In response, Allison bit her lower lip and gave a little innocent shrug. Josh's attention was suddenly drawn elsewhere.

Jess sympathetically asked her friend in earnest, "But you don't, like, like him, do you?"

Allison's face reddened. Because of the strappy green halter exposing her chest and breasts, Jess saw the tomato red flush of embarrassment spread to her chest, too, bringing a pink hue to her cleavage that stood out compared to her head-to-toe neon green.

"No, No, No, I'm trying to ditch him, but he's so nice, I don't want to hurt his feelings."

Allison waved her arms back and forth, dismissing her friends accusations. Jess noticed that as she did, her breasts bounced up and down in place. She noted that her friend didn't need to wear a bra to keep her boobs in place if she so chose. A stark difference to Isabel's fake breasts, which Jess imagined wouldn't have moved at all had she made the same hand gestures.

"So, he's a nice guy, is he?" Josh asked, distracted as he stared off somewhere in the distance.

At that moment, they all turned to see Bobby pushing through the crowd, shuffling towards them, carefully balancing four drinks in his hands.

Bobby smiled brightly as he approached the three slowly, careful not to spill a drop. He carried with him three glasses full of clear liquid and one brown beverage.

"Hi guys," Bobby greeted them enthusiastically. Before either of the girls could grab their vodkas, Josh quickly tipped the rum and coke out of Bobby's hands.

"Hi Bobby!" Josh greeted him equally cheerfully.

"Hey, that one is mine..." Bobby's protests were cut short when Josh slammed his closed fist into Bobby's jaw, literally sending him flying off his feet before landing square on his back. Three cups full of clear liquid fell all around him.

Bobby did not move once he hit the ground, nor did he open his eyes. As soon as Josh made contact, both Jess and Allison covered their mouths in a gasp. Jess pulled her boyfriend away from the man he just assaulted for fear he would somehow get in trouble. Josh, in response, cooly sipped Bobby's rum and coke.

"Josh, what's gotten into you?" Jess punched his arm repeatedly, and not in a playful way.

Allison, meanwhile, just stared in disbelief with wide eyes, unblinking.

People were starting to crowd around. Josh gestured with his hand, holding the drink at the man on the ground.

"As soon as he got our drinks," Josh explained calmly, "I saw him put some white powder in all three of them."

Jess saw him hit the floor. Allison blinked, then punched Josh in the same arm that Jess was repeatedly punching just moments ago.

"Well, what if I wanted to get roofied, dick!" Allison cried as she pulled Josh.

Jess and Josh laughed, though they were unsure if she was kidding or not.

"Who said it was roofies," Josh started catching Allison's incoming fists in his defense. "What if it was, like, arsenic and I just saved your life from the festival serial killer?"

"Either way, let's get out of here." Jess pulled both of them by their elbows away from Bobby, who still appeared to be unconscious and gathering a larger crowd with every passing minute.

"And, Josh, dump out that drink, will you?" Jess said with an index finger pointed at the drink in Josh's hands.

Reluctantly, Josh took one more sip of the rum and coke before emptying the contents of the cup in the general direction of Bobby.

Jess continued to pull them through the crowd at a fast walking pace with the tenacity of someone fleeing a crime scene. Allison finally tore her arm away from Jess's grip.

"Jess," She started to say. Jess noticed the start of tears welling up in the corners of her friend's eyes. "What am I going to do now?"

Seeing her best friend's distress, Jess ran instantly there, holding her in a consoling embrace with her arms around Allison's tiny waist. She gave a little squeeze to let her know that everything would be alright.

"Oh, Ally, don't you worry," She said, looking her friend in the eye with a warm smile on her face.

The warmth of Allison's breasts pressing up against her own much larger breasts felt good amid the cold night air. Jess's smile was contagious, and it started to spread to Allison.

"I think I've got everything worked out, and I promise that you'll be happy."

Allison looked up into her friends eyes. Her tears were gone. "Really?"

She sniffled hard, whether it was the disappointment of losing Bobby, or the chill in the night, it was hard to tell.

"Yes, Ally, I promise I'll make it up to you." Jess let her go and took a step back, dragging Allison forward by the hand. "We just need to make one quick stop back at camp first, okay?"

"Okay!" Allison's face brightened.

Chapter 5: Free Love

Finding their way back to camp in the middle of the night proved difficult.

Everything was thrown into darkness. Thankfully, Josh remembered to bring with him a small LED pocket flashlight which, while not incredibly bright, did manage to illuminate their path just enough to see where they were going.

With Josh leading the way, the three, holding hands, merrily dance-walked past the stages, past the carnival rides, into the campgrounds where they finally came upon their canopy and tents. Upon seeing their camp, the girls exploded with excitement.

"Here it is! We're back!" Allison did a cartwheel.

"Just the way we left it!" Jess spun around to stand on her tippy toes and give Josh a kiss. "You did it baby, you found our way back."

"As if there was any doubt," Josh said, waving a hand dismissively.

"Now before I reveal your big surprise, Ally, let's do some shots!"

Jess pulled a bottle of Grey Goose from their tent.

"Thank God!" Allison said. "After tonight, I need to get fucked up!"

While Jess poured out three shots, Josh had a sudden stroke of brilliance. He disappeared inside their tent for a moment. Allison drained her shot and made Jess pour her another one.

"Hey, we were going to do those together!" Jess insisted.

Allison grabbed Jess's shot that was intended for her and threw it back.

"Uh, then it sounds like you need to catch up, bitch." Allison said, not looking up from the liquor.

Jess giggled as she poured out more vodka for them.

When Josh finally emerged from the tent, "Ladies, who wants another roll?"

Allison slammed down the shot glass she had in hand with the vodka still in it.

"Oh my god, you read my mind. Mine is almost completely worn off." Allison said.

She and Jess jumped in front of Josh like two puppies begging for a treat. He handed each of them one capsule full of white molly powder.

"Are you sure this is safe?" Jess asked.

Allison had already swallowed hers.

"I measured these out myself," Josh replied. "Just go easy on the alcohol, girls."

"Thanks, dad, I think I'll be fine." Allison had the Grey Goose bottle clutched in both hands, taking a few very large swigs.

Jess and Josh exchanged cautious looks. Only then did it really sink in for Josh exactly what his girlfriend had been plotting ever since he knocked out the guy who tried to roofie the three of them. Josh wrestled the bottle away from Allison.

"Can I get some of this? Thanks, Ally." He smiled, then poured another two shots for him and for Jess.

"It burns, but it goes down sooo smooth," Allison was starting to slur.

They had to do this now or never.

Jess looked to her boyfriend for approval. He gave her a small nod.

"Ally," She started. "Can you come into the tent for a second? I want to talk to you about something."

Allison was looking for the Grey Goose bottle. She forgot that Josh took it away.

"I want to hang out here and dance to the music," she slurred, doing a tipsy, swaying dance. "Besides, you were supposed to find me a man."

"Well, that's what I want to talk to you about."

"Ok, Jess, well where is he? I don't see anyone unless you're hiding him in your tent." Allison was dropping it like it's hot. They could still hear the distant music from one of the stages, "All I see is your boyfriend that you love to fuck in front of everyone." She said, referring to the incident earlier that night.

Jess walked over and took Allison gently by the hand. "That's exactly what I'm talking about, Ally."

Allison froze.

Josh's face was expressionless.

"I want to make up for hurting you, but I also want you to understand what I feel. Ally, I want you to fuck my boyfriend so you know how much this means to me."

"I want you to experience the same level of pleasure that I feel," Jess led Allison over to a folding chair where Josh had made himself comfortable. "Please, Ally?"

Jess was immediately self-conscious when Allison didn't say anything back, but she started to feel the molly kick in even harder than last time. Suddenly, the only thing Jess was driven by was a seemingly insatiable lust.

Jess got on her knees, fiddled with Josh's pants zipper, then pulled free his rock-hard dick. She was surprised that it was already rock hard. Jess guessed that the molly had hit him the same as it had hit her.

She wasted no time running her tongue up the length of his shaft, then pushing his tip past her wet lips and into her mouth. Jess let out small moans of delight every time she took his cock deep into her mouth.

It felt good having Josh's dick in her mouth, but she didn't want Allison to miss out on any of the fun. This was, after all, supposed to be for her benefit, for her enjoyment.

Jess tugged on Allison's hand, and she finally settled on her knees next to her best friend. Jess held Josh's fat dick at the base, waving it teasingly in Allison's face. Although at first, the look on Allison's face was that she didn't know if this was a trick or not.

Then, after a bit of coaxing from Jess, Allison ultimately gave in to her desires and fully took Josh into her mouth.

Jess's jaw dropped as she watched her friend suck on her boyfriend's cock with a hungry zeal and eagerness that she had never before witnessed. Not even porn stars enjoyed sucking dick as much as Allison passionately devoured Josh's shaft.

As Allison made noises similar to what she imagined a fat kid must sound like when presented with an endless supply of his favorite chocolate, Josh's own moans began to draw the attention of passersby and neighboring camps.

Jess suddenly remembered that this must be the very first dick that her friend has had in her mouth since her terrible breakup so long ago.

Allison had been starved for cock, and now that she finally had one, Jess would make sure she had her fill.

She had to admit, though, that watching Allison slide Josh's entire dick all the way down her throat, and the hungry moans she kept making, were really making Jess wet. When she slipped her fingers down her panties on a mission to find out exactly how wet, she found that they didn't want to leave.

While she was still crouching on the ground, balancing herself with one hand on the folding chair Josh sat in, her other hand to massage her clit, adding her little moans to Allison's hungry ones. In the otherwise dead quiet camp, the three of them were making quite the ruckus.

Just like when they were on the dance floor in front of one of the stages, people who were walking by started to stop and cheer them on.

"Oh my God!" said one incredulous woman.

"That's so hot!" said another.

"Whoa!"

"Fuck yeah!"

"Damn, look at her go."

And yet another, "Why can't you suck dick like that!"

Finally, with a dramatic scream of satisfaction, Josh came. There was a thunderous sound of applause as Allison swallowed every drop. When she finally pulled Josh's hard cock out of her mouth, she looked sheepishly at Jess, like she got carried away in the moment and didn't mean to take it that far.

But Jess wanted her to know that it was alright. That this is what she intended. That Allison hadn't yet gone far enough. She wanted her to know all of this, but Jess was chasing an orgasm of her own.

With one hand stuffed down her neon pink panties, hard at work massaging her clit in a circular motion. Jess stood up and, with her free hand, helped Allison to her feet, holding Allison's hand above her head.

She twirled her friend until her back was to Josh. Confused about how to process this situation, Allison eagerly complied with Jess's unspoken directions.

Jess did not say a word, her breath quickening, panting just as fast as her little fingers could move.

Jess reached down with her free hand and took the thin green strap of Allison's G-string in her thumb and index finger, gently moving it to the side of her firm ass cheek and exposing her friend's glistening pussy to the cold night air.

Allison did not say a word when Jess pulled on her thong strap, forcing her ass backwards.

Allison was forced to take three or four baby stutter steps backwards before the crooks of her legs met Josh's knees, thus forcing her to lose her balance and fall backwards onto Josh's lap.

He was already holding his throbbing member in position in anticipation of what Jess intended. Allison fell back, but caught herself on the armrests of the folding chair, where her hands rested just on top of Josh's. Allison was able to catch herself as soon as Josh's tip fell into her tight, wet hole, giving Allison a sensation she hadn't felt in nearly a year.

But just like riding a bike, no matter how long you stop, you never forget how to ride a dick.

Allison made an "O" with her lips as she narrowed her eyes, flapping her big, beautiful eyelashes in the process. She moved her bottom around in slow, circular motions as she tried to grind her hips into Josh's lap, working his large, erect penis deeper and deeper into her a little bit at a time.

Meanwhile, she had a small crowd of her own gathered to watch the show, and making a show of it she was.

With one of her hands overlaying Josh's hand in a death grip on the arm rest, and her other hand palming her tight tit, kneading her breast like a soft lump of dough, Allison let out exaggerated, porn-star-sized moans of ecstasy as she bounced her ass up and down on top of Josh's dick, taking a little bit more of it into her tight pussy with each downward swivel, then taking back up, just to the point where the tip of his throbbing cock parted the entrance to her pussy lips, then again squeezing it back inside of her, before taking him a little deeper, then pulling out completely.

She repeated this motion over and over with increasingly louder moans, much to the enjoyment of the dozen or so people standing on the walkway in front of their tent, cheering them on.

Not to be outdone, Jess found herself another folding chair around their campsite, sitting on the opposite end from Josh, where she plopped down with one leg slung over the armrest and her other leg resting over the other armrest, bending her knee so she sat spread-eagled. She slumped down so her ass cheeks were flush with the edge of the seat.

Jess pulled the front of her pink thong panties to the side of her thigh, revealing a perfectly smooth and tight little pussy, with her eyes locked on her best friend and her boyfriend fucking passionately in the chair, maybe a yard away from her. Jess licked her middle three fingers and parted her pussy to reveal an engorged clit, just as pink as her neon G-string and the heart-shaped pasties covering her nipples.

Jess's own moans were nearly loud enough to rival those of Allison's; only Jess knew that the noises of stimulated sensual satisfaction coming from her mouth were authentic.

People had phones in their hands now. Jess had no doubt that they were taking videos of her.

That's fine, she thought. In a way, it was flattering, and she would give these spectators something that they themselves could masturbate to for the rest of their lives.

She looked over at Allison. Sweat beaded down her creamy white skin. Allison had her head tilted all the way back with her eyes closed. Her dirty blonde hair's curly ringlets and curls bounced up and down in sync with her booty slapping against Josh's thigh.

It took all of her willpower to take all of Josh's rock-hard cock into her tight, wet hole. Despite all of the whooping and hollering, Allison had her eyes closed and didn't even seem to notice.

When Jess closed her eyes, it was like she was in a different world. Lost in a world of heated passion. She could feel a sensation on the horizon. A wildflower blooming between her legs.

She pictured Josh's perfectly handsome face, his chiseled muscles, and his strong arms wrapped around her. She imagined what those arms felt like, holding her tight in a safe and loving embrace.

As she thought only of Josh, she continued to work her fingers through her pussy, vigorously massaging her clitoris in little circles. She suddenly felt a gushing wetness between her legs as the thrill of climax took her.

"Oh, shit! She's a squirter!" someone yelled.

Jess opened her eyes to see dozens of aroused faces she had forgotten about staring back at her.

Jess suddenly felt her face redden a bit to match her pink outfit. She was a little embarrassed to be sitting spread-eagled in front of all these people.

Where did they come from? Why were they all here? There was no doubt that they all saw Jess with her pussy hanging out. Christ, they all watched her cum and squirt, no less.

Jess looked over at Allison and Josh. Her friend was no longer bouncing on top of her boyfriend's dick. Instead, she was just sitting there on his lap, jaw slack, just as star-struck as Jess was that all these people were there watching them with their phones out.

She didn't know whether Allison had cum yet or not, but she knew what she was going to do next.

Jess shot up out of the folding chair, replaced the front of her pink panties, fluffed her black hair behind her, then went to grab the hands of both her boyfriend and her best friend.

"Alright, show's over, get out of here and get those phones out of my face!"

The crowd of idiots did none of those things. They continued to gawk and record with their phones. Jess, meanwhile, led her two friends out of the limelight and into the big tent.

Once inside, Jess stopped only to make sure the flap behind her was fully zipped up, then the fun could really begin.

Josh reached up to the top of the tent, where there was an LED color-changing light attached with a carabiner. He switched it on, and the entire tent was painted in a soft purple light. Josh jumped to the far end of the king-sized air mattress as the lights in the tent gently shifted to pink. then blue, then back to purple.

Even in the darkness of their tent, Allison's outfit glowed a deep neon green. Jess looked down and saw that her pink heart-shaped pasties covering her nipples were glowing as bright as ever.

Allison looked up and over at Jess with half-closed, innocent eyes, looking up at her from her long, beautiful eyelashes. The light illuminating the tent bounced off her breasts, her shoulders, her cheeks, softening every feature. Jess thought the light that brightened the tent, though still very dark, reminded her of a strip club.

Through the closed canvas tent, they could still hear the bass coming in. Jess could feel it in her body. She didn't recognize whoever was performing on the main stage at this point in the night, but based on how late it was in the evening, she guessed that it had to be one of the headliners.

The bass thumping over uplifting trance melodies had her in a heightened state of arousal, although all of the ecstasy and vodka surely helped too.

Jess felt her eyes flutter closed, and her jaw hang slack, just opening her lips the tiniest amount. Jess suddenly felt very sexy. She could feel the tightness of her muscles, the way her chest would rise and fall with each breath. She slowly cupped her own breasts in her hands, squeezing them, feeling the softness of her own skin, the supple feel in her hands.

Jess enjoyed playing with her boobs whenever she was turned on. She also liked the reaction she got from Josh when he watched her play with her large, natural breasts. For a moment, she entirely forgot there was someone else watching her with stimulated arousal.

She felt another pair of hands covering her breasts, hands too small to belong to Josh.

Jess opened her eyes to see Allison standing before her, pressed up against her body, exploring her friend's curves with wandering hands.

In the many years that Jess and Allison had been friends, they had shared bodily contact often. The two friends had regularly and casually seen each other naked when trying on clothes or getting ready for a night out, but never have they had never shared an intimate touch like the way that Allison was rubbing up on her body right now.

It was a sensual touch, and very different from the way Allison was touching Josh just moments ago.

In the long history of Jess and Allison's friendship, she couldn't deny that she had fantasized about her friend on more than one occasion.

But this was no fantasy. The way that Ally erotically dragged her fingers over Jess's body, cupping her breasts Jess, was very much turning her on. And she wanted more.

She suddenly forgot about her plan to get her friend to fuck her boyfriend in favor of her own wants, needs, and desires.

Slowly, cautiously, Jess brought the tips of her fingers to the sides of Ally's hips. Upon making contact, Allison's face contorted in ecstasy with closed eyes and pursed lips, not unlike the face she made when Jess watched her orgasm earlier in the night.

Jess liked the effect her mere touch was having on her friend. With her fingernail tips, gently floating on top of Allison's skin, she moved her delicate fingers up the sides of Ally's abdomen and up to her shoulders.

Allison, who never stopped playing with Jess's breasts, shuddered under her touch.

Looking her friend in the eye at long last, Ally draped her arms around Jess's neck and pulled her close. If the two women hadn't both had such large breasts, their shoulders would have touched.

Jess thought Allison was pulling her in to kiss her, so she closed her eyes and pursed her lips. Her breath rapidly increased.

In nervous, jagged, and shallow panting breaths, Jess was anxious, and while she never would have had the confidence to initiate the kiss herself, she willingly surrendered her inhibitions to this wild and raw moment of passion.

With her eyes shut tight, Jess was surprised when no kiss came.

Instead, she felt a hot breath on her ear as her friend whispered in a barely audible voice just enough for her to hear, "How do I get this off?"

Jess's eyes shot open, and a sudden smile grew on her lips. She tried to stifle a laugh, but she couldn't stop a small giggle from escaping her mouth.

It wasn't what she thought at all. Of course, Allison wouldn't know how to get her outfit off. Jess had designed it specifically for her.

Although the strappy green halter and garter tied into one was very easy to remove, Jess had to admit that it did look a little intimidating for someone who wanted to quickly disrobe without ripping anything.

Even though she was denied the kiss that she was expecting, when Jess pulled back to look her friend in the eye, Allison brought her cheek next to Jess's neck and ran it up the side of her face in an erotic nuzzle that sent shivers down her spine, all the way down her spine and ending in between her legs.

When she again looked into Allison's beautiful, hungry eyes, she saw the soft, pink light reflecting off her skin and her glistening, quivering lips.

It was almost too much for Jess to bear.

Never before had she felt such an incredibly strong yearning for another woman, least of all her friend. Not in a very long time had she felt so nervous getting naked in front of another person, least of all her best friend.

Again, Jess ran her fingers up the sides of her friend's soft, warm body, barely making contact as her nails and fingertips glossed over her glowing skin, caressing her shoulder blades before gently resting on her neck, mirroring the way that Allison had wrapped her arms lovingly around Jess's shoulders and the back of her neck.

Jess delicately hooked her thumbs underneath the high-neck band Allison wore and moved both hands around the sides of her neck so that they finally rested in front of Allison, on her collar bones, just above her breasts that still pushed into Jess's own chest.

Jess pulled on the front of Allison's neck band, stretching the elastic out until it was nearly touching her own collarbone, then brought the stretchy band over Allison's head and behind her bouncy hair, which looked to be much more blonde with tinges of pink and blue, pink and purple reflecting beautifully in the dim light of the tent.

Jess brought the stretch of fabric down, behind Allison to the small of her back, but went no further. All of Allison's straps of clothing fell to her waist, where Jess held onto the rest of it, preventing her garter from falling to the floor as well.

It seemed like a lifetime ago when Jess and Allison were getting ready for the rave, and Jess excitedly helped Allison into the outfit she had custom-made by hand, exclusively for her best friend.

But never did the thought cross her mind that she would be the one undressing her, certainly not in this circumstance. A million thoughts were running through Jess's mind at once.

Then she felt a force on the back of her neck pulling her closer to Allison. Their flesh pushed against one another. Jess could feel the heat of Allison's body flesh against her thighs, stomach, breasts, and shoulders.

When Allison's soft, wet lips pressed delicately against her own, her mind suddenly went blank. Jess forgot all of her stressful and nervous thoughts the moment her best friend parted her lips with her tongue, finding her own tongue.

All she could think of was the playful dance of the wet kiss they were sharing.

I love this woman. This is love, Jess thought, as she licked Allison's lips with white hot need. *Funny how much love tastes like Burt's Bees lip balm.*

Her muscles in her hands relaxed and the rest of Allison's outfit fell to the rug on the floor.

Now the only thing Allison was wearing were her glow in the dark green fishnet stockings, G-string thong, and the two neon "X" shaped pasties covering her nipples.

Allison started kissing Jess more and more aggressively. The quiet little moans she was making were becoming noticeably louder.

With one arm still hooked behind Jess's neck, her other hand brushed the side of her face intimately, then started trembling in nervous jitters as she caressed Jess's cheek.

Jess was about to ask her what the problem was, why her friend who moments ago showed such cavalier confidence, was now trembling like an anxious chihuahua puppy, but before she could say anything, it was Allison who opened her eyes and pulled back from the kiss first.

Allison placed her palm on Jess's shoulder and pushed her back a couple of feet. The front of Jess's body was suddenly cold without Allison's body pressed up against her.

She didn't like it one bit. A nervous moment passed as Jess looked her in the eye, then, finally, Allison's eyes darted down to Jess's pink pasties and back up again.

She spoke at last, "I wasn't talking about mine, you know."

Allison beamed a lustful smile, but Jess could only stand there and blink. It took a few long seconds for her to understand what Allison was talking about, but as soon as she did she felt her face go crimson red.

Allison must have seen the mortified look on her face because she started giggling immediately. Jess felt mortified. Allison wanted to take off all of Jess's clothes, but she thought her friend was asking her to undress her.

"Here, let me do it," Allison whispered in her ear. "I think I've got this figured out."

Similar to Allison's outfit, Jess's was held up in place by a single pink plastic strap. The only difference is that with Jess's outfit, the strap ran behind her neck instead of a band in the front, like Allison's.

With her hands wrapped around Jess's neck the entire time they were making out, Allison did quickly figure out how Jess's outfit came apart. She hooked both thumbs on the strap behind her neck. Jess helped her by pulling her long black hair to one side as Allison lifted the strap over her head.

Unlike how Jess simply dropped Allison's outfit and the entire thing fell to the floor, Allison pulled the elastic strap connecting all of Jess's outfit and holding it together. Allison got on her knees as she peeled off each piece of Jess's wardrobe.

She pulled the halter straps down to the garter, unhooked Jess's glowing pink fishnet stockings, so that they would stay up by themselves.

She reached around so she had on firmly on Jess's bare ass cheek with a loud spank, then she peeled off the rest of her outfit, including the garter and, to Jess's surprise, her thong panties.

Surprised or not, once they were around her ankles, the only thing Jess could do was step out of them. She kicked everything off to some far off corner of the tent, and then she was completely naked, or at least, she felt completely naked. She was still wearing her hot pink fishnet stockings and heart pasties.

From her position still on her knees, with one hand wrapped around Jess's butt cheek and the other pressed up against Jess's flat stomach, Allison was able to steer Jess backwards onto the air mattress with surprising power and maneuverability.

Jess let out a little scream of mock terror when she fell backwards, bouncing in the air a few inches before settling on her back with her legs dangling off the front of the mattress. She couldn't help but giggle at the absurdity of what was going on.

How far was her best friend willing to go? How far was she willing to go?

She felt Allison's tiny hands running up her legs. She would soon find out.

The warmth of the molly and alcohol were really starting to sink their teeth into her now.

Allison ran her fingers up her thighs as her head bobbed up and down between her legs. Her warm hands ran up the length of her stomach until she at last clutched each of Jess's tits in her hands.

When Allison's fingers danced over Jess's nipples, even over her pasties, her touch made Jess tingle inside. As soon as Allison started playing with her nipples, Jess instinctively raised her legs, bending them so that her feet touched the mattress, spread-eagled.

At that moment, Jess felt like the sexiest, most desirable woman on earth. She didn't think it could get much better than this, but then again, she has often been criticized for not being imaginative enough.

She felt a familiar warm wetness in between her legs followed by a growing surge of pleasure. Jess propped herself up on her elbows so she could see Allison's crop of blonde hair, looking up at her, smiling with her tongue stuck deep in Jess's pussy.

This is it, Jess thought to herself. It's finally happening.

Looking up at her with those big, beautiful eyes and luscious, luxurious eyelashes with her smiling face planted between her legs, Allison whispered to her, "Jess, you taste just like I always imagined you would."

Then, after dragging her tongue all the way from Jess's asshole between her cheeks, up her gash, over her moist pussy, teasingly across her clit, and up to her belly button.

"Thank you for finally making my fantasy come true. I don't know how you knew, but thank you."

Then Allison returned to burying her face between Jess's legs, putting all of her concentration into licking away and causing Jess to let out a loud and unexpected moan.

A hand brushed her shoulder, pulling back Jess's hair. It was at that moment that she remembered that Josh was there in bed with them. She jumped a little until she looked up to see her boyfriend's handsome smiling face staring back at her, comforting her.

While the girls had been busy, it was clear that Josh had been busy, too. He had pulled off his shirt, revealing his lean, muscled chest and tight six-pack abs. In the shifting light of the tent, Jess could see the various tattoos running up his arm and part of his chest in red and black ink.

With his brown hair, light eyes, chiseled chin and jaw line, he looked like a modern day Ken doll.

She thought of how lucky she was to have him in her life. His smile never failed to make her smile, but right now her smile was contorted in pursed lips of pleasure as moans of ecstasy escaped her lips.

It took but a moment for Jess to realize that he had his jeans pulled down to his thighs, freeing his massive erection. Josh slowly stroked his throbbing shaft as he watched Allison eat out his girlfriend's pussy. He had clearly been enjoying the show.

Jess's mind briefly turned to a few moments earlier, outside the tent, where Allison swallowed all of Josh's cum. Just the thought of that got her really wet and lustful for more of the same.

Remembering the sensation of her boyfriend's dick in her mouth, the taste of him shooting his hot wad down her throat, and her eagerly swallowing every drop of his cum had awakened a new desire in her.

Jess pulled on Josh's legs, but instead of moving him further down the bed like she wanted, his pants came down further when she tugged.

This would work, too, Jess thought to herself as she continued pulling at Josh's jeans until finally she had pulled them entirely off his ankles. Jess blindly threw them to the opposite side of where she sat, then continued to pull at Josh's bare legs until she was able to get him to scoot down to the middle of the air mattress, with his hairy legs strewn parallel to Jess's body.

She finally had him right where she wanted him-within dick sucking distance. She found it extremely difficult to focus on her best head game while Allison's expert lounge flicked her clit at speeds she didn't think were humanly possible.

From experience, Jess knew that Josh was very much turned on when she moaned while his dick was in her mouth, which was not very difficult for her to manage.

In fact, with Allison at work between her legs, moaning with Josh dick in her mouth was pretty much all she could do. Despite her best efforts, she knew by the look on his face that Josh was a little disappointed his dick wasn't getting more attention.

When he pulled his cock out of Jess's mouth, she guessed that he was more than a little disappointed. But Josh had always been more than a generous lover, so this apparent tantrum was more than surprising to Jess, although nothing as surprising as what he was about to do next.

In one swift, fluid motion, Josh swiveled around on his ass, whipping his legs behind him and above Jess's head while his arms and head now extended hanging over the same edge of the mattress as her feet and her pussy.

Allison didn't even seem to notice, not looking up even once as she continued to lap up Jess's sweet juices with her knees bent on the rug at the edge of the bed and her face buried deep into Jess's pussy.

When Josh reached over and picked Allison up at the thighs, using her green fishnets to get a grip, She was so concentrated in her task she almost didn't notice at first as her world got turned upside down literally.

Josh pulled Allison onto the bed with them and positioned his head between her thighs. Josh wasted no time in ripping the green thong panties to shreds, completely exposing Allison's smooth, hairless pussy for the taking.

Allison, meanwhile, hooked an arm around Jess's knee, where before she was in between her legs, and playing with her tits, now Allison's head rested on Jess's belly as she sat face down with her mouth between Jess's legs and her thighs covering Allison's ears like ear muffs.

Jess now saw the masterpiece stroke of genius that Josh intended.

While Allison returned to eating out Jess's pussy like it would be her last meal on earth, Josh now comfortably rested his face between Allison's legs, and from the indiscreet, non-stop moaning coming from Allison, it seemed like Josh had already knocked the dust off her pussy and was putting it to work.

Jess looked to her left to see Josh's throbbing erection that looked like it was asking for attention so badly that it might explode at any second. And Jess would make sure of that - and that when it did explode, she would be nearby.

Leaning over to her side, Jess was able to take his cock well in hand and began playing a game she was very familiar with called "How much dick can you fit in your mouth?" She was very good at this game and won every time, only sometimes it took her much longer to get to the end of the game.

It took a lot of concentration, need, and patience to fit all of her boyfriend's massive cock into the back of her throat. And although she was highly motivated to do so, she found it extremely difficult to focus on the task in hand (and mouth) with Allison tongue-punching her clitoris like it was a punching bag.

Still, she eagerly took him into her mouth as best she could, and from the sound of Josh's moaning, albeit muffled with a mouth full of vagina, he was very much enjoying it.

Then something amazing happened.

The three of them started breathing as one, their heartbeats completely synced up. Suddenly, every flick of the tongue was completely synchronized. And, as one, each of them began to unconsciously increase their pace.

Allison took the back of Jess's thighs in her hands and pulled her face deeper in between her legs, while she started using more pressure with her tongue on Jess's clit.

Josh caught both of Allison's ass cheeks in his hands and used them to steady himself as he began licking faster and with much more ferocity.

Jess used her hand on the base of Josh's shaft to take as much of his dick into her mouth as fast as she could.

And the three of them continued to increase their pace to impossible speeds until - *BOOM-BOOM-BOOM* - All three of them came at the exact same time to a thunderous scream of ecstasy.

As the three of them collapsed onto the air mattress, Jess had the strangest thought pop into her head: *This is exactly what the Human Centipede should have been.*

Jess was still rolling hard by the time she caught her breath. She enjoyed sitting there, more or less completely naked, listening to the far-off bass from a performance on the main stage.

Josh was the first of the three to move.

With a great sigh of relief, he slid out from under Allison's legs and sat up on the bed, sitting back on his haunches, with one hand casually resting on the small of Allison's back. He pulled on Jess's elbow, urging her off her back.

Jess sat up on the bed. One look in Josh's eyes and she knew what he wanted her to do. Their bond ran so deep, and they understood each other so well, that much of their communication was unspoken, non-verbal, and conveyed by either body language, situational context, or a simple, knowing look.

Even though she considered herself to be fucked up on molly and vodka, she still knew just by the way Josh was looking at her that he wanted her on her knees.

Right now, his look told her that he was going to fuck her from behind.

Allison, who was already on her hands and knees, did not react when Jess pulled her pussy out from under Allison's face. She let out a deep whining noise, like a dog that just had its dinner pulled out from under it.

But when she saw her friend assume the same position as her, on her hands and knees right next to her with her ass sticking up in the air, Allison, too, understood what was going on and made a face that looked like it was anticipating what was to come.

The two best friends both sat on their knees and elbows, holding their asses high in the air and teasingly shaking them left to right in front of Josh. Jess looked over at Allison with a mischievous smile that she shared.

Her friend returned the smile, albeit a nervous one. Knowing her friend as long as she did, Jess recognized the subtle look of anxiety behind her beaming smile. Jess reached over and gave Allison's hand a comforting squeeze.

Josh rested his right hand on the small of Jess's back, his left on Allison's. He gave Jess three quick spankings to her left butt cheek, each one harder and louder than the last.

Jess was not surprised. In fact, she savored the red-hot sting where Josh had slapped her ass. Even afterwards, she could still feel the tingling of the spanking, envisioning the pink hand outline on her ample, milky white cheeks.

Josh rubbed his left hand in small caressing circles on Allison's right butt cheek three times, as if to soften up her flesh for what was coming.

Allison looked anxiously in Jess's eyes and bit her lower lip, steeling herself for the blow. To her fright, Jess gave her friend a relevant smile, telling her that everything would be alright, that she would enjoy the spankings, she had thought.

That smile held a twinge of jealousy, too, for Jess would greedily take all of the spankings that were meant for Allison, and any more Josh was willing to administer.

Slap-slap-SLAP.

Allison's mouth fell open, eyes wide.

Jess could tell that Josh had spanked her with all of his lustful power - much harder than he had given her.

Jess looked upon her friend's face as she processed that erotic threshold between pleasure and pain. She was secretly jealous of what she must be feeling, of what Jess envisioned Allison's ass must look like right now with its stinging, bright red handprint against Allison's creamy buns.

The thought of what Josh must be seeing right now really turned Jess on. She could physically feel herself getting wetter when she pictured Ally's perfectly firm and bubbly ass side by side with hers, with their tight, dripping wet pussies between their legs.

She had always admired her best friend's ass, especially when Allison wore a thong that revealed her entire perky butt cheeks.

But she also wondered who had the better-looking ass - her or her friend. Jess knew that either way, the sight of both of their bare rear ends was enough to give her boyfriend a raging hard-on.

In her mind, she could envision the decision Josh was weighing up with the glorious buffet that was presented before him. It was something that she knew other men would kill for - two perfectly supple libertine asses in their sexual prime bent over before him, presenting, and much more than willing - eager for attention, two smooth, hairless, tight little pussies dripping wet because of their hunger for a fat and juicy cock - their need to be penetrated.

If he so chose and if the mood should strike him, two perfectly delicious and tight little assholes starting back at him, vying for his attention not to be overlooked.

Jess would just as happily be fucked in her ass as she would her pussy, for she truly enjoyed both on different levels. To her, anal and vaginal were like Mexican and Chinese food, both of which she very much enjoyed for different reasons and at different times. Should the mood strike her.

Based on a few stories that Allison had told her, she knew that her friend felt the exact same way.

Jess was jostled out of her fantasy when she noticed Allison's face contort in surprise for a moment, then quickly switched to one of sheer unbridled pleasure as she heard the unmistakable sound of Josh's thighs clapping against Allison's bare ass.

He wasted no time in driving his huge cock deep into Allison's tiny pussy. Jess wondered how he had managed to get his big dick all the way into Allison's little hole when she seemed to have an incredibly difficult time of it only moments ago when they were on the folding chair outside the tent.

She didn't know the answer to that, but what was evident to her was that Josh was clearly not holding back. He was fucking Allison's pussy with the lustful enthusiasm that he used to show her when they first started hooking up.

Lying flat on the bed so her large, supple tits lay flat on the mattress, face down and ass up, she stared at her friend with a Cheshire cat smile.

Her plan was unfolding exactly how she envisioned it.

She knew, based on the type of guys that Allison dated and from the stories she had told her, that she never had the luxury of taking any dick quite as nice as that of her boyfriends.

It was big enough to be what Jess considered the perfect size, but if she was being honest with herself, there were often times that it was too big. Yet he wielded it skillfully, and that was what really mattered.

He always seemed to know when to go fast, when to slow down, the right time to be gentle and was aggressive when she wanted it. He knew how to match the pace of his thrusts so that they were in tune with her breathing, her heartbeat, and sometimes she felt that he could match the very rhythm of her soul.

That's why she was happy to see him attacking Allison aggressively and lustfully instead of the tender love making that he knew Jess liked so much. Allison hadn't been fucked in a very long time - not properly fucked, anyway, not like the way her boyfriend could do it.

No one deserved this more than Allison, so if she had to share her boyfriend's skilled cock with her best friend in order to get her out of a rut and back on her feet, she was more than happy to do this small act of charity and in the name of friendship.

Jess couldn't help but to smile lasciviously as she watched her boyfriend pull on her best friend's hair so that he could fuck her even deeper, even harder than ever. Although her face looked paralyzed, caught in the sensual delights, Allison was just starting to get vocal with them after she realized that not only did Jess approve of her fucking her boyfriend - she grossly encouraged it.

At first, it was just "Yeah, Yeah, Yeah, Oh God, oh fuck yeah."

Then she added a bit of direction, "Fuck me harder, yes, fuck me deeper, like that. Fuck me harder. HARDER! Oh, yes, just like that. Right There. Fuck me like that."

With renewed vigor and aggression, Allison voiced her satisfaction with the type of loud screams you would expect to hear on a roller coaster at an amusement park. Jess imagined that for Allison, getting fucked like this for the first time was very much like riding a roller coaster, or at least like riding some kind of ride that should be at an amusement park for adults.

Jess had to admit to herself that watching her boyfriend fuck the shit out of her best friend was really turning her on. Desperate for attention, she abandoned her hope that Josh might start fucking her pussy, too, and instead of sitting with her face down and ass up on her knees and elbows, Jess flipped herself around so that she was now lying on her back.

From this position, she could comfortably slide her head underneath Allison's. Although Allison could hardly catch her breath with how hard she was getting fucked, as soon as she saw Jess's beautiful green eyes, shiny, shimmering black hair, and full pink lips being wet by her tongue teasingly, she wasted no time in tilting her head angled down so that her wet, bloated lips met her friend's.

Jess shared in her passion with a kiss that absolutely stole her breath-or what was left of it anyway. Although it was clear that Allison had trouble concentrating on making out with Jess. The way that Josh was fucking her, she would have forgotten her name had someone asked her

But Jess more than made up for that by throwing all of herself into a kiss that was so hot that it could even steal attention away from Josh. Jess pulled the back of Allison's head closer to hers. Josh had released Allison's hair in favor of a much tighter grip on her hips, where he was able to also spread her ass cheeks further to allow for deeper penetration.

All attention was on Allison.

Though her face said that she was in the throes of the molly and rolling really hard, you could see the unbridled passion, joy, and pure ecstasy that she was enjoying every second more than the last.

With Jess's mouth fully covering Allison's, and with Allison's tongue eagerly exploring every inch of her friend's, Allison let little moans of pleasure escape her throat each time Josh drove his hard cock deep between her legs.

Jess eagerly swallowed all of the sexy little noises she made, drinking them out of her mouth like a baby bird. Every moan of satisfaction, every noise that Allison made, caused Jess to become more and more horny until finally she could stand it no longer.

Jess's free hand wandered down the length of her own, hot, sweaty body, down her neck, caressing her breasts, pinching her nipples, pushing up on her flat abdomen, and finally finding a home between her legs. It wasn't until Allison's vibrant blue eyes followed Jess's wandering hand and saw her playing with herself that her whole demeanor changed.

Josh continued to squeeze Allison's perfectly round ass cheeks apart so he could get a better angle as he thrust his stiff shaft into the tight, wet hole between her legs.

Although this was what was creating the soft moans that came from her throat with each deep, penetrating thrust, and although it was the sensual kissing that Jess had her head pulled into, with her hand on the back of Allison's neck, that was really what got Allison's pussy so dripping wet.

It wasn't until Allison saw Jess playing with herself that she felt like she was going to come.

The thought that Jess was so turned on by making out with Allison that she had to touch herself was what turned Allison on the most. When she saw that Jess was masturbating to her made Allison feel sexy.

It was such a huge turn on to her that, even though she was getting fucked hard from behind by Josh's huge cock, and even though Jess and her friend never stopped their intimate tongue wrestling competition, it only took a few seconds of watching Jess fingering herself as she simultaneously played with her clit for Allison to start cumming long and hard.

She opened her mouth as wide as it would go as Jess nibbled her lower lip before gently kissing her friend all down her neck. The light kisses over her sensitive skin only worked to increase the intensity of her orgasm.

Josh greatly increased his pace, ramming his cock into Allison's pussy as his hips slapped against her ass cheeks. The sound of flesh slapping against flesh was drowned out by Allison's screaming orgasm.

With her eyes shut tight, Allison screamed her climax release directly into Jess's face in front of her.

Jess imagined that her friend's orgasmic shrieks as well as the distinct sound of skin pounding against skin, and possibly even Jess's own loud and primal moans that she only just realized she was making - she imagined that all of these sounds and intimate little noises probably echoed throughout the camp.

But in the privacy of their massive tent, she would not be embarrassed.

Although she had hoped that the crowd that was watching Allison get fucked in the folding chair outside, underneath the canopy, had dispersed, she convinced herself that she didn't care. She erased the mental image of the dozen or so people who had seen her playing with her pussy standing outside the tent.

She would not restrain herself for them, if they still lurked outside of the tent for some reason. She would not restrain herself for anyone. This was a music festival after all, and Electric Love was, above all things, a celebration of love.

But if Jess was being completely honest with herself, the thought of all those people watching her touching herself while Josh and Allison were fucking just a few feet away had really turned her on.

All of those eyes, the eyes of complete strangers, looking her body up and down and cheering while she was masturbating, was empowering.

But were they cheering for her, or Josh and Allison? Or both?

Part of her really wanted to be the one getting fucked raw in front of a bunch of strangers just so she could feel that way again.

Still, none of that made her quite as horny as being just a few inches from her naked best friend when she just experienced what was probably the best orgasm in her entire life, up until that point at least, Jess thought to herself.

After all, there are still two more days left of Electric Love, and who knows what could happen?

The moment Josh pulled out of Allison, She collapsed on wobbly knees, trying her best to catch her breath. Allison may have just had the best orgasm of her life, but it was clear that Josh hadn't even cum yet and was still as horny as ever.

He gave Jess this devilish look that she recognized immediately, with narrowed eyes and wrinkled nose, anyone else might easily mistake that look for one of anger - but Jess knew better. She had been on the receiving end of that look only a handful of times, but there was no mistaking it.

His maniacal eyes hurtled well over lustful and into the realm of testosterone-fueled fueled unrelenting sex junkie on a mission to fuck until either his dick falls off or he collapses from exhaustion.

Every time Jess had seen Josh get like this, it was the best sex she had ever had-but she had also been sore for days afterward. Being on the receiving end of this man possessed both excited and scared her, and it looked like allowing him to put his dick in Allison's tight pussy had awakened a primal animalistic need inside of him.

It was as if Jess could see her boyfriend's dick going Super Saiyan before her very eyes.

Jess had never stopped rubbing her clit, and although it felt good, it wasn't getting her anywhere.

Taking her in, Jess could see the fire in his eyes as he let himself be seduced by his girlfriend's perfect body, her hot pink fishnets, her very closely matched the color of her full lips, and her glistening clitoris. Josh knocked her hand away from her pussy, then dragged her a few feet across the bed by her thighs until she lay directly in front of him.

Jess let out a playful scream when she slid on her butt over to him, then started playing with her boobs-just to give her hands something to do. She started pinching the edges of her pink pasties, trying to get the little vinyl hearts off of her nipples. Josh wasted no time in sliding his hard cock inside of her, holding on to her thighs for support as he started fucking her as hard and fast as humanly possible.

Jess instantly lost her grip on the heart pasties when her D-cup tits began bouncing out of control.

"Oh My God!"

The sudden momentum of her getting fucked up and down on the bed caught her off guard.

Jess pushed her tits together as close as they would go just to get them to stop bouncing, but then another hand reached over and slapped her hands away, freeing her boobs to once again bounce uncontrollably up and down at the pace that Josh was fucking her.

To her surprise, the hand belonged to Allison.

Allison's tiny hands reached over and firmly squeezed Jess's left tit. As Allison lay naked and parallel to her friend, she leaned over on top of her and began trying to peel off Jess's pink heart pasties with her mouth.

Josh lifted both of Jess's legs up and propped them on his shoulders, all the while pounding her pussy harder, deeper, and faster than she thought humanly possible.

"Oh fuck, right there, Daddy. Oh, fuck me like that." Jess was surprised to hear the words come out of her mouth just as Josh started hitting her G-spot.

She knew it wouldn't be long now before she would be gushing all over their covers.

Thank God we brought a spare set of linens, she thought.

It was all she could do to dig her fingers into the sheets and pull hard.

To her surprise, Allison was able to completely peel off one of her pasties using only her mouth, which Jess knew was by no means an easy task - sometimes she had difficulty peeling them off herself with just her own fingers.

Now that Allison had liberated one of her nipples, she had Jess's tight titty in a firm grip while she licked the edges of the vinyl heart, trying to get it up enough to pinch in her teeth so she could then just rip off her nipples with one swift jerk of her jaw.

Allison had the second one off in record time, and judging from the ear-to-ear grin on her face, she was quite proud of herself.

Jess's toes curled as her friend took her newly liberated nipples in her mouth, pushing her tongue into Jess's areola, savoring every lick, then sucking on them as if they contained the cure to cancer.

While Josh continued to jackhammer her G-spot, Allison was sucking on her titties as if she were a 15-year old boy.

All of this attention on her was pushing her to the limits. She didn't want to cum. She wanted this warm, tingling, feeling all throughout her body to last forever. She loved the feeling of primal ecstasy leading up to the orgasm and never wanted it to end.

Man, she loved getting fucked.

And, still, she didn't want to cum. not just yet. A little bit longer. But at the moment she could hold it back no longer, she felt overwhelmed by climactic ecstasy.

A chill ran across her entire body, she felt a hot gushing roar in between her legs, she gave in to the rush of dopamine and serotonin exploding in her brain.

"Oooohhh!" A passionate scream overtook her.

She lifted her hips to better receive Josh's dick. Then she realized that he was slowing down.

"Uh, shit. Did you just cum too?" she asked her boyfriend who had suddenly lost that animalistic look in his eye.

"Yeah" he finally said between panting breaths.

"We came at the same time."

Jess didn't even realize-she was so caught up in what she was feeling. Josh was still thrusting his dick in and out at her pussy, albeit at a much slower pace than before-almost at the same pace he used when he and Jess made love in stead of just fucking like crazed animals.

"Thank God you're on birth control." Josh smiled, "I just shot enough cum in you to put out a small forest fire."

"How fucking romantic." Jess pulled away from him, then got up off the bed to clean herself up.

"By the way," Allison said as she sat up on her knees, "I'm not on birth control. But I do love to swallow."

Cautiously, she eyed Jess, then looked at Josh, then glanced down at his still hard cock, dripping with Jess's juices. "Can we please just not talk about this tomorrow?"

Allison bent her back down at the hips, got on her knees and elbows, then took Josh's dick at the base of his shaft. It hardened up after only a few tugs, at which point she licked the tip of his cock. After seeing it harden even more, She went ahead and started sucking on his whole dick eagerly.

"I think we're going to be talking about this for a long time to come, Ally," Said Jess.

After she finished cleaning herself, Jess's attention was brought back to the bed after she heard a long moan coming from Josh.

Jess was surprised to see her friend again sucking on her boyfriend's dick, but she decided to let it slide. This was, after all, supposed to be her comeback weekend. Josh could hardly be blamed for a smoking hot woman like Allison having her mouth tightly wrapped around his shaft after only just having his dick inside of her not more than a few minutes.

Allison needed this, so Jess decided to give her all the sexual healing she desired. Naturally, Jess knew that her boyfriend would be on board with whatever she decided, at least as long as the body was willing.

"Ally, Can I get some of that?"

Jess crawled onto the bed towards Josh on her hands and knees. Jess pulled up right alongside her friend, lying flat on her belly propped up by her massive tits.

Seeing this, Allison did the same. Although her C-cup breasts weren't big enough to completely support her the way that Jess's boobs did, Allison leaned with the support of one elbow on the bed with her other hand wrapped around Josh's fully erect penis.

Allison pulled his dick out of her mouth.

"Of course," She licked his tip. Josh's penis quivered at the sensation of the soft, wet tip of her tongue against the most sensitive part of her body.

"It tastes like you," she added, then pointed it in Jess's direction. Allison's tiny hand wrapped around the base of Josh's cock made it look even more huge than Jess was used to.

With her hands flat on the bed, folded in front of her, Jess placed her lips around the tip of the dick that she had sucked on so many times before. This wasn't exactly a thrilling new experience for Jess, although she had never sucked a dick in the presence of her best friend, despite them having talked about it many, many times.

Then a thought popped into Jess's head.

With Allison holding her boyfriend's cock in front of her face, Jess propped herself up on her tits a little bit more, making sure she was in the right position for what she was about to undertake.

She again wrapped her lips tightly around the tip of his hard cock, feeling it inside her mouth with her tongue.

Josh let out a small noise like he was enjoying a fine steak, followed by a much louder moan after what Jess did next.

Straightening her throat, she moved her lips as far down Josh's cock as she could, deep throating most of his dick until its tip hit the back of her tonsils. She could take no more of his cock into her mouth.

Jess was only able to fit about three quarters of his entire dick into her mouth. All the same, with a cock as long as Josh's, this was still a feat.

Upon seeing this, Allison gasped. "Oh my god! How do you even do that?" Allison still had three fingers wrapped around the base of Josh's dick, but Jess could go no further.

"I want to try!"

Jess slid his dick back out of her mouth, looked at her friend and smiled proudly.

"See?" Jess said, "I told you I was good."

In the time Jess and Allison have known each other, they have had many conversations about their dick sucking prowess, although, admittedly, Jess would often embellish.

Allison scoffed, "I could suck more dick than that in my sleep."

Allison let go of Josh's cock and Jess grabbed it at the same place she had been holding it. Allison talked a big game, but when she looked over the length of Josh's cock and realized how monstrously big the thing was, she looked intimidated.

Jess held his dick steady in front of her face. Allison opened her mouth wide, went down on his dick a little over half way, then pulled her head back in a coughing fit.

Jess laughed openly, but could see that this only made Allison more mad.

As soon as she stopped coughing, Allison cleared her throat, then wasted no time in throwing her open mouth down on top of Josh's dick. This time she only got about half way down his shaft before she pulled her head back, retching.

"Sorry. Gag reflex." Allison took a deep breath, then in a very serious tone, said, "Let me do this one more time. I got this!"

It sounded like she was trying to convince her self more so than Jess.

"Take your time," Jess told her friend encouragingly. She looked up at Josh and smiled the smile she gave only him.

He returned their special smile.

Imitating what she had seen Jess do, Allison first wrapped her lips around only the very tip of Josh's cock. Again, he made a noise like someone had just given him his favorite candy.

At a turtle's pace, Allison's lips marched further down his shaft, then retreated back so that she held only the tip in her mouth. Jess thought for a minute that she was about to give up, but to her surprise, Allison slowly went back down, taking more of him into her mouth before again retreating back to the safety of his tip.

Once more, she slid her lips slowly down Josh's cock, further and further inching towards the base. Jess had a look of shock on her face when she had to move her fingers from the bottom of his cock so that Allison could fit even more of it in her mouth.

Sure enough, Allison was able to deepthroat more of her boyfriend's dick than she was by about the width of one finger. Although when she pulled back to pull his dick out of her mouth she fell into another coughing fit, "Oh my God, you did it!" Jess laughed as she pat her friend on the back.

"That was so fucking hot." Jess leaned in close and whispered in her ear.

Allison stopped coughing the moment she heard these words. Allison looked up at her friend, pushing a loose strand of hair out of her face. A sheepish smile spread on her face. Jess could tell that Allison was still pretty drunk.

Both the girls were laying on their stomachs, with their tits pushed out in front of them. Their legs kicked idly behind them in their respective neon fishnet stockings. Their bare bottoms swaying back and forth lazily.

Allison closed her eyes and leaned forward with pursed lips in a drunk attempt to kiss Jess. Jess planted a simple peck on her lips, though it was clear that Allison wanted much more.

She opened her eyes, smiling dumbly, then her attention was diverted elsewhere.

"Can you take these off me?" Allison pushed her tits together, squeezing hard. "They're starting to hurt." She whined in reference to her pasties.

Jess knew that Allison knew how to take them off herself and just wanted Jess to do it for some reason.

"Turn over," Jess instructed.

Allison eagerly flipped over so she was laying on her back. ."Hold them steady," Allison pushed up her breasts from the bottom, making them appear much bigger than they actually were.

"On three."

Allison grit her teeth.

"One." Jess counted, then fast as lightning, ripped both of the green 'X's off of Allison's nipples. She began crying in mock agony at this deceit.

"Why? Why would you do that?" Allison whined. "Now kiss them and make them better."

Although Jess thought this would be hilarious, she quickly realized how mean this was. Jess complied, lying down beside her again, Jess began licking her friends nipples like a puppy greeting its master.

Allison reached behind her and wrapped her hand around Josh's dick, tugging him down toward the bed, on her other side.

"You too," She instructed him, "You need to kiss it and make it better."

Josh wasted no time laying down alongside Allison, taking her breast in his big hand. Josh began licking Allison's other nipple much more aggressively than the soft, subtle and sexy way that Jess was licking her friend's tits. Josh was sucking on them much in the way that Allison was sucking on Jess's breasts as soon as she removed her pasties with her mouth.

Allison gently brushed the backs of both Jess's and Josh's heads while she closed her eyes and made faint, little moans with her throat.

"Mmm. Uh-hmmm." Allison cooed.

Josh soon fell into the same pace as Jess, realizing that he had at first attacked Allison's tits too aggressively.

The tent soon fell silent, with the only noises being Allison's very faint moans and the little sucking sounds of the couples wet lips and tongues against Allison's hard nipples.

"Hey, the music stopped!" Josh eventually pointed out.

Neither of them had realized when it had happened.

Jess, who was starting to really enjoy sucking on her friend's tits, pointed out, "Hey, I think she fell asleep."

Sure enough, Allison's arms fell limp at her sides. Jess and Josh shared a special smile that they only gave one another. The smile that meant all was well in their relationship. That all was well in life.

Using Allison's tits as a pillow, Josh and Jess laid their heads down and fell fast asleep. The three of them lay completely naked on top of the covers of their air mattress in the tent, illuminated by the ever shifting shades of lights.

Chapter 6: The Shower Stage

The heat and humidity trapped inside the tent is what awakened Jess. It had to have been the mid afternoon.

She could already hear the distant dubstep beats from the main stage as well as the laughter and chatter of people outside the tent as they walked to wherever they were going to party on that day of the festival.

Jess sat up on the air mattress. Josh still lay asleep on top with his head nestled comfortably on top of Allison's chest.

She stood up off the bed and instantly her head spun. God, it was hot. Where did they put all the waters they brought in?

Jess frantically looked around the room. The heat was stifling. It was all she could do to find the zipper to the tent flap and yanked it up, just enough for her to crouch down and slip out.

Even with the hot afternoon sun on her skin, it wasn't nearly as oppressive as the sauna in the tent.

Jess spotted the ice chest underneath the canopy in the common area. She ran over and flipped the lid open only to find nothing but beer and vodka floating around in melted ice water.

With a heavy sigh, Jess grabbed one of the beers, cracked it open and chugged half of it down. At least it was still kind of cold. Thank God.

She held the open can of beer to her head, letting the coolness soothe her hangover. Only then did she realize that not only was she covered head to toe in sweat, aside from her pink fishnet stockings, she was entirely naked.

She looked out to the trail beside the canopy they had set up as a common area. It was a choice location because it was positioned right on the corner of one of the main walking trails in and out of the festival, on the way to the main stage.

As groups of people strolled by on their way in to the festival, some looked at her and smiled, but most kept on walking.

Jess then realized that she didn't need to be ashamed or try to cover up her nakedness. This was a music festival after all and she was around her people.

Jess calmly and casually picked up a pair of red tinged heart-shaped sunglasses laying on the dirt path in front of their tent. Some one must have dropped these, she thought, but it's their loss because they would probably look a hell of a lot better on her anyway.

She wiped off the sunglasses and put them on. Suddenly everything had a beautiful red tinge to it.

Jess casually raked her fingers through her hair - it felt a mess but there was nothing she could do about that now. All Jess could do is sit back in her reclining folding chair, cross her legs

(She was, after all, a classy bitch), and sip her beer until the others woke up.

As small groups passed her by and she caught their eye, cheering on her casual nudity, she would raise her beer in a toast.

By the time she opened her second beer, she was starting to enjoy herself.

By her third beer, the concept of "self-consciousness" and "modesty" were completely unknown to her.

As she sat in the mesh and aluminum folding chair, completely naked from head to toe, with the exception of her hot pink fishnets, guys would occasionally stop to compliment or cat call her.

"Holy shit, check out her tits! Those are much better than any of the tits we saw last night!"

A young looking guy, no older than 14, wearing a backwards baseball cap and white tank top with scrawny, noodly arms awkwardly flapping to his sides, remarked to one of his similarly dressed friends as he slowed down to a snail's pace in front of Jess's canopy.

"She can hear you, you know. And if you come back for my performance in an hour, I'll have a fog machine, too!"

All of the boys' friends let out a playful "OOHH!" and laughed at him.

His face turned bright red. He continued down the path, embarrassed like he couldn't get away from her fast enough.

An equally young man desperate to impress his friends approached her. He was not bad looking, and looked a lot like a young Will Smith from his Fresh Prince days. Only much younger.

"Dayum, girl, why don't you come over here and park that beautiful white ass on my face?" Jess stared at him over the brim of her heart shaped glasses with a look that said, "are you kidding me?"

"Oh, please, kid. My ass is way too hot for the likes of you. If I sat on your face, it would leave a permanent brand."

His friends busted up laughing as he walked away, hanging his head in shame.

A group of guys and girls dressed in their bathing suits passed by. One guy had an inner tube around his waist while a woman in a red bikini was holding a giant inflatable duck.

As soon as the woman in the red bikini saw Jess, she was smitten. "Oh my god, I love those glasses!"

"Thanks, they were a ground score," she replied honestly.

The group of pool-goers cracked up in laughter. When it died down, Red Bikini complimented her, "Wow, you have really nice tits."

Jess looked down at her chest.

"Oh my god, thank you!"

Then Red Bikini asked, "Are they real?"

Jess laughed. "Yes, my boobs are 100% organic." Then she added, "Got them from my Mother."

Red Bikini gasped in mock excitement. "Can she get me a pair?"

Jess laughed so hard She almost dropped her beer. "Sorry, but they're a family heirloom." She used her free hand to push her left breast up, making her large, natural boobs look even bigger. "And I plan on passing these down to my daughter if I have kids."

Red Bikini feigned her extreme disappointment. "Okay, well if you change your mind come find me and I'll gladly take them off your hands - or in my hands!" She blew her a kiss and they continued on their way.

The next group of people to walk by were, to Jess's surprise, also all completely nude. Three women and two men walked down the dirt path without a shred of clothing other than the sunglasses worn by two of them - one of the men and a woman who wore Aviators.

Each of them was holding a towel. As soon as they saw Jess, a woman with long blonde hair that went all the way to her ass (which, Jess noted, was disappointingly flat). As soon as Jess saw her massive Double D tits or very possibly much bigger, she felt like her own breasts were small in comparison.

"Did you just get back from the shower?" the blonde with huge tits asked Jess.

"There is a shower?" She asked, incredulous.

She laughed, not knowing if Jess was serious or not. She quickly understood that Jess knew nothing about any shower.

"Yeah, it's an awesome co-ed shower right in front of one of the stages," She explained. "I just thought because you were sunbathing that you had just come back from the shower."

Jess pondered this. "Oh, that's awesome. That actually sounds really nice."

"Yeah!" The blonde woman smiled an authentic smile and said with a sugary voice, "I love that you're so comfortable with your nudity, you should come with us!" The invitation was also authentic.

"Thanks, but I should probably wait for my friends to get up first. But I'll definitely see you down there!"

"I hope so!"

As they walked off, Jess got a good look at them. Both of the men were lean and muscled. The other two women, aside from the blonde she spoke with, had tiny breasts, although they seemed to suit them pretty well.

A few of them had tattoos, mostly of writing that was too small for Jess to read. Jess noticed as they were walking away that every single member of their nudist group of 5 were sporting some level of pubic hair. With one of the women with small boobs having a full, untamed bush.

Hippies, Jess thought, *hardcore hippies, one and all.*

She finished her beer. By her fourth beer, she was growing impatient, frustrated, and hot. And this shower suddenly sounded like a really refreshing idea.

She set her beer down and ducked back in the tent to see why Allison and Josh were still sleeping. But no amount of beer could have prepared her for what she saw when she went back inside the tent.

She drew the zipper to the main entrance flap all the way up to get some air circulating in the hot tent that otherwise trapped the heat from the sun like a sauna.

She found Josh and Allison's naked bodies still lying on the air mattress where she had left them.

When she got up over an hour ago.

Both of them still had their eyes closed. Josh's chest was pressed flat against Allison's back, and they both lay on their sides facing the same direction. Josh's arm closest to the bed lay out stretched in front of him. Allison laid her head on his bicep, like a pillow. Josh's other hand was wrapped around Allison's breast, pulling her closely to his chest. Allison's arms mirrored that of Josh's, with one stretched in front of her and the other covering the top of his hand over her breast.

Jess's eyes slowly moved down their torsos which were so close that she wasn't sure where her boyfriend's flesh stopped and where her best friend's body began. They were spooning, exactly like how Josh and Jess would start their days out spooning in bed.

And exactly like how Josh and Jess liked to spoon every morning, Josh slowly and intimately slid his fully erect cock in and out of Allison's pussy at a casual rhythm.

Seeing this made Jess drop her beer. It splattered on the ground with a loud clink that caused Josh and Allison to open their eyes. Josh stopped fucking Allison but didn't pull out.

They both looked up at Jess, standing there, naked, with their jaws hanging slack.

Allison continued to hold Josh's hand on her left tit for a few awkward moments.

No one moved.

Jess saw from the suddenly terrified look on Josh's face that he knew he was in trouble. But still, he didn't pull his dick out of her best friend's pussy.

Jess could feel tears welling up in the corners of her eyes. Before she started crying, she turned and walked back out the tent.

As she stepped out to the light of the day, a thought occurred to her. She was with her boyfriend all night when he was fucking her.

Not only that, but she encouraged it.

In fact, if it weren't for her approval, Josh never would have fucked Allison in the first place.

Somewhere in the back of her head, a voice was screaming at her that she was being irrational that she was being a silly, emotional, possessive, drunk little girl who had no right to be mad at her boyfriend for fucking her best friend.

But that didn't make it hurt any less.

Then she knew why. What she saw him doing to Allison - she felt like that was *their* thing.

She immediately dismissed this and laughed out loud. You can't *own* a certain sexual position.

She began laughing and cackling. The people who were walking by and saw her standing there naked and laughing maniacally surely thought she must have been an escaped mental patient.

Josh came running out of the tent without even waiting for his massive erection to go down. He put his hands on the back of Jess's shoulders in an attempt to comfort her.

"Oh my god, baby, I am so sorry!" He started. She could tell from the shaking tone of his voice the way it was about to crack that he was authentically distraught.

Good, Jess thought to herself. *Let him sweat.*

"I honestly thought that was you, Jess. You have to believe me, I was half asleep."

She turned around, stood up on her tippy toes and planted a kiss on his lips to shut him up.

"I know. I believe you." She saw Allison standing in the doorway of the tent. A look of terrified sorrow plastered on her face. Allison looked like she was about to burst into tears. She looked like she had just lost her best friend.

Jess forced a smile in her direction. "It's okay. I'm not mad."

Allison's frown did not fade. Jess walked over to her equally nude friend, stepped over a pool of spilled beer on the rug at her feet, and embraced her in a bear hug, pressing their boobs squished together tightly. Jess knew this would make Allison smile. When she pulled back from the hug, she saw that it did.

"Wow, you've really been up partying, huh?" Allison raised an accusative eyebrow, desperate to change the subject from Josh's infidelity.

Jess giggled and her giggle turned into a hiccup. This did not help her case. "Maybe a bit." Then she turned to Josh and punched him in the shoulder. "Why didn't you pack any waters, like I asked? There is only beer in the cooler!"

Josh shrugged. "What are you talking about? I bought a shit ton of waters."

"That would be my fault." At that moment, Jon walked out of his tent dressed in, of all things, a plush navy blue bath robe.

He walked into the common area and immediately his gaze fell upon Jess and Allison. She couldn't help but feel like Jon was eye fucking her without her consent. She suddenly felt very self-conscious and folded her arms over her breasts, covering her nipples.

Seeing this, Allison did the same.

"Damn, Josh! I had no idea you were hung with a horse cock." Jon pointed at Josh's dick and laughed. "Do you have a license to carry that thing?"

"Eyes up here, buddy!" Josh, with all of his confidence, was never one to be embarrassed. "How was your night?"

A wicked smile appeared on Jon's face. "Wish I could remember!" Then he returned his vulgar gaze back to panting. Jess's nude body up and down. "I had to toss all your waters in the trash to make room for more beers."

Without breaking his eyes off of Jess, he walked to the cooler and took out a beer.

"Sorry," Jon opened the beer and gulped down half. "But you're all welcome to as much beer as you like."

Jess suddenly wanted to be out from under Jon's gaze, and she thought of the perfect excuse to do so.

"Josh!" Jess started without unfolding her arms. "Someone told me about a shower they have here that's right in front of one of the stages!"

Josh turned around to look at Jess. For a second, she thought he was going to knock the beer out of Jon's hands with his massive cock, even flaccid.

"I could use a shower," Josh smiled, trying to comfort Jess. As soon as he saw her and Allison covering their breasts in front of Jon, he knew what was going on.

"It's badass, dude!" Jon smiled a lascivious grin. "Isabel and I just came from there!"

"That explains the robe," Josh said at the same time Jess thought it.

This is why they were such a perfect couple, she thought.

Jon at last turned towards the dirt road. "If you keep going up this road and turn left at the festival entrance, just keep going straight and you'll see the shower stage on your right hand side." He gestured with the beer in his hand.

Jess wasted no time walking down the path where he was pointing.

"Thank you," she muttered weakly to Jon as she passed him by.

Allison followed closely at Jess's heels. "Thank you," she muttered without looking Jon in the eye.

Jon craned his neck as the two women scurried down the dirt trail and around the corner so he could get one last look at their rear ends.

"Damn, Josh! You didn't tell me you were hitting both of those tight little asses! I had no idea you were such a fucking pimp, bro!"

Jon put his fist out for Josh to bump, which he did.

"Yeah, neither did I, man. It kind of just happened," Josh shrugged.

"Hey, before you go, can I smell your fingers?" Jon asked.

Josh laughed.

Jon did not.

"Listen, I better go catch up with the ladies," Josh hooked a thumb in their direction. "Can't let two beautiful women run around a festival completely naked. Lots of creeps running around here, after all."

Josh turned to leave without waiting on a response from Jon.

Over his shoulder he heard him say, "Don't hurt Thor's Hammer in the shower!"

As Josh turned the corner, he heard Jon cracking up at his own joke.

He was walking so fast that he almost ran into Jess and Allison, who were standing just around the corner and a little up the dirt road, just far enough away so that Jon couldn't see or hear them.

Both Allison and Jess wore a frown and were still covering their breasts, but when they saw that it was just Josh, coming down the trail without Jon, their demeanor changed completely. Their worried frowns turned to excited smiles. Their defensive body language turned to eager acceptance as their arms fell to their sides.

"What was that about?" Allison was the first one to speak.

Josh kept walking, leading them down the path to the shower stage. He knew it would be a long walk and in addition to wanting a break from the hot afternoon sun, he also wanted to limit his time walking around in public stark nude.

"Listen, Jon is my co-worker, but he and I were roomates back in college. Part of me still thinks he is stuck in that fratboy mindset. It's been years since we've hung out like this. I had no idea he was such a creep."

Jess and Allison just stared at Josh for a moment as they walked, barefoot, down the dirt path with other festival goers, most of whom didn't give them so much as a second look.

Josh had basically just explained all of the questions that Jess had for him.

"So, you felt that, too?" she asked.

"I'm so sorry you girls feel uncomfortable around him. I'll have a talk with him about it later. For now, let's just enjoy a nice afternoon shower in front of a bunch of strangers!"

Allison and Jess chuckled. Jess adored her boyfriend's sense of humor. "Well, we can also enjoy Jon's beers while we're at it!" Allison held up four beers - two in each hand. Jess was aghast.

"Ally, honey, where were you hiding those?"

"Like herself, Allison wore nothing but a pair of fishnet stockings!" she said dismissively, handing a beer to Josh and one to Jess. She winked a hand at her friend. "Thanks, but I already had, like, three beers. Plus, I spilt one with the tug in our tent earlier, remember?"

Allison shrugged, handing the other beer to Josh. Him and Allison drank the cold beers quickly while they walked.

As they walked the road to the shower stage, they could hear the trap music from the main stage, and another star that was playing drum and bass. The three of them dance-walked back and forth across the width of the road, trying to get other people to dance with them.

When they got bored with that they tried to get strangers to decide which of the three of them were the hottest. Jess saw another nude couple headed to the shower stage and one of them joined in.

Unlike the hippie nudist that Jess had met earlier, this couple was strikingly gorgeous and surprisingly well-manicured. "Hi, my name is Cherette, but my rave name is Cheetch!"

The gentleman with dark features introduced himself, with parted black hair, a handsome manly face with just enough stubble to darken his full jaw and chilling brown eyes that gleamed in the sun so much that it appeared to Jess as though they were sparkling.

He was much smaller than Josh, but equally lean and maybe even more muscular for his size. His forearms were covered with tattoos of typical guy tattoos - skulls, flames, cars, naked women. And Jess had to pry her eyes from his well-defined six pack ab show casers and well hung package.

She would only sneak a peak when she was sure that both Cheetch and Josh were looking the other way, and even then, she could feel her face visibly redden when she caught a glimpse.

One look at Allison and it was obvious that she was finding it incredibly difficult to not stare as well. Jess had to elbow Allison in the tits to remind her to stop to stop staring more than once.

"This is my beautiful partner, Chyvonne," Cheetch said by way of introduction to the woman walking beside him, holding his hand.

While chewing on a piece of gum, she said, "Howdy, ya'll can call me Crystal. I go by my rave name, too."

Her face was bright, bubbly, and brimming with a tide of content, self-assured confidence that Jess felt a twinge of jealousy for.

She was surprised when she heard Crystal talk—She did not expect that southern twangy voice to come from someone like her.

Crystal had bright red hair that flowed to just past her shoulders and a pale complexion with little freckles dotting her entire body. She had the vivid green eyes of green lush Irish fields—something they had in common—Crystal's face looked like she had never stopped smiling even for a moment her entire life.

That's not all she had in common with Jess—her ample breasts appeared to be about the same size as her own—a natural D-cup—with small, quarter-sized nipples that stood at attention in the warm summer breeze.

Jess was very much impressed by Crystal's behind. It looked like her ass was considerably bigger than both hers and Allison's. For someone so pale, Jess thought, She has the amazing ass of a black girl in a trap music video.

And she told her so.

"Oh my God, Crystal, you have such a nice ass!" Crystal, still chewing her gum, looked over her shoulder as if nothing to it, for the first time ever.

"Oh, thank yew so much," she said with even more twang than before.

Then she let go of Cheetch's hand and turned around, so her ass was pointed at both Jess and Allison, with Cheetch and Josh standing in front of her. Crystal bent over, and put her hands on her knees, and started bouncing her ass up and down.

As she twerked her ass cheeks up, Jess could see her pink, hairless pussy in between her legs. Then when her ass cheeks fell back to planet earth, it was gone. Watching her twerk was like a peep show peek-a-boo that made Jess's jaw drop.

Her crazy ass was literally stopping traffic along the festival walkway as everyone walking in either direction stopped what they were doing, ended their conversations, and started cheering Crystal on. Cheetch wore a proud smile and Josh was clapping along with everyone else, but Jess and Allison were mesmerized.

Almost as soon as everyone started whooping and hollering, Crystal stopped and waved her hand dismissively, as if to say, "ain't nothing!" Even long after she stopped, there were still creeps about, following close behind her staring at her ass.

Crystal humbly took Cheetch's hand once more and the five of them kept walking. "That was incredible," Jess finally found her words, "Can you show me how to do that?"

Again, Crystal waved her hand dismissively. "Oh, ain't you sweeter than a bee in tea!" Jess and Allison exchanged looks of confusion. "I tell you what, I'll teach you girls how to twerk when we get to the shower stage, if y'all let me wash y'all titties." She pointed an index finger, as if she were counting both Jess and Allison's boobs. Jess was a little taken aback. She did not expect this sweet southern belle to say something bordering on vulgar. "What?" Crystal changed defensive. "Y'all got some really nice titties. And if I'm going to teach y'all to twerk like that, that is my price!" She said firmly. Cheetch was wearing an ear-to-ear smile. Josh seemed to find this interaction equally amusing.

"Hell yeah you can wash my tits!" Jess pushed up her milky white breasts, pressing them together to make them look even bigger than they were.

"My boobs are pretty filthy, so you'll really have to get in there." Allison smiled, looking down at her own breasts, which were clearly the smallest among all of the women, but suited her very well.

"Then, I want to wash yours, too!" she was referring to Crystal.

"Whoops, sorry, darlin, but that's his job." She pointed at Cheetch.

Allison suddenly looked very disheartened, like her puppy got stomped on.

Jess knew that she was slightly insecure because of her breast size, despite Jess constant reassurance that her tits were world-class.

But because of this, Allison had developed an obsession with big breasts—and specifically with Jess's big breasts—and although she never said anything to her friend, she knew Allison fawned over her supple boobs at every chance she get.

"Ally, could you please wash my boobs, too?" Jess asked.

This simple gesture put a smile back on her face.

"Okay!" she said brightly, then took a large pull on the vodka bottle before turning to Crystal.

"Want some?" Allison waved the bottle of Grey Goose in front of Crystal.

"Oh, thank yew," She took the bottle in hand and poured a bit in her mouth like it was water before offering it to Cheetch, who politely declined.

It wasn't long before the entire bottle was gone between the three nude women and Jess was feeling pretty buzzed.

Jess went back to getting strangers to decide who among them was the hottest.

She stopped a group of three nerdy looking guys, because Jess thought that they looked like they had only seen a pair of tits before in porn and she wanted to give them some thing memorable to think about.

"You three pick which of us is the hottest?" Jess smiled, then struck a pose with her hair brushed over her shoulder as she bent slightly at the waist so her ass was sticking out and her breasts dangling forward.

To her surprise, the three nerdy looking guys wasted no time in judging them.

"Well, you're obviously the hot brunette of the group," one said to Jess.

Another pointed to Allison, "She is the sexy blonde one."

Then Crystal, "She is the red head smoke show!"

The three nerds all nodded their heads in agreement. "Yeah, are you girls, like, Charlie's Angels or something?"

The girls all busted up laughing.

No matter how many people she asked, the answer was always the same—all three of them were individually the hottest of their respective hair color.

With the shower stage in sight, Jess stopped one more person and asked them who among the three of them were the hottest.

"Well, you clearly have the best set of tits," He pointed at Crystal. "She has the best ass," then Allison, "And her, well, fuck, she has the whole package going for her... Damn, what do you say, gorgeous?"

Jess was happy the stranger singled out Allison. That was the whole point in her engaging people in this exercise—to boost Allison's self-esteem.

Crystal abruptly pulled one of the women who had just come from the shower with a towel wrapped around herself, and asked her the same question about Josh and Cheetch.

"Excuse me," Jess found her southern twang alluring to no end, "which of these fine gentlemen would you say is the hottest?"

She moved behind Cheetch with all the grace of Vivanna White. "EXHIBIT A!"

And in an instant she floated over behind Josh, "or EXHIBIT B?"

Holding her towel in place over her ample cleavage, the woman put her other hand to her chin, deep in thought. She grinned as her eyes groped up and down over Josh and Cheetch's entire bodies, a few times, clearly enjoying taking in their masculine nudity.

"Well, they both have really nice butts."

That was true, Jess thought. They most certainly did.

"And they both have big old dicks."

This was also true.

"Damn, and both of you have that six pack muscle thing going for you!"

Jess was also enjoying objectifying both men.

"But he is bigger," She pointed to Josh. "But I do like me some dark meat!" She pointed to Cheetch, which Jess thought made no sense because Cheetch was only slightly more tan than Josh.

And then, after all of that, she finally turned back to Crystal and says, "I don't know, but I sure could sit here and look at them all day long!"

And then she turns back to the guys, who started making goofy muscle-man poses, and she very obviously starts staring right at their dicks.

"But if you guys are headed into the shower I might just go back in myself." The girls laughed, but were unsure if she was serious or not. "Anyway, thanks for making a deposit in my spank bank!" And then she trotted off with a renewed confidence.

The five of them started to dance-walk their way to the Shower Stage. Jess was beaming that she was able to facilitate their brimming with confidence right before they all reached the Shower.

The entrance to the shower stage was a gigantic wooden cut out of a water drop. They passed a wall of cubbies and something resembling a coat check, where people kept things. "Um, were we supposed to bring clothes?" Allison asked when She saw the cubbies. Every one looked at one another, confused and shrugged.

"Fuck it!" Josh said, leading the way into the stage area, which was essentially one huge tarp on the ground covered in soap and bubbles.

The DJ at the Stage was showering them in up beat, booming, shaking House music beats. There were two people waiting by the entrance to shower them in bubbly suds. All three of the women yelled in glee as soon as they stepped into the shower stage. Like any other stage at the music festival, it was a densely-packed afternoon set full of nude and partially nude dancers, all looking like they were having the time of their lives.

Jess was taken aback by how awesome the glory and brilliance of the shower stage truly was. They took one of the most annoying and troublesome things at any music festival—taking a shower—and made it a fun experience that everyone could enjoy. Jess had never in her life seen anything like it. Dozens of beautiful naked people around her own age, dancing and having a good time, completely comfortable in their own skin and not at all self conscious.

The three girls squealed with glee as they found the nearest foam cannon to jump in front of, with Josh and Cheetch closely in tow behind them.

It was a veritable feast of flesh for the eyes.

Jess couldn't turn around in a circle without seeing bouncing butts dancing and shaking to the beat in every direction. Booty shaking and sudsy bouncing boobs gyrated against one another in the suds, everyone smiling and having a good time. To both the right and left of the stage, foam cannons blasted dancers from the front to the back.

Crystal, Jess, Allison, Josh and Cheetch all got the front of their bodies doused head to toe in soapy bubbles. Jess was jumping up and down screaming along with the rest of them having the time of her life.

When she saw Josh dancing in her peripherals, Jess instinctively ran her hands down his chest, with his entire body soaped up she could feel every muscle against his hard body. Jess ran both her hands down his chest, clawing his abdomen, tagging at his tree trunk of a cock as she bent at the waist, poking her ass out. As she walked her finger tips up over Josh's muscles, she felt someone slap her ass HARD.

As she looked over her shoulder with a lascivious smile and bubbles all in her hair, she saw Allison "whooing" behind her, grabbing her hips and ramming her pussy into her rear end, pretending to fuck her doggystyle.

Turning around to "whoo" back in Allison's face, Jess straightened up, then pressed her back into Josh's chest.

He grabbed her by the hips and started bumping and grinding behind her.

Meanwhile, Jess poked her chest out in front of Allison and shook her shoulders, making her enormous tits shake back and forth, side to side.

Allison caught hold of them, trying to take as much of Jess's ample breasts into her tiny hands as possible and gave them a firm squeeze.

Jess winced—it kind of hurt. Jess knocked Allison's hands away by slapping her wrists.

The look on Allison's face was mortified. Jess thought to give her friends tits a consolation squeeze instead. As Jess was feeling up Allison, Crystal walks over to the two of them with Cheetch hugging her from behind with his hands on her boobs.

"What the fuck is going on here," Jess thought to her self.

"Y'all ready to learn how to twerk?" She screamed loudly so that the two women could hear her over the loud music.

Only then did Jess realize how close they were to the speakers, and that the foam blasters were located next to the speakers. Before Jess could answer, all of them got pelted with even more soap. The second time around, it was not as fun and more of an awful surprise.

"Can we move a little to the back first?"

At Allison's suggestion, the three women shook the soap from their eyes, nodded in agreement, then pushed their way past a dozen gyrating naked bodies towards the middle-back of the stage. Where they found a clearing in the shower stage.

All five of them were still covered in white foam. "Don't you want to wash our titties before you teach us to twerk?" Allison asked Crystal, presenting her sudsy boobs to hers.

"Nah, I'll collect my payment from ya'll down the road," Crystal waved her hand dismissively, sending white foam flying. "Now, show me what yew gals got."

She assumed the standard twerking position.

'Now, stick ya'll's booty's out like you're bending over to milk a cow. Goode. Now get your hands on your knees like you're picking the brambles from ya'll's yard."

The girls copied what they had seen Crystal do earlier, but exchanged very confused looks.

"I'm just messin' with ya'll. I'm from Nashville. I've never even been on a farm."

They all giggled for a moment. Crystal smiled an innocent smile as she chewed her gum and continued explaining, demonstrating.

"Now, just arch yer back an' pop yer hips. Like dis. Slowly now," she said, "Slowly at first, ya'll."

Both Jess and Allison imitated Crystal and although neither of them had quite the same caliber of booty as Crystal.

Both Jess and Allison unquestionably had ass. Allison, more so than Jess, although both of the women had frequently heard others-most commonly refer to their booties as "cute and bouncy" and/or "Bubble Butts," both by their significant others as well as by complete strangers.

Jess would classify what Crystal was working with as a "Monster Dumpar" or "Crazy Ass." Certainly in anoth

er level than their own, however, they all had what was most commonly referred to as "Incredible asses for three white girls," or at least, those were the words they heard most frequently from strangers as they were learning how to twerk.

"Gewd! Now yer gettin' it!" Crystal cheered them on as Jess and Allison gradually increased the speed of their ass popping twerking.

As a small crowd of nudists began to encircle them, Crystal jumped in and the three of them danced in a circle, pushing their asses together and twerking right next to each other, giggling the entire time.

After a few songs of incessant booty shaking, the three girls were tired and ready, happy to take a break from the dancing.

The five of them hosed off all of their soap and went to hang out in the very rear of the Shower Stage.

"Hey, take a look around here. Are any of you getting weird vibes?" Josh asked the group.

Jess looked around the back of the stage was filled with more naked people, some much older than the dancers toward the front. But some of them didn't even look like they were wet.

"I'm getting kind of a creepy vibe back here, too." Allison's comment mirrored Jess's own feelings.

"Me too," she said.

Then Cheetch pointed it out. "Yo, the freakin' creepers are just peepin' on everyone else, dawg. They all just standing around eye fucking everyone while they shower." He held up a hand, gesturing to a group of twenty old guys lurking in the back.

"Shit aint right, mon. Yo, lets get out of here, Crystal." He took Crystal's hand, and immediately started for the exit.

"Yeah, I think we should leave as well," Josh said.

"Yeah," Jess and Allison said simultaneously.

Once they were aware of the prying eyes, dancing naked in front of a bunch of strangers was no longer erotic. It was creepy, and the three women did their best to cover up their private parts until they cleared the Shower Stage exit.

Crystal let out a big sigh as they left, visibly leaving the stress of the creepy vibes behind. She smiled and flapped her arms up and down like a penguin.

"AH! Well, I feel much more refreshed now."

Her positivity was infectious and soon Jess found her self smiling just as wide.

"Ey, you guys seem pretty cool..." Cheetch spoke up before anyone else could. "You want to come to our camp and get high?"

"Yeah!"

"Hell yes!"

"Oh my God, Please."

The three of them agreed all at once.

"Ey, cool, man. Yeah, I've got some sativa and dabs and stuff back at our tent this way." Cheetch pointed ambiguously toward all of the tents, but they were all off following him anyway.

"Shouldn't we stop by our camp and grab some clothes first?" Allison asked as if she just realized for the first time that all she had on were green fishnet stockings from yesterday, which were now completely soaked.

"Nah, you don't need no stinkin' clothes. Clothes are overrated." It was Cheetch who waved his hand dismissively this time. Jess could see where Crystal got it from.

"Yeah, I have a few things I know would look just so hot on ya'll." Crystal took Jess and Allison by the hands, walking faster with renewed vigor.

As Jess passed Josh on the dirt path, she gave him a side long glance that said, "HELP!"

"That's kind of you Crystal, but we can only stay for like, a hit or two, or a few minutes. There is this one performance that I think Jess is dying to see today," Josh, to her rescue.

"Nah, what you want to see in the afternoon Jess? Everyone knows all the best sets are always after sundown." Cheetch smiled at Jess as he noticeably picked up his pace.

"Yeah, Jess, we have the set list back at our camp. I'll show yew." Crystal's smile widened.

Dear Lord, Jess said a silent prayer, *please don't let these two hedonistic stoners murder me today. I'm too young and beautiful to die. And also, I actually haven't seen the one set I'm looking forward to this weekend.*

Chapter 7: Hedonistic Hippies

Cheetch and Crystal lead them around the campgrounds with all of the tents (including their own) and to a part of the festival that they had never been to before.

With every passing second, with every step, Jess was more sure that this couple would try to murder them.

As Crystal tightened her grip on Jess's wrist, the only thing that kept her from screaming and turning to run for the hills was the thought that Josh was by her side to protect her. She knew that nothing bad would happen as long as she was with Josh. He made her feel safe, and no amount of homicidal hedonists could change that.

"Ey, our camp is right around here."

"Yep, almost there, ya'll."

The two sounded more excited than they should be to get high with strangers, stoners or not.

"Yeah, so, it's not much, but this is the camp Crystal and I bring with us wherever we go to music festivals, you know. And you guys eem pretty cool, so our camp is yer camp."

As the five of them stepped around a pair of canopies, they came to a clearing with a silver Airstream trailer, complete with an awning, grill, and outdoor kitchen.

Audible gasps came from Jess, Josh, and Allison.

"This... Is this an Airstream camper?" Josh asked, fawning his eyes over every bit of shiny chrome.

"Yeah, you know, I wanted something big enough for Crystal and me, plus if we want to entertain guests, you know," Cheetch actually did speak exactly the way you would expect Cheetch Marin to sound.

"Bruh, these things are like two hundred thousand dollars."

"Ey, I'm no dummy, mon. I got it used for like a hundred eighty."

"Thousand Dollars?" Josh was aghast.

"Cheetch, what do you do for work?" Jess asked.

Cheetch emerged from the Airstream with a bong in one hand and a dab rig in the other.

He looked at Josh and shrugged, "I sell drugs."

"Oh, okay," Josh seemed content with that answer.

The five of them got into the Airstream and Cheetch ushered them to sit at a bench style table.

"Don't you want to put down like, I don't

know, cushions or a table cloth?" Josh asked.

Again, Cheetch shrugged this away, "For why? We all just got out of the shower."

"Ah, boy." Jess, and Josh piled onto one side of the booth table and Cheetch and Crystal sitting across from them on the other side.

Cheetch packed the bong full of pungent sticky greens and handed it to Allison first. "For our guests," He said simply.

Allison lit the bong with a butane torch provided to her by Crystal, cleared the stem, cleared the chamber, then a moment later she was coughing up the sweet smelling smoke everywhere.

Handing the bong to Jess next, she repeated the process. Then Josh.

Meanwhile, Jess almost didn't realize that while they were passing around the bong, Crystal and Cheetch were ripping dabs.

Every time they cleared the bong, Cheetch just kept adding more weed to the bowl and handing it back to either Jess or Allison.

The dab rig went around, too, but after only one hit of wax, Jess thought that she would never stop coughing.

Suddenly, everyone was laughing and laughing and Jess couldn't remember what they were all laughing at.

Zoning out, Jess kept staring at Crystal's tits. No matter what happened, she just couldn't seem to look away. Even when it became very clear that everyone else at the table were very aware that Jess was starting at Crystal's chest.

Cheetch did another bong rip, and although the door to the Airstream was still open, the room was thick with smoke.

Jess heard smacking sounds, then through the smoke she realized what it was. Across the table, she was watching Cheetch and Crystal passionately make out.

And then Cheetch was sucking on Crystal's nipples and she threw her head back and started moaning.

Jess was suddenly aware of some thing warm and tingling between her legs. Jess blinked and Allison was sitting across from her, biting her lip and playing with her pussy underneath the table.

Jess blinked and it was Josh sitting across from her. She didn't see his mouth move, but he was asking her what they were doing there on this Airstream with a complete stranger when they could be in bed, when he could be making love to her the way she likes.

Then Jess blinked and Crystal was leaning over the table asking her if she was alright.

"What?" Jess raised her head, breathing heavy.

"I asked if yew want to try on some of my clothes, darlin'?"

"Oh..." Jess looked to her left.

Allison stared at her.

On her right. Josh stared at her.

"Oh... Yeah,"

Crystal laughed, "Well, okay, let's go."

They all got up out of the booth and Crystal showed them to the bedroom of the Airstream while Cheetch asked Josh if he could talk to him about something in the other room.

The bedroom of the Airstream was laden with elegant and modern wooden paneling with a shelf top where the headboard should have been and two pine wood cupboards above that.

The queen mattress was low to the ground, but made neatly. Aside from the bed, there was barely enough room for a set of pine drawers off to the right side, opposite the entrance, and a 65" Roku flat screen TV mounted facing the bed.

The red, orange, and pine wood paneling motifs of the room, similar to the rest of the interior of the Airstream, had a very 70's vibe, but more modern luxuries Crystal lead the two women by hand to the set of dressers and sat on the bed.

She delicately slid the bottom most drawer open and began rummaging through it. Jess saw that Crystal did indeed have quite the cache of rave clothes. Neither Jess nor Allison said anything while Crystal hummed a little tune and began separating the clothes into small piles on the bed.

Jess watched her as she separated tops from bottoms and untangled some of the fishnet outfits.

"No! I don't do that." Jess turned her head to the other room where she heard Josh in a heated conversation with Cheetch. "You'll have to ask them!"

He sounded angry. Jess wanted to get up and see what was going on, but Crystal used her thumb and index finger to move Jess's chin back in her direction, acting as if the disturbance never happened while trying to get Jess's attention back on her.

"Now wouldn't you look good in just about any of these little numbers?"

Jess turned her head back to where Josh and Cheetch were having some sort of argument, but Jess couldn't make out what they were saying.

Again, Crystal placed her fingertips on Jess's cheek and turned her face back towards the clothes she had piled up on the bed. Jess was finding it difficult to concentrate.

"You pick," she said and smiled politely. Inside, she was worried about Josh.

This was apparently exactly what Crystal wanted to hear because less than a moment later she was on the bed, sitting directly behind with a white bikini top with Hot Pink trim and straps.

"This would look just fabulous with your fishnets, darlin'."Crystal had her hands on Jess boobs, holding the top in place with one hand as she tied the strings with the other - a feat that Jess knew was certainly not easy.

Jess looked down. The bikini top was several sizes too small and her breasts poured out of the sides. She could easily see her own nipples through the white fabric, however, the Hot pink color of the trim was the exact same shade as her fishnets.

Crystal gasped "Oh my word! That looks so gewd on yew! Oh, and for your little blonde friend,"

Crystal pulled another bikini top from the pile. This one was black with the same shade of green trim as Allison's fishnets, but it was even smaller than Jess', and would certainly never fit on Crystal herself.

Jess couldn't help but wonder where, then, she got it from.

As she held the top over Allison's breasts, Crystal gave them a little squeeze before tying it around her neck and back. When she was done, Crystal leaned back to admire her handy work.

"Oh, yew two look so dang hot!" Allison, like Jess, was literally spilling out of the bikini top that was obviously made for someone several sizes smaller.

"What about you?" Jess asked as she stared at Crystal's large, freckled breasts.

At that moment, before Crystal had a chance to answer, Josh and Cheetch walked in, both still as naked as when they left the shower.

Josh had this look on his face that looked like he had just lost a bet. Cheetch wasted no time in looking Crystal in the eye and giving her a curt nod.

Less than a moment later, before she had time to react, Crystal had roped her arms around Allison's neck and started making out with her.

Jess looked from Allison, to Crystal, to Josh, who was now climbing across the bed towards her. Jess wanted to ask him what was going on but before she had the chance to, his lips were on hers, his tongue in her mouth, his hands on her neck and her cheek, kissing her tenderly.

Smoking all of that weed left Jess in a state of confusion. She didn't know what was going on around her and everything was happening like a dream. But more than confused, the weed had left her high and horny, and kissing Josh felt really good, so she didn't stop to question it and she didn't slow down.

In fact, whatever was happening, she leaned into it. This sudden burst of intimacy felt so good.

Suddenly, Jess was thinking about watching Josh fuck her friend this morning, about all of the lustful looks she got when she was sitting under the canopy, about all of the people staring at her, that told her how hot she was, she was thinking about all of the booty shaking and bouncing titties and flying cocks at the shower stage, and about the creepy old men hanging in the back, starting at her longingly like they would cut off their left hand just for a chance to fuck her.

All of the day's events flashed through her head all at once, filling her with this primal, animalistic need. And as she kissed Josh back, biting his lip, pushing her tongue as deep into his mouth as it would go, she ran one hand through his hair on the back of his head, pulling his face into hers.

With her other hand, she grabbed Josh's shoulder and pushed him back onto the bed with all of her might. She was on top of him, her legs wrapped around the outside of his thighs.

Her hands found him, their fingers laced together intimately as she pushed down hard, pinning him to the bed, holding him down.

Her breasts, popping out of her new white and pink bikini top, pressed up against Josh's chest. Jess turned her head side to side so she could switch up her approach, making out ferociously with her boyfriend.

She unconsciously fucked side to side, up and down. Jess's moist slit slid up Josh's lower abdomen; she was grateful she didn't put her panties back on this morning, and almost regretted letting Crystal put a top on her tits. Clearly aroused by Jess's sudden ravenous desire, Josh's cock stiffened.

Although he couldn't take hold of Jess's hips with her pinning both of his hands restrained to the bed with Jess's legs parted at either side of his hips, all he had to do was thrust his hips up in order to rub the tip of his hard dick along Jess's pussy.

Her womanly juices helped guide his member into her tight, little hole. Her pussy wrapped tightly around Josh's thick cock, conforming to every inch of flesh, molding tightly around every vein.

The surprise of her boyfriend's huge cock pushing into her made her jaw go slack. Her breath caught in her throat. She let go of his hands pressed against the bed, all she could focus on was how good his huge cock felt inside her and her pussy tightly wrapped around him.

His dick seemed to stun her, leaving her temporally paralyzed. In that instant, Josh swung his hands around to Jess's hips, lifting her, guiding her, so that he might plunge his dick deeper and deeper still inside her as she sat there atop him, panting.

Allison fell on her back, bouncing on the bed right next to where Josh was laying, and Crystal wasted no time crawling on top of her.

The two women were making out much like how Jess and Josh were moments before they started fucking. Jess heard Crystal making small, guttural moans into Allison's mouth as she jerked back and forth.

When Jess looked behind her, she was not surprised to see Cheetch with his dick in Crystal's ass. He was squeezing one of her cheeks while slapping the other.

Because her face was right next to Crystal's, she heard her whisper into Allison's ear, "Do you want to get fucked?"

When Allison gave no answer, Crystal asked her again, louder, and through her own moans of pleasure.

This time, Allison replied with a weak, "Yeah," although she looked confused as to how Crystal was going to fuck her, Jess knew exactly what she meant. Crystal once more asked for her consent.

"Do you want to get fucked?"

This time Allison's answer was "Fuck me. Yes, fuck me." It came out as a demand.

Jess didn't have to look behind her in that instant to realize that Cheetch pulled his dick out of Crystal's ass and started fucking Ally hard in her tight, little pussy.

Jess knew first hand the look on Ally's face when she was getting her pussy worked over, and her being stoned seemed to accentuate all of her senses and kick her libido into overdrive. At least, that's the way it was for Jess.

After smoking more weed than she could remember, all of her bodily senses were heightened and she was more horny than she could ever remember being.

Once she got over her sexual hangup, Jess found that she was really enjoying getting fucked by her boyfriend while she watched her best friend getting fucked simultaneously.

This is just so hot, Jess thought.

Watching her friend getting the shit fucked out of her was turning her on in ways she didn't think possible.

Crystal was just sitting there on top of Allison, staring down at her and smiling. Although she was probably enjoying the view as much as Jess, it somehow bothered her that Crystal just sat there.

Jess suddenly felt like she was in a porno, and in the pornos, the girls never just sat around.

Jess thought that, if this were really a porno, Crystal would be getting her pussy eaten out right about now. Jess felt like she should be going down on Crystal while Josh was fucking her, maybe that was just because she was high, but she felt like that's what she was supposed to be doing right now.

Jess tugged on Crystal's shoulder, getting her attention, but how would she convey to her that she was supposed to be going down on her without words? She couldn't, even if that's how they did it in the porn movies.

"I want to eat your pussy." Jess leaned close and whispered in Crystal's ear.

After hearing this, a big, toothy grin appeared on Crystal's beautiful, freckled face.

She immediately flipped off the side of the bed to her left, then ran around the room gleefully to the side of the bed across from Jess, with Josh under her, still holding onto her waist, taking Jess from beneath her.

Crystal jumped on the bed and suddenly her face was right in front of Jess.

"I have a bright idea, darlin'." Her face lit up with a smile. Then she leaned in and planted a kiss on Jess's lips and crawled around the bed on all fours, like a dog desperate to earn a treat.

Jess leaned down horizontally to give Josh a big wet kiss, her tits pushed up firmly against his chest while he continued to rhythmically slide his cock back, stick in and out of her while giving her ass the occasional hard and loud *SLAP*.

When Jess looked up, Crystal was backing her massive, rap video booty up into her face like a dump truck.

And she continued to back that ass up until her swollen pussy found a new home right on Josh's face.

Jess felt a tinge of anger, but silenced it immediately. Crystal was a nice enough person and everyone deserved the right to carnal pleasure.

In her heart, she had enough confidence in her relationship with Josh to know that even if he ate a hundred pussies today-even if he fucked a thousand other women, she knew that he loved her and she loved him and that was what mattered above all else. And she was confident enough in their love to know that it could withstand anything. And she knew Josh well enough to know that there was no way he would be disloyal to her. Nor even give the time of day to those thousands of pussies.

Jess knew at the end of the day, there was only one pussy that he truly loved, and thankfully, it was firmly attached to Jess and currently being repeatedly filled with his own delicious cock. And that was why when she saw Crystal park her pussy right on Josh's face, she did not get mad.

In fact, she fully embraced it.

And so did Josh.

Even Crystal's enormous ass was covered in freckles, which gave her tight and smooth pussy an orange hue.

Jess immediately thought of a peach upon seeing what was between her legs. And as soon as Josh started gobbling up her peach cobbler, she cried out loud enough to get the attention of everyone in the room.

Jess knew how good Josh's expert tongue could work its way around a clit, she knew firsthand the power hidden in his mouth and what it could do.

And now Crystal did too.

After the initial shock of Josh's mouth in between her legs, Crystal started working up to twerking her fat ass back and forth, grinding her hips, rubbing her pussy in small circles all over his face. Seeing that luscious peach bouncing in front of her was all too alluring to Jess. To Josh's credit, he never once slowed down or changed his rhythm fucking Jess the entire time Crystal started twerking on his face.

The enticement was too much for Jess to stand. Without knowing what she was doing, she bent at the waist and dipped down to get a taste of the delicious bouncing peach before her. From her position. She was able to run her tongue where Josh's chin started.

Jess ran her soft, wet tongue into Crystal's vagina, wrapping her mouth around her pussy and pushing her tongue in as far as it would go. But that wasn't what she had her eye on. She continued to lick upward until her tongue ran around the rim of Crystal's asshole.

The way she cried out told Jess that she was not expecting this.

The way she moaned told her not to stop. Jess wanted to make her moan like that again and again.

With Josh's tongue whipping her clit, Jess started to lick Crystal's ass as well as she could for a moving target, but the sensation was so good that Crystal soon stopped twerking and started moaning even louder.

Jess had never eaten ass before, but she has had her ass eaten more times than she could remember. So she just did all of the same things to Crystal that Josh did to her when he was able to make her cum just by sticking a tongue in her ass.

And from the way Crystal was reacting, it was clearly working.

"Oh-Oh my Good!" Crystal was frozen, but her thighs were convulsing.

Jess immediately recognized the symptoms for what they were.

Multiple orgasms.

Just like how seeing other people butt naked sometimes have the odd effect of getting other people to take off their clothes, watching Crystal cum in front of her-sitting on her boyfriends face, with her tongue stuck in her ass, made Jess cum at that exact same moment.

"Oh fuck oh fuck oh fuck!" Jess cried.

Hearing her words, feeling her pussy tighten around his rock hard cock, Josh started to cum, too.

Jess could always tell when Josh was about to cum because he started to breathe a lot harder, which, even with a mouth full of pussy, she could easily spot his quickened breathing.

His other tell was that he always changed tempos right before he was about to cum — either much faster or much slower. While Josh was typically extremely skilled at keeping a consistent rhythm going when he was fucking, this time his thrusts became much deeper and much slower.

Also, Jess and Josh were so much in sync that they almost always came at the same time — unless Jess made it clear that she wanted to keep fucking. But without fail, every time Josh came, so would Jess. And right now, she could feel him filling her up with his white, hot love.

She savored every millisecond of their twin orgasms.

"Oh my God, oh my God. Oh fucking God," Jess looked over at Allison, whose bikini top had come off at some point, leaving her tits to bounce around freely.

She was on her back, rubbing her clit, with Cheetch holding one of her legs upright as he jackhammered her with his cock.

"I'm cumming!"Allison threw her head back, squinted her eyes, and rubbed her clit as fast as she could.

Jess's orgasm had just ended, but Allison's eyes looked so wide that she was actually jealous.

As Cheetch's breathing quickened, Jess watched him pull his dick out of Ally and stroke it until he shot one, two, three... ten ropes of cum directly on Ally's tits.

Holy fuck, Jess thought to herself, *that was so hot.*

As Allison lay in bed moaning softly, "Hmmmm, oh, hmmm, ohh," she still had her eyes closed as if she was reliving the orgasm she just had.

Allison idly started pushing her tits together and playing with all of the semen all over her chest.

"Ey, let me get you a towel. What did you say your name was again?" Cheetch said, going through the drawers until he produced an off-white towel and threw it at Ally.

"Hmmm, don't worry about it." Allison was still high on the afterglow of her orgasm, she made no haste as she wiped all the cum off of her.

Jess, meanwhile, got off the bed and was looking for her clothes, only to remember that she wasn't wearing any when they came into this stranger's camp.

"Um, could I please borrow something to wear?" she asked politely.

"Oh of course!" Crystal sprang up from the bed and helped Jess and Allison find their too-small bikini tops she had dressed them in earlier. This time, Jess was able to put it on herself without any assistance.

The demeanor in the bedroom of their Airstream changed the second everyone had now finished cumming. It almost seemed like how Cheetch and Crystal were rushing them out the door.

Jess didn't see it happen, but when she turned around she saw that both Cheetch and Crystal were now fully dressed. Cheetch, in a simple black banana hammock that was barely more than a G-string with a large pouch on the front where his package bulged out. Jess watched him throw on a black and white vest that looked like it could have been a Chip 'n Dale's work uniform. Crystal had somehow found the time to put on a matching cheetah print bra and panties in the same amount of time it took Jess to tie on the white and hot pink bikini top Crystal had given her earlier. Jess wasn't sure of the exact moment when it happened but it had completely fallen off at some point when Josh was fucking the shit out of her. Maybe he untied it— or maybe Crystal untied it. Or, for all she knew, it could have been Cheetch since he was standing behind her while he had his dick in Allison, the only one not laying on the bed after all.

Cheetch cleared his throat loudly. "Well, we're going to go to the drum and bass stage." He moved to the entrance of the Airstream bedroom. "So, uh, maybe we'll see you guys down there?"

Jess didn't have to be sober to understand what was happening. They were being rushed out.

Allison was busy trying to fix her hair in the mirror at the head of the bed. She already had the black bikini top with neon green ties tied on, even though it was so small that her boobs looked like they would topple out at the moment she raised her hands above her head.

Jess looked at Josh. "Ummmm..."

He knew what she was thinking.

"Crystal, do you have something that Jess and Ally could borrow to, you know, cover up their pussies?"

Even though he said exactly what she was thinking, hearing the words aloud still made Jess blush.

"Oh!" Crystal cried.

The red head was standing next to Cheetch by the bedroom entrance ready to leave, looked down at Jess, then over to Allison, as if she was just noticing their vaginas for the very first time.

"Oh, yeah! Of course, darlin'. Of course..."

She pushed past Jess and back over to the corner of the room with the set of drawers. Without giving much thought to her selection, Crystal opened the bottom most drawer, pulled out two items at random, then shut the drawer, all in the span of a second.

Although she politely handed both Jess and Allison a pair of booty shorts, Jess thought that Crystal would have thrown them at the girls if it would have gotten them out of the Airstream sooner.

Jess unfolded the booty shorts, both hers and the one she handed to Allison were both black and, like the bikini tops, appeared to be several sizes too small. Jess couldn't help but wonder why Crystal had all of this different clothing that there was no way of her fitting into.

Jess mentally sighed, but outwardly smiled politely and thanked the green-eyed red head. Jess laid on her back and swung her feet and ass up into the air so she could thread her legs into the shorts.

That was the beauty of booty shorts— small as they were, they were always stretchy.

Both Jess and Allison were suddenly standing on the bed, checking out the way their asses looked in their new shorts. They both stood facing the TV looking over their shoulders at the mirror. Only then did Jess realize that both of the shorts Crystal gave them had large writing on the back. Jess's ass said "SLUT" while the writing on Allison's ass said "GET".

The two girls instantly fell on the bed giggling and only stopped when Josh asked, "How does this look on me?"

Jess and Allison turned their heads to see Josh wearing a black and white tuxedo banana hammock identical to the one Cheetch was wearing. In fact, Jess had to check to make sure that Cheetch hadn't taken his underwear off and given it to Josh to wear.

He did not.

Jess did a double take. Were they actually both wearing identical banana hammocks?

While Allison again collapsed on the bed and started rolling around, laughing so hard that her boobs fell out of her top, Jess turned to Cheetch with a wry smirk, "Did you get these at a Thunder Down Under Fire Sale?"

Cheetch offered a shrug and deadpanned, "I used to work at Chippendales."

Well, Jess thought, *he has the body for it.*

"Ey, we've got to hurry to the drum and bass stage to catch Andy C before his set is over," Cheetch reminded them.

Jess read the message loud and clear. Cheetch might as well have told them, *Now that we're done fucking, you can kindlt get the fuck out.*

After that, they left the Airstream, which Cheetch locked behind him and placed the keys into the pouch of his banana hammock

Josh visibly cringed at watching this.

Crystal gave Jess and Ally a hug, Josh and Cheetch fist bumped, and they parted ways.

For whatever reason, Jess got the feeling that Crystal and Cheetch did not want to see them ever again.

But it was fun fucking in a stranger's bed, and at least Allison finally got that strange dick that she had been after.

Chapter 8: Get Slat

The three started down the dirt trail back into the music festival in silence before Josh finally turned to the two women.

"So, where to now, ladies?" He asked.

The question seemed to linger for a moment, hanging in the air before Jess finally answered.

"I'm still high as fuck. Let's get some food," Jess said.

At the mention of food, Allison, who until that moment had almost seemed like she was in another world, perked up.

"Oh my god, yes! I'm starving!"Allison said, jumping up and down until her tits popped out of her bikini top, which she promptly fixed.

"You read my mind." Josh flashed Jess the private smile that was just for her. "I think I see the food trucks right over there."

They made their way to the small fist of people crowding around a semi-circle of trucks selling every type of food that the three of them could possibly imagine, and many more that they couldn't possibly imagine eating, like bacon wrapped cauliflower, sauerkraut flavored ice cream, and salmon sea salt taffy. The same truck also sold caramel dipped sardines.

The smells ranged from mouthwatering to vomit-inducing when the three were able to take in the. of food options, they quickly realized that each of them wanted different things.

Jess wanted a chicken shawarma gyro from a Mediterranean truck called Greek 'n Fleek.

Josh wanted a cheese burger from a truck called Meat in your Mouth.

Allison wanted pizza from a truck that was shaped as a pair of lips with the actual words, oh the top that said Mouthgasm Pizza.

As the three were finalizing their orders and each explaining to the others why their food selection was inferior, something occurred to Jess.

"Shit. How are we going to pay for this?"

The three of them were hardly wearing clothing, let alone no cash or cards, or even their phones were all safely back at their campsite, which was now a seriously long walk away.

Their spirits visibly sank. Just as Jess was preparing herself for a long and hungry walk back to their tent, then back again to the food trucks, Josh spoke up.

"I've got an idea. Wait here. I'll be right back."

As Josh disappeared into the throng of people waiting in line for food, Jess and Allison found a vacant and relatively clean picnic table to sit at.

"Where did Josh go? Do you have any idea what he went to go do?" Allison asked impatiently.

Jess could only shrug, as both of the women's stomachs began to growl.

Allison let out a heavy sigh and slumped over the picnic table.

Jess had no idea how long Josh had been gone. If he really did go back to camp to grab money, they would be waiting for a good long time, plus, the food truck lines were LONG.

After some time, Allison stood up impatiently.

"Okay, I have an idea!" She said suddenly, then got up and started off in the direction of the food trucks, "And mine will actually work!"

Jess watched her disappear in the crowd of people. Then Jess was alone, thinking about how hungry she was and wishing that she, too, would get struck with an awesome idea that was guaranteed to get her free food.

Less than a minute after Ally had disappeared, Josh sat down at the picnic table next to Jess, his hands full of all types of food.

He set down burgers and fries and pizza and falafel and Jess's chicken gyro.

"Where's Ally?" he asked as he delicately spread all of the food across the table.

It was a veritable food truck feast and the smell was driving Jess absolutely wild.

But there was one burning question in the back of Jess's mind. "My God, Josh! This is so much food! How did you pay for all this?"

Josh gave her a smug smile, looking into her eyes as he dug into his banana hammock and produced a small, clear zip sealed bag with something in it that Jess couldn't tell what it was at first.

Upon a closer look her mouth gaped at Josh. "Wax?"

He grinned a toothy grin. "Got it from Cheetch. He gave me so much that I knew there was no way we'd ever smoke it all. I traded a bunch to get our food." He pointed at the bag on the wooden picnic table. "That's what's left." It wasn't much. "So where did Ally run off to?"

Jess already had the gyro in her hand and had just taken a massive bite. "I don't know," She said with a mouthful of food, she said she had an idea and ran off." She took another bite. "Fuck, that's delicious.

"And you didn't try to stop her?" He sounded angry.

Jess looked at him and shrugged. "You said the exact same thing." She took another bite of the succulent chicken and white sauce gyro. "Am yee er ung yee."

Josh rolled his eyes and finally sat down next to Jess, casually picking at french fries. "I know you're hungry. I get it. But I hope she's okay, dressed the way she is."

Jess swallowed the mouthful of chicken. "What the fuck does that mean?"

"I just mean that she's a good looking girl in a sea of randos and she is high as fuck right now." Josh held up his hands in surrender.

Jess's eyes narrowed.

"Not as hot as you, though!" He quickly amended.

"Josh, Ally is a strong girl and she can take care of herself." She popped a falafel ball in her mouth. "Besides, I'm the one with 'SLUT' stamped on her ass." She smiled with a mouth full of food.

"Yeah, about that..."

Josh was interrupted by Allison sitting down at the table with a fist full of pizza and three shakes.

"Sup, Slut?" Allison set a drink down in front of Jess, one in front of Josh, and one in front of herself. "Uh, where the fuck did all of this food come from?"

"Josh magic'd it down for us." Jess eyed the pepperoni pizza sitting in front of Allison.

"Well, I hope he didn't get it the same way I did." She picked up the cup in front of her and took a long, hard pull. Jess saw thick white stuff slowly making its way up her straw and into her mouth. Allison saw the way Jess was looking at her. "Vanilla shake," she offered. "They wouldn't give me the Oreo one, but it's better than nothing."

"Okay, Ally, I'll bite." Josh said, folding his arms. "How DID you get the pizza and shakes?"

The lascivious smile that appeared on her face told Jess everything she needed to know.

"Oh, no, Ally, you didn't." Jess put her hand on her friend's shoulder consolingly.

"Look, the truck is called 'Mouthgasm,' so that gave me the idea, alright? See that one guy behind the counter? The Italian-looking one?"

Jess looked. She could barely see his dark face, black hair, and big nose inside the food truck. He was busy making pizzas and had a huge smile on his face. "Well, his Italian Sausage was a little premature, but very creamy." Allison burst out laughing while Jess quietly sipped the vanilla shake in front of her.

"Um, thank you?"

Allison looked at all of the food on the picnic table. "But apparently I just blew that guy for nothing because Josh beat me to it."

Josh raised his hands defensively.

"And I didn't even have to suck a dick to get it! Imagine that!"

"Oh, don't be jealous. Besides, with your lips, Josh, you'd be lucky to get half a slice."

The three laughed and talked about music while they ate. Then, when they were just about done. "Oh, Ally! Before I forget." Allison slurped down the last of her shake and looked at her friend. "Josh wants us to trade shorts." Jess said nonchalantly.

"I never said that!"

Jess looked at him and said evenly, "No, but you were thinking it."

By the way Josh's mouth just hung there, she knew she was right. All he could say was "You know, it's very eerie that you can always read my thoughts. I don't like it."

"Well, don't you ever forget that I CAN read your mind at the time of my choosing." Jess already had her booty shorts off and held them in both hands. She shook them out a couple times, meaning to loosen any debris that she may have sat on on the picnic table.

Jess held the shorts out to Allison to take. "Well, I guess 'SLUT' suits me a little bit better than 'GET.' Just what is that supposed to mean, anyway? Like, GET this ass?"

Allison looked over her shoulder at her own booty, but couldn't see the writing. She started turning around in circles like a dog chasing its own tail.

"I think it might have been part of a two piece set with another pair of shorts." Jess leaned on one leg while she bent one knee, looking off into the distance, deep in thought. "You know, like GET MONEY or GET FUCKED."

Allison stopped moving in circles and pulled her booty shorts off so she could look at the back, swaying slightly dizzy from spinning. She held the back of her shorts up to her face, examining them. "Yeah, or like GET your taxes done here, or, GET ALONG LITTLE PONY."

"GET Shorty, remember that movie?" Jess's face brightened as she looked at Josh.

He did not look entertained.

"GET a haircut, you hippie!" Allison yelled and pointed at a nearby white guy with dreads.

The two bottomless girls were starting to get the attention of everyone within the semi-circle of food trucks, everyone in line, everyone eating, as well as the food truck workers themselves.

"GET a life." Jess shouted.

"GET GONE!" Allison yelled. The girls were now worked up into a frenzy.

"GET ON UP like a sex machine!" Jess twirled.

"GET DOWN!" Allison dropped it like it's hot.

"GET in line, soldier!"

"GET IN MY BELLY!" Allison did her best Fat Bastard's impression, which was actually pretty good.

"GET OVER HERE," Jess, with her best Scorpion.

"Get well soon, Sweetie."

"Get some!"

"Get in touch with everyone you've had intercourse with in the last six months because you have chlamydia."

That last one sent a shock wave of silence across the entire food truck area, all of whom were now staring at Allison's and Jess's bare asses. The two had been walking around completely naked for the majority of the day, so when they stripped off their booty shorts, they didn't think much of it. But from the looks of everyone's faces, other people certainly did.

"Would you two please just switch shorts, already?" Josh asked them in a loud whisper.

The two women answered at the same time and in an equally nonchalant manner, "Yeah, sure." Jess and Allison shrugged, traded bottoms, then stepped in to each other's booty shorts.

Now Jess's ass read "GET" and Allison's ass read "SLUT."

After they had pulled up their shorts, both women were looking over their shoulders at their rear ends, then slapping each others' asses at the same time. Again and again and again,

Jess and Allison smacked each others' butts while chanting at the same time. "GET SLUT! GET SLUT! GET SLUT!" while jumping up and down.

Josh pinched the bridge of his nose as if he suddenly had a terrible headache.

"GET SLUT! GET SLUT! GET SLUT!"

Josh could only fathom what other people standing around the food trucks were thinking, but he took the hand of both of the women and started leading them away. Josh, only wearing a black Chippendales banana hammock, pulling on the hands of Jess and Allison, who were leading them through the crowded music festival while they jumped up and down screaming "GET SLUT!" over and over was certainly a sight to see—even at a music festival, and especially when both women's tits had spilled out of their hilariously small bikini tops almost as soon as they started jumping up and down. Although Josh thought that maybe his girlfriend had literally lost her mind, Jess continued to up the ridiculousness only because she knew it annoyed Josh.

Determined to put an end to their antics, Josh led the women by hand over to the parallel rows of festival vendors.

Or, from the perspective of a festival vendor, an angry white stripper in a black banana hammock dragged two hysterical topless maniacs, probably all on drugs, down the street.

Some passersby smiled at the trio. Some laughed, some leered, while others ran in the other direction as soon as they saw them coming. Either way, Josh was determined to get them new clothes.

By the time he reached a vendor who sold steampunk style clothing, Jess and Allison's mantra had turned to mush in their mouths and sounded more like "Coleslaugh" than "GET SLUT."

Josh approached the clothing vendor still holding both of their hands. "I need new clothes for these lunatics."

He let go of their hands, and, as if for the first time awake of their sort-of-drugs, both Jess and Ally immediately started browsing and holding up different outfits to each other to see how they would look.

The shop owner was a gentleman not much older than Josh with a thinly black moustache that made him look like a cartoon villain who tied women to train tracks. And he was VERY into steampunk.

From his long, dark brown top hat, complete with a pair of gold trimmed goggles strapped to the base, fingerless gloves with gaudy rings that adorned every finger, high-top boots, and a brown leather vest, opened to show his surprisingly lean, cut, and hairless chest. Jess noticed Allison's eyes taking up and down his open vest, painting the shop owner's skinny, muscular frame and well-defined ab muscles with a lustful look as she passed him by.

The look did not go unnoticed, and when Josh saw that the vendor saw, he rolled his eyes, expecting more trouble. And when the steampunk guy read what was printed on Allison's ass, Josh knew was sure of it.

"Can I help you..." He drew out the word "you" in a way that made Josh and Jess's skin crawl, but Ally seemed to find it charming— or at least she pretended to.

One look at Josh's face and Jess could tell what he was thinking—*Thank God they put their tits away before going into this shop.*

But Jess was in a mood to make mischief, which was typically the case anytime she knew her mischief making would vex Josh. Especially when he was in one of his serious moods.

Making sure she had eye contact with Josh, Jess waited until the steampunk shop keeper turned around to show Allison some leather harnesses, then, as soon as he wasn't looking, Jess pulled down the white bikini top and pushed her tits together while doing her best Gene Simmons with her tongue.

She only pulled her top back up and put her tits away after she saw that they had the desired result of further vexing Josh, who shook his head at her and put the palm of his hand in his face. Seeing what was going on behind the vendor's back, Allison couldn't help looking at Jess and giggling.

The vendor, who was in the middle of explaining to Ally how each harness was made, looked behind him to where she was looking just in time to see Jess simply adjusting her bikini top. He looked back to Ally, confused.

"Uh, maybe you could help my friend find a new top." Ally gestured with her chin in Jess's direction.

Of course, the vendor was all too eager to assist. And as he took Jess into another corner of the store, Allison whispered Josh's name to get his attention.

The moment Josh looked up, Allison ran over to the other side of the shop so she was standing directly behind the steampunk guy now. As silent as a stoned raver could manage, Ally pulled her booty shorts down to her ankles, and, with her ass pointed at Jess and the steampunk vendor, she started to twerk exactly the way Crystal had shown her. Only she didn't have anything to hold on to in front of her, so as Josh shook his head disapprovingly, Allison's hands slipped off her knees and she fell forward.

Her face broke her fall— and not quietly, so as the steampunk vendor whips around to see what the commotion is, he is greeted by Allison on all fours with her ass sticking up high in the air less than a foot away from him. Before he can even react, Josh sprints across the store to help her up to her feet.

Naturally, her tits fell out of her bikini top yet again.

Allison whined while dusting off her scuffed knees, "ow, ow, owie-e-e!"

Jess appeared by her side to pull up her shorts over her ass while Josh tried to cover Allison's boobs with her black top, but it was so small and Allison stumbled again which, of course, freed her nipples once more.

Josh and Jess each grabbed a hold of one side of Ally's top and together they were able to pull it back in place without her breasts spilling out again, but not before the vendor saw every inch of Allison's supple, naked skin in the low light from white LEDs lining the ceiling of the shop's canopy.

It was clear that he liked what he saw because he made a canopy of his own in his tight leather pants. Worse yet, he made no move to hide his missile erection. Jess breathed a little sigh as soon as she saw it.

I'm sure this is exactly what Josh was trying to avoid, she thought to herself. *He probably thinks that was intentional and that Ally is actually coming on to him.*

Jess rolled her eyes.

"I'm fine. I'm fine." Josh and Jess released Allison, who did her best to regain her composure after her face turned bright red.

Jess was surprised at how well Ally composed herself after her little spill, but shocked at what her friend did next.

Allison raked a hand through her hair, then patted the end of it where her hair fell on her back, to give it a tussle of volume.

Oh, no, Jess thought as she watched her friend primp herself, hoping that she wouldn't do what it looked like she was getting ready to do.

Allison made sure that both Jess and Josh were at least an arm's distance away before diving straight into the act that Jess had seen her perform a handful of times before. Jess knew the game well, as well as most young women did, but no one played it better than Allison.

She tilted her head up at the steampunk vendor, batting her long eyelashes at him as she made eye contact. The initial eye contact was essential to the rest of the performance. Ally took one step in the opposite direction of the vendor, then tripped on her flip-flops and fell— right into his arms.

He caught her at the waist, and as Ally gave him a girly little giggle that sounded closer to something you would expect to hear from a dog's squeaky toy. She gently caresses his arms, and, in the case of Mr. Steampunk, his exposed chest.

Allison laid her head on his chest and whispered something to him that Jess couldn't hear, though she was certain it was some variation of, "I'm so clumsy," and/or, "What big muscles you have."

After seeing this much, Jess took her boyfriend by the hand and dragged him over to the front of the store. She had seen this show before, and it was painful to watch.

Once the couple stood at the front of the shop, giving their friend plenty of room to do her thing, Jess turned to Josh and in a low voice she said, "Pick out a couple of things you want from the store."

Josh looked at her incredulously. "I'm not shoplifting from a small business like this— it isn't right."

Jess looked at Allison then back at Josh. She was still pawing at his chest. "Shhh! It's not shoplifting. He is going to give us a few things for free."

Josh raised one eyebrow. "Babe, have you seen the price tags on a lot of these clothes? All of these are handmade."

A knowing smile spread on Jess's hot pink lips. She wanted to tell him what a silly, naive boy he was. Instead she said, "Just trust me on this, okay? He's going to comp Jess a bunch of clothes for free. For Christ's sake, pick out a pair of pants. No, wait. I'll pick one out for you. Best if you just stand outside. No, further out, you know what? Just go wait at the booth across the street."

Like a good boyfriend, all he could say was, "Okay," then he gave her a quick kiss and started to walk away. He only took one step forward before he whirled around to ask her, "She's not going to... you know..." His eyebrow was in the air again.

Jess smacked him on the shoulder. "Ew! No! But if she wanted to, it would be none of your business."

Josh nodded in agreement and started for the vendor booth across the street, which sold Kandi bracelets and glow toys. The way Josh bussied himself playing with flashing string LEDs reminded Jess of a 9-year-old.

She smiled amorously at the man she loved before returning to the shop to see how far Ally's seduction was coming along. She saw her friend standing in the middle of the shop holding a few items on hangers with the steampunk guy standing right in front of her.

Jess was excited that she arrived just in time for her favorite part of the show— the breaking of the male spirit.

"Please?" Allison begged with seductive puppy dog eyes. "You can pick out anything you want me to wear."

Allison was leaning forward so her tits were right in the vendor's face, just on the cusp of falling out of her top, but not quite. Looking into the vendor's eyes, she could see it, the exact moment a frown turns into a smile, the moment of resignation, of male dominance being subjugated by female seduction.

Jess couldn't help but crack a smile.

"Oh, okay!" He said at last, and Allison rewarded him with a giddy smile.

"But, I don't have a changing room," He shrugged and lifted his hands above his head.

Jess thought about chiming in with a facetious, "Oh no, what are we ever going to do?" But Ally had already gotten to the end game and she didn't want to blow it.

"That's okay!" Ally, with a victorious smile on her face, handed all of the hangers in her hands over to the shop worker, except for one.

Allison eagerly pulled her bikini top over her head and handed that over to the vendor, too. "Hold this, please."

He was just as eager to receive Ally's top as she was to try on her new, free one. It was another strappy tie-on bikini top, only this one was made of some sort of soft felt-like material, soft and durable, and made to look like animal skin, triangular in shape. The top was a near identical match to Ally's dirty blonde hair color. Best of all, it was an appropriate size for Ally's C-cup breasts.

"What do you think?" She was facing the vendor, but she was really asking Jess.

All in all, Ally was only topless for about three seconds while she was juggling the two bikinis, which seemed much to the steampunk guy's chagrin, although he stared at Allison blankly, holding his head like an idiot.

Only when Jess gave her friend the thumbs up did Ally continue.

"Oh, and my friend here would look so sexy in the black one! don't you think?" Allison cooed, rubbing his arm.

While he continued to nod his head, Ally took two more hangers out of his hand and handed one to Jess. It was indeed a very sexy looking black leather top with silver hoops and studs.

The vendor wouldn't take his eyes off of Jess—it looked like he wouldn't even blink, and although Jess definitely did not feel comfortable changing in front of him, she convinced herself that it was a small concession for free designer clothing.

She thought briefly of the shower stage and the creeps that hung out in the back, leering at all of the naked dancers having a good time. Jess was sure that this guy must have been one of those creeps. Even though she was happy to walk around naked for most of the day, that was on her terms.

As Jess untied her white and pink bikini top, she suddenly wished that she wasn't so sober.

The top was so small in the first place that her tits didn't even move when she took it off. It was pretty much there just to cover up her nipples, not unlike the heart-shaped pasties she wore the previous night.

Jess crumpled up the top and threw it at the creepy store clerk. She squeezed into the black leather top with silver hoops connecting it in the front and in the back. It was a much better fit and offered much more support.

Ally actually got her top size right on the money— and the shiny black material matched her hair color.

Instantly, Jess saw the look that Ally was going for. When she looked back over at her friend, Ally was already completely dressed. She had replaced the black stretchy booty shorts with tan colored cut offs that had little pockets in the front and back while still managing to expose plenty of her robust booty.

Jess saw her adjusting a brown leather harness that went from her daisy dukes cut off, over her breasts and around her shoulders. She knew exactly what type of look Ally was going for.

"Bitch, are you Lara Croft or what?" Jess teased.

"Do you like it?" Ally modeled her new clothes, striking a few different poses before at last she handed the booty shorts with "SLUT" on the back to the Steampunk Guy.

He held only one more hanger in his hands and it was a black leather low rise bottoms with a zipper that went all the way around— from the front of her pussy to the crack of her ass.

How do you even put that on? Jess wondered.

She snatched them out of his hands while he was distracted by Ally's shorts, but he was not distracted for long.

Shit. Ally waited until he was watching Jess's tits as she changed tops, using that as a distraction while she changed her shorts, both eyes perving all over her.

Now all of his undivided attention was on her.

If he's going to eye rape you, lets just get this over with, Jess thought. *I've got to change somewhere, and if this creep will enjoy watching me change, it might as well be here.*

When she unzipped her leather pants, she realized that it had a flap on the inside to prevent it from catching skin.

Thank God, the last thing I need is to get my clitorous stuck in a zipper.

She turned around so the only thing the guy could see was her ass, then she stepped out of the "GET" booty shorts.

In 5 seconds, she had her new black leather low rise shorts zipped up and the steampunk guy was happily fondling his two pairs of still-warm booty shorts.

"Hopefully he doesn't have a collection of these to add to," Ally whispered in Jess's ear as the three of them walked up to the cash register.

"Hopefully we didn't just give him a reason to start collecting women's used shorts." Jess added.

The two girls giggled amongst themselves, then as the vendor was ringing up each item and camping every single one individually. Jess grabbed a pair of pants displayed on a wall.

"Oh, I almost forgot. These, too." She said, holding up the pants.

He complied without question. The women did not get to keep any of the garments they came in wearing— that was part of their creepy-ass deal.

Although he was generous enough to give each of them a tote bag.

Before they left, Jess and Ally asked if they could say their farewells to their dear friends, "GET" and "SLUT."

Allison gave the eulogy in a solemn voice, "Oh, Get Slut. Although our time together was very short, the memories we made together will be with us always. Like that time I slapped Jess's ass, and in return, she slapped my ass."

Jess could have sworn she was hearing pipe organs somewhere in the distance.

"You were with us when we got super faded and I fucked that random couple we met. You were with us when we helped kidnap Liam Neilsom's Daughter. You were our only friends while Jess and I were stranded on that desert island and were forced to cannibalize that bag of children. As you pass from this life of keeping our vagina's warm, into your next life as some sort of weird trophy for this totally creepy cosplay pilgrim vampire..."

"It's steampunk," he said, but Jess shushed him.

"We hope that you are in a better place now where you can roam free-forth in an endless, lush green field and valley with all of the other women's booty shorts in this guy's collection, where you will be happy—"

"I don't—" Jess slapped him again.

"Shh! Rude..." Jess held out one open hand to Ally. "Please continue."

"We bid you farewell, Get Slut, and rest in peace. Amen."

"Amen." Jess bowed her head, then clasped Ally on her shoulder. "It was a beautiful service."

Both girls sniffled as they somberly walked away from the steampunk shop.

Over her shoulder, Jess heard the vendor in the top hat say to himself, "What the fuck just happened?"

Jess couldn't help but feel like he would be asking himself that question for a long time to come.

His boss also would be asking him that question for a long time to come.

Chapter 9: Cocaine Cowgirls

Jess saw Josh in the booth across the street still entertaining himself with different LED toys. She signaled for him to come join them as they walked away from the vendor village and back into the festival grounds.

"Oh my God! You two look HOT!"

Josh took Jess by the hand and gave her a little twirl. She giggled girlishly. She was excited about her new outfit, and so was Josh.

"What's the damage assessment, Mistress Allison?"

Ally held up the tote bag. "Plus the pants. $580."

Jess jumped up and down screaming. "$580?" Her energy was so infectious, she got Ally to jump and scream with her.

"That's what the clothes cost!?" Josh was outraged.

Jess ran a soothing hand through his hair and held it on the back of his neck.

"Baby, that's what it costs to look this good." She pulled his head down to her height and gave him a kiss.

"Yeah, but not for you two."

Jess beamed a smile ear to ear. "No, not for us."

"Well, what happened to the clothes you were wearing?"

"We traded them in!" It was Allison who answered. "It was an upgrade." Then she turned to Jess, "Shit! I wish I had grabbed those sunglasses on the way out."

"Oh, I know. Those would look so good on you."

Josh blinked. "Why? It's getting dark out fast!"

Both women rolled their eyes simultaneously.

"Don't you know anything about fashion?" Ally was incredulous.

Jess put a comforting hand on Ally's shoulder. "He's learning."

"Did you get my pants? I'm freezing my balls off in this thing." Josh rubbed his hands together for warmth.

The three stopped walking and Jess handed Josh the pants in the tote bag. He wasted no time in putting them on over his banana hammock.

"How do they look?" He moved around so the girls could get a good look.

Both of them put a hand to their mouths as they tried to restrain laughter, and failed.

"Hey! What the Hell?" Josh looked over his shoulder and his face immediately reddened. "You got me assless chaps!?"

At this both Jess and Ally were falling on the ground, laughing themselves to tears.

"Not cool! I'm still cold!" Josh cried.

Sure enough, the pants that Jess had picked out for Josh were made of the same animal hide material as Ally's Tomb Raider top and shorts, only Josh's pants were tight in the crotch and opened up at the legs with fringe on the very bottom of each leg and zebra fabric on his rear end, like authentic cowboy riding chaps—exposing Josh's defined and now well-tanned butt cheeks.

"Well, I guess they look alright," Josh finally admitted as soon as the three started walking again, "they are kind of growing on me."

This comment sent the girls spiraling into yet another fit of laughter.

"I'm not happy you both chose to strip down in front of that creep, but by the way," Josh tried to change the subject.

"Oh my God, you *were* watching us!" Ally punched Josh in the ass cheek.

"I'm very protective," he said defensively.

"Oh, relax. You're the one we're fucking tonight, not him." Jess pulled his head down in another kiss.

We're fucking...

Too late did she realize her mistake, and now it seemed to hang unspoken in the front of each of their minds.

When Jess said, "We" did she just commit Ally to having sex with her boyfriend two nights in a row?

Jess looked at her friend's face, but it betrayed no reaction to her just volunteering her pussy to Josh.

Instantly, she changed the subject. "Let's go see The Glitch Mob."

Jess held Josh and Ally's hands and started running in the direction of the stage where she could hear The Glitch Mob's "Animus Vox" being performed.

By the time they got to the outskirts of the people who crowded the stage, they had already gone through their songs "RISE" and "West Coast Rocks."

Jess, Josh, and Ally were somehow able to push their way through the thick crowd of people while head banging to a lot of their songs. Jess volunteered Josh's head to the front of their line to act as a wedge while Jess draped her hand over his shoulder and Ally's hand on Jess's shoulder, and together they formed a "Shoulder Train" to dance and headbang their way, slowly but surely and as politely as they could for a group of people, trying to politely shove people out of the way so they could get a head of them.

After pissing off an untold number of people, they made it to the barricades backing the crowd from the stage in the very front row. By the time they got to the front row, Black Tiger Sex Machine had taken the stage and whipped everyone into a frenzy.

Being packed elbow to elbow, it was all they could do to lean forward against the barricade and fist pump and headbang.

Josh stood directly behind Jess, hugging her from behind, wrapping his hands around her waist. Jess felt safe, she felt his love, she felt like nothing in the entire world existed except for her and Josh and the music.

Despite how cold the night was, Josh was right there behind her, taking her in his warm embrace.

This is true love, she thought, *and life doesn't get any better than this.*

Jess never wanted this night to end— She wished to live in that moment forever, to live in his embrace, for all time. Her only wish was that her best friend, Ally, could also feel this way.

Jess occasionally caught a glimpse out of the corner of her eye of Ally staring at the two of them, with a look of tired longing in her eye. Jess's heart hurt for her.

They stayed for the next and final performance on that stage for the night— Excision.

Both Jess and Josh had been to many Excision shows in the past, so they knew exactly what to expect. Although both avid Excision fans and expert headbangers.

The three began the long journey of pushing back through the same crowd of people so they could escape the ensuing chaos before it began.

With Josh in the lead creating the wedge, they shuffled back and forth through the crowd, trying to reach the back, until Jess gave a tug at Josh's shoulder, bringing there train to an abrupt halt as soon as She heard the first notes to "VAULT," a hard hit from Excision collaboration with Subtronics, who took the stage alongside Excision to thunderous applause.

"OH MY GOD!" Jess and Ally screamed in each other's face excitedly.

The song was one of both Jess and Ally's favorites and they didn't hesitate to shout every word at the front of the stage.

Jess had never been more grateful that she wasn't carrying a handbag, because as soon as the breakdown dropped a mosh pit broke out, then all hell erupted.

Jess, Ally, and Josh were among the first three in the pit, pushing, shoving, dancing, head banging to the bass-ridden dubstep beats.

For 40 exhausting seconds, the three of them were part of a sacred brotherhood that only a mosh pit can create.

As if in a trance, it was all over in an instance, just as it had begun. By the end of it, Jess had only a few more bruises, a lot more sweat, and one maniacal smile gracing her face, as did all of them.

As the mosh pit eventually caved in, and more ravers filled the vacant circle, the three were separated. Jess pushed through the sea of people, continuing toward the back of the stage as she had been previously, all the while her eyes roving over everyone in sight to try and find a glimpse of Josh or Ally.

When she finally reached the end of the tightly packed people and found her way into a clearing, it was much easier to search, and although she could see no sight of Josh or Ally, what she found next surprised her.

She was surprised at who she did find among the crowd.

"Jess? Jess!"

It was Isabel, Jon's wife.

She was wearing blue denim jean cut-offs that were meticulously designed to reveal as much of her ass as possible and had a bunch of iridescent crystals adorning her chest, covering her nipples and spread out across her fake boobs, cleavage, and lower neck that were arranged to create a glittering butterfly pattern.

Jess wanted to roll her eyes at the sight of Isabel, but she looked really good. And she was all alone.

"Isabel, where is your Jon?" She asked.

The two women hugged and Jess could feel the hard crystals all over Isabel's chest press up against her skin uncomfortably.

"We came to see Excision and I lost him." Isabel gave Jess a sad look for but a moment before her face turned to one of curiosity.

"What happened to Josh?" Isabel asked.

Jess gave her a fake smile. "Same thing."

"I'm sorry." Isabel frowned, then looked in the direction of the stage, "For two tall guys, it sure is easy for them to disappear."

Jess nodded to her, then.

"Oh my God, Jess!" Ally came running up to the two women, pushing people out of the way, and forcing one small woman to the ground. "Where are the boys?"

Jess and Isabel both shrugged at the same time.

The three women turned back to the crowd in front of the stage.

"You know, for being so tall they sure do blend well."

Isabel smiled humorlessly. "I just said that."

The three women scanned the crowd as they called Josh and Jon's names, but they quickly realized that competing with an Excision show was completely helpless.

After less than three minutes of searching, or the length of one Excision song, they decided the search was futile.

"Let's just go back to camp, I guess," Isabel suggested. "It's late, and Jon and I were about to head back that way anyway."

Ally and Jess nodded their agreed.

"They might already be there." Ally pointed out.

To prevent getting lost again, the three women held hands on their walk back to camp.

On the way back, Jess and Ally regaled Isabel with stories of what they did that day. Isabel seemed very entertained and even a little jealous at the telling. When they got to the point where they lost Josh in the mosh pit, Isabel wore a bright smile.

"Wow, that sounds like a legendary day. unforgettable."

"What did you and Jon do today?" Jess asked brightly.

"Well, you know, it's my first time at a festival, right?" Isabel began, "Jon and I went to the Shower Stage, but he didn't like me dancing naked with everyone, so we came back to camp. Even with these crystals I bought specifically for the festival, he didn't want me wearing these." Isabel shook her tits back and forth and the iridescent crystals all over her chest shimmered.

"What? That's crazy! Your tits look beautiful, by the way." Jess thought that Allison was about to reach out and motorboat Isabel.

"Oh my God, thank you! After the Shower Stage, I worked really hard putting these on, well, then, to be honest, Jon and I got really high after that, then I don't remember much of the day, but Jon was being kind of a big dick all day to me."

Jess shuddered at the words big dick, remembering what she saw between Jon's legs on the drive into the festival.

"To be honest, I'm really glad I found you girls when I did. It seems like I've been trying to get Jonny to fuck me all day but he just wasn't interested. Oh, is this our camp?"

The girls abruptly stopped walking. If Isabel hadn't said anything, she thought that her and Ally would have walked right by it.

"Oh, that's terrible." Ally patted Isabel's shoulder consolingly. "He's crazy not to be all over you! I mean, look at you."

Isabel looked like she was going to suddenly break down in tears. Actually, Jess thought she might have seen Isabel's eyes tear up right then.

"I just try so hard to look good for him, and I throw myself at him. And nothing," Isabel sobbed. "Yet he checks out every rave slut that walks by."

Allison covered her backside with both hands, where the word "SLUT" was written.

Isabel turned her face up to Jess. Those were real tears. If she were wearing makeup, it would be running, but Isabel looked gorgeous without a dab of make up.

"Then I hear about how hot your day was and all the attention you girls got, and how much Josh loves you, Jess," Isabel added as she took Jess by the hand. "It all sounds so much like what I expected to happen to me when we all drove in here together."

Jess hugged her, the small, iridescent crystals all over her chest prickling Jess's skin. Jess's heart and she wanted to cry with Isabel.

Then Isabel's tears faded as she regained her composure almost immediately. "Thank you, Jess, you're a good friend."

Suddenly Jess felt terrible about all of the negative thoughts she had about Isabel.

Isabel wasn't a bad person. She was actually a lot more like Jess than she realized. She felt bad that she hadn't seen it earlier.

"Oh, before I forget. I want to share something with you girls."

Isabel walked right into the large tent she shared with Jon without looking behind her to see if Jess and Ally were following. The two girls exchanged looks that told one another that they were both feeling the same thing for Isabel.

As Jess was one step away from entering the tent, she saw the entire thing light up from the outside, illuminated by a swirling spray of colors.

Ducking under the tent flap, she saw why.

A black ball with dozens of colorful lenses was plugged into a small electric generator. The rotating ball of rainbow color lights cast every color on every surface within the tent all at once. The spectacular light display was something that Jess expected to see as part of the lights show at one of the festival stages rather than used to light up a tent, but the effect was profound.

Set against the music of Excision performing at the far off stage, it definitely gave off party vibes.

Inside Isabel and Jon's tent, there was no air mattress like in that of Jess and Josh's.

Instead, there were dozens of small throw pillows that littered half of the tent. Although Isabel's tent was the exact same size as Jess's without the enormous air mattress that her and Josh slept on, Isabel's tent seemed quite roomy indeed.

Aside from the pillows, there were two folding tables with an ornate table cloth thrown over the top, a couple of backpacks, and various electronics plugged into the generator so they could charge.

After Isabel flipped on the multicolored party lights, she gestured for the other two to join her next to one of the folding tables. There was nothing sitting on the oriental patterned table cloth when Jess and Ally wordlessly joined Isabel at her side, but she bent over, busy rummaging through one of the many bags strewn throughout the tent.

"I love your tent," Jess said, just to say something positive.

"Thanks," Isabel said distantly while she dug through the backpack.

A few seconds later, she pulled out a tin container and set it on the table. It was the type of tin that was always sold at Christmas time and had those terrible, hardly edible Christmas cookies in them that Jess hated.

This is what she wanted to share with us, Jess thought to herself. *Holiday cookies? And just when I started to like the girl, she pulls some weird grandmother shit out like this.*

"Oh, no thanks, Isabel. We actually just ate not too long ago," Jess did her best to keep her tone as even and polite as possible.

"Are you sure?" Isabel looked Jess in the eye as she pulled the top off of the tin cookie container.

Immediately, a sharp and caustic smell flooded the tent. Though Jess couldn't identify it by its signature sharp, sweet, and chemically scent, she most certainly knew what it was as soon as she saw it.

Both Jess and Ally's jaws fell open.

Inside the cookie tin was the most cocaine that Jess had ever seen in one place. One massive white rock, like a snowball the size of a child's fist, sat to one side of the container, while many much smaller white balls littered the rest of it, with white powder covering every inch of the bottom in a thick layer.

Isabel carefully placed the top of the container next to it and pulled out the tiniest spoon that Jess had ever seen, along with a small cut of straw, out of the backpack. She scooped a couple of spoonfuls of the powder from the tin over to the lid, then carefully pulled at a razor blade, appearing in her hand from where Jess did not know.

Still polarized, Jess and Ally watched Isabel methodically scrape the powder on the tin into three long, thick lines, then looked up and with a sad sort of smile, she handed the straw to Jess.

"I don't want to feel anything anymore tonight. Will you girls stay with me?" Isabel asked.

How could she say no to that? Jess felt like taking the straw into her hands was like entering into a contract with Isabel, a contract she didn't really want to sign but was being forced into.

But she still took the straw from Isabel and heard herself say at the same time as Ally, in a consoling tone that women use when they lie to other women.

"Of course."

Then the next thing Jess knew she was snorting the most coke that she had ever done at one time.

And as soon as she had finished doing the massive lines that Isabel had laid out she quickly realized why all those pillows were there.

She collapsed back into a puddle of clouds, of softness everywhere, of rushing euphoria, and suddenly she was a melting, giggly mess. Jess was rolling on her back, laughing hysterically, at what she did not know, then Ally fell onto the pile of pillows next to her.

Sniff. Sniff.

Then Isabel fell on Jess's other side, all three of them laughing like they had gone mad.

Jess had found a frilly pillow with red tassels all over its sides that she was clutching close to her chest. She hugged the pillow tightly, and the tighter she squeezed it, the more comfort it brought her.

Isabel finally broke the hysteria by getting the girls to sit upright with her, still among the pillow puddle.

"Check this out," Isabel hollered down with her arm motioning to her chest.

There, amid the iridescent crystals stuck to her body were two white lines of powder delicately going up and over each crystal, held up by the top of her tits.

"I've always wondered if other women could do this." It was a challenge.

Ally handed the straw again to Jess who wasted no time snorting the coke off of her fake tits. Ally did the same.

"I don't see what the big deal is. Do one off of me next."

Ally jumped up to the coke table where she scooped a large spoonful of coke, then held it in the air hesitantly, lost in thought.

"What's wrong Ally?" Jess asked as she picked up the same pillow as before and got it in a death grip. Ally set the spoonful of coke back down on the table.

"I don't want to mess up this expensive new top," Ally started undoing the tan bikini top. Jess laughed at her.

"Bitch, it was free. What, are you afraid your top is going to get all coked out and run away?"

With her breasts freed, Ally threw the top into the pile of pillows.

"It's still more expensive than I'll ever be able to afford."

She picked up the coke spoon again and began dusting her tits with coke like she was adding spice into a soup. Almost all of the cocaine fell off of her chest and onto the ground.

"Damnit! I'm sorry, Isabel."

"What are you sorry for? Did you see how much cocaine is in that container? Besides, I didn't pay for it!"

The girls all laughed.

Ally tried again to sprinkle coke on her tits, this time by pushing them up from below, creating a bigger shelf for the powder to sit on.

"See? Not so hard."

Isabel went in closer for an inspection.

"That's cheating!"

She still snorted the small amount of coke that rested on her chest.

"I can do it because of my implants, but I've never known if other women can balance enough powder on their tits to snort," Isabel explained.

"Ah. Now we know!" Jess offered.

"Oh, no," Ally pulled on Jess's hand, "You're not getting out of this either. You have much bigger boobs than me, so I'm sure you could do it."

Isabel filled the spoon full of more white powder.

"Come on Jess. For science." Isabel gave her a cute little wink.

Jess seemed unwilling to part with the pillow she was holding, but Ally managed to wrestle it from her hands. Then, as Jess was staring at the spoon, deep in contemplation as to how she was actually going to make this work, she felt her black leather top being ripped off her body.

"Hey!" Jess was not surprised to see Ally holding her clothes.

The next thing she knew, Isabel was dabbing a spoon full of cocaine on her tits, just above her nipples. A considerable amount fell onto the floor, but to Jess's surprise, enough of it stuck to her skin to make a sizable line, which Ally wasted no time in snorting up.

Isabel giggled at her enthusiasm.

"That settles it," Jess said with an air of finality. "Your tits must be magic or something, Isabel."

"Is that why they sparkle like that?" Ally joked.

"Yeah, right," Isabel said sadly, "If my tits are magic then why doesn't my husband want me?"

Before the vibe in the tent had a chance to 180, Jess blurted out, "Oh my God, how ever will I get all of this cocaine off of my body?" In her best phony, lascivious voice, "Ally, Isabel, any ideas?"

That was all the invitation Ally needed, though it had really been meant for Isabel. Ally ran her tongue over the length of Jess's massive right tit, from bottom up to her collar bone.

Thankfully, a beautiful smile once again adorned Isabel's face as Ally compelled her to follow her lead. The two women began lapping up all of the remaining powder on Jess's chest like dogs with a mouth full of peanut butter.

After only a few seconds, all the coke was gone, but they continued to lick Jess's breasts anyway. Jess started laughing, half at the awkwardness and half because their tongues tickled.

When Ally pushed the bottom of Jess's titty up and started sucking fiercely on her nipples, Jess fell on her back into the pile of pillows.

Jess knew that Ally always loved Jess's tits and would worship them at any opportunity she got. But Isabel grew weary of sucking on Jess's tiny nipples, so after her entire chest was covered in the two women's saliva, Isabel gently caressed the side of Jess's cheek so that she would look in her direction.

The two women's faces were less than an inch apart. Their faces numb, her nipples numb, her mouth numb.

Jess lost herself in Isabel's beautiful brown eyes, full lips, and grossly enchanting smile. Her smile looked so inviting, her lips so full and soft.

She never wanted Isabel to ever feel pain ever again. She wanted to be her source of pleasure, and Isabel hers. As if in slow motion, both women's soft, wet lips met.

Once, they pulled back to look each other in their eyes again, to smile that playful smile, to share a painful look of longing, to silently give their consent, their need, their lust for one another.

And when their lips met next, a shivering tingle of pleasure and burning satisfaction swept through both women, starting at their lips and continuing throughout their entire beings, ending in between their legs.

They both closed their eyes as their tongues danced in slow motion, a romantic, slow dance. With every movement, every flick of the tongue, every lick of the others' lips, every playful little bite, a growing warmth bubbled in between either woman's legs, stiffening their loins, until finally the white hot magma of their passion erupted to the surface and their lust for each other could no longer be denied.

A ravenous, primal lust that nothing on earth could get in the way of. Isabel and Jess could not keep their hands off of one another.

Jess had never wanted another woman the way she wanted Isabel at that moment. Although she was absolutely certain that the way Ally was licking on her tits and playing with her nipples, undoubtedly had a role in the insatiable lust she now felt, just as much as she was sure all of the coke she snorted played a role in it, but none of that changed the way she felt now.

At that moment, she could no longer contain her desire.

Jess pulled back from Isabel and lifted her ass up so she could wiggle out of her shorts.

"I want you so bad right now," Jess heard herself whisper lustfully underneath.

Ally lifted her head abruptly, thinking that Jess was talking to her. She didn't want to hurt Ally's feelings, either.

As soon as Jess had wiggled out of her tight leather bottoms, she pedaled her feet until she was completely free of them and completely naked once more, taking Ally's head in both her hands. Jess pulled her face up to hers to offer her the same hot, passionate kiss she had planted on Isabel.

Meanwhile, thinking she was taking a cue from Jess, Isabel slid down between Jess's legs to play with her freshly liberated pussy.

As Jess and Ally shared what was unquestionably the steamiest make out session in their long and complicated friendship, Jess could feel Isabel sticking her tongue all over her vagina and it wasn't great.

She eats pussy like a teenage boy, thought Jess.

Although she reckoned that this must have been the first time Isabel ever had a mouth full of pussy, that's no excuse for not knowing how to make one feel good. Especially considering Isabel had a vagina of her own.

After a few minutes of Isabel clumsily poking at Jess's pussy with the tip of her tongue, she could stand it no more.

Allison was still playing with Jess's boobs when Jess whispered to her friend.

"Can you go down there and help her? She really has no idea what she's doing," she pleaded.

Ally silently and incredulously mouthed the word, "What?"

Jess went on, "I know it's bad."

She lifted her head to see Isabel running her tongue up Jess's thigh the type of way you might lick grease running down your fingers while eating chicken.

Jess looked at Ally with a disappointed look on her face, "Please help her."

Jess could tell by the look in Ally's face that she thought the idea of training Isabel how to lick another woman's pussy seemed like more of a chore than a sensual experience.

Ally frowned at her friend, "If you make me cum while I'm teaching her."

This was not what Jess was expecting to hear, but she agreed all the same, "Okay."

Jess knew how she felt. After doing all of that cocaine, she would do just about anything for an orgasm.

Just then a thought occurred to Jess, *this must be why everyone's always saying how cocaine is addictive.*

Ally brought a fist up to Jess's face with only her pinky sticking up.

"Pinky promise me you'll make me cum."

"If you pinky promise me the same," Jess replied.

The two girls locked pinkies, and at the same time said "Okay."

As she watched Ally shimmy out of her leather harness and shorts, all Jess could think was how that was by far the strangest pinky promise she had ever made.

It only took Ally a few seconds for her to shed every bit of her clothing and flip into a fluid 180 degrees on the pillow puddle.

Jess could hear Ally whispering to Isabel below her, "Pst! Do it like this!"

Then she could feel Ally take her entire clit into her mouth and start sucking and licking hastily.

At last Jess thought as she let out a moan of relief, my poor neglected clitorus.

Right on cue, Ally began inching her smooth and glistening wet pussy over toward Jess, also refusing to be neglected. Jess knew all too well what that felt like, and although she was having trouble concentrating with the sudden surge of pleasure between her legs, Jess hooked one hand around Jess's inner thigh to lift one leg up high into the air, and dove face first into her best friend's pussy.

She wrapped her entire mouth around Ally's little pussy and started stabbing her tongue at her clit, licking her pussy. It was easy for Jess to tell whose tongue was between her legs at any given time.

Every now and again she would hear the two women whispering to each other. It seemed like Isabel was a slow learner, and what was supposed to be an intimate and sexy experience was quickly becoming frustrating.

Jess suddenly found herself wanting more coke, but she realized that the only way out of this was to get Ally off first.

Then something happened to bring everything to an abrupt stop.

As Isabel was sucking on Jess's clitoris, she suddenly felt a sharp sting on her soft, pink, super sensitive clit. Isabel had accidentally scraped her tooth against the most sensitive part on her body.

Jess immediately jerked upward and crawled away instinctively.

"Oh my God, I'm so sorry!"

Isabel looked like she was going to cry.

Jess sat up. She took Isabel's face into her hands to calm her.

"It's okay. It's okay," Jess assured her.

She kissed Isabel on the lips, then looked her in the eye. "Listen, I have an idea, but first I want to snort more of that coke off your tits."

Isabel flashed a profane smile. "Only if you let me do a line off your ass," Isabel rebutted.

Jess nodded in agreement.

Isabel disappeared for a moment, then returned to the pile of pillows with the entire cookie tin full of coke. Isabel dumped a heaping spoonful on the top of both her breasts. This was much more than Jess had anticipated or ever wanted.

"Have as much as you want," she told Jess after handing her the straw they all used to do the coke with while she leaned back on her haunches.

Jess took the straw but wasn't sure how to proceed. The two clumps of cocaine, sitting atop both of Isabel's tits looked like fresh snow that capped a ski resort mountain.

"What's the matter?" she asked when Jess sat motionless, starting at Isabel's chest.

Jess blinked, trying her best to compose herself. "Uh, I really like your boob job."

"Aw, thanks." Isabel swayed her chest side to side.

While her boobs hardly moved at all while she was showing them off, small amounts of the glimmering coke covering them fell every time she moved. Jess involuntarily shrugged, then leaned forward with the straw held to one nostril and the other end hovering above Isabel's left tit.

"Whoa!" Jess dropped the straw and clutched her nose.

She wasn't even able to make a noticeable dent in the abundant amounts of cocaine that Isabel piled onto her breasts.

Both Isabel and Ally giggled at Jess's pain.

"It'll be numb soon enough, love," Isabel propped up the straw and handed it to Ally.

As soon as Allison took it in hand, she blurted out what Jess was thinking. "Holy Shit! Isabel, that is way too much coke for me today! I'll never be able to do all of that."

"Well, not with that attitude you won't," Isabel said encouragingly.

This answer seemed to be sufficient for Ally, who shrugged and dived right into the tower of coke piled on her tits, nose first.

Neither Allison nor Jess were experienced coke users. In fact, the two girls had only ever done cocaine while at music festivals. The girls had been in each other's presence each time the drug was offered to them, and even then, it was only a couple of bumps or a line here or there. While neither of them were avid drug users, they did not shy away from recreational drugs, such as weed, coke, molly, or mushrooms.

Jess and Ally shared the same philosophy when it came to their drug use - as long as it was a fun drug used to enhance an activity - typically music or sex - then it wasn't a problem.

While festivals were also known to be magnets for peddlers of more sketchy drugs, things like meth, heroin, PCP, or opiates, the two friends had no problem turning down such offers, which unfortunately seemed more and more abundant at recent festivals.

But since neither Jess nor Ally had ever done this much coke, or even close to it, neither were not prepared for how horny it would make them.

As an unpleasant chemical taste dripped down the back of her throat, Jess gave serious consideration to humping some of the softer looking pillows in the pile.

She suddenly felt Isabel tugging at her legs.

"Flip over so I snort this off your ass. You promised!"

Damn. She did promise.

All of Jess wanted to simply luxuriate in the pile of pillows on the ground that, while she remembered coming into the tent not understanding - only made too much sense now.

With considerable effort, Jess pushed off the ground with her hands and flipped over, one leg over the other, one arm over the other, until she was laying flat on her stomach. She pushed up on her pillows so she wouldn't be crushing her massive boobs underneath her weight. Then she found her pillow once more and clutched it to her chest, comfortable again at last.

Jess looked back at Isabel standing over her and shook her ass back and forth teasingly, a devilish smile on her lips.

Isabel stared at her a moment appraisingly, before giving a small nod. She bent over Jess and, pushing her nipples into her ass cheeks, then brushed all of the remaining coke off of the top of her tits onto Jess with her index finger.

The white powder came raining down and went everywhere. Despite only having to travel a short distance from Isabel's fake boobs down to Jess's bubble butt, Isabel clearly imagined the transfer going a different way.

The coke did not fall into a neat pile, like it was when Isabel had scooped it onto her chest. Instead, it coated not only Jess's ass but her entire back side, up her lower back, and even on a few of the surrounding pillows.

The way Jess was sitting with her naked butt sticking up in the air and her legs slightly parted, some of the coke even found its way into her pussy once it became airborne.

"Whoopsie," was all Isabel uttered once she realized her mistake.

"What? What happened?" Jess asked, trying to crane her neck around to see what was going on while still sitting flat on her stomach.

Ally and Isabel surveyed the white sheen that painted Jess's entire backside. Then erupted in uncontrollable laughter.

"What?" Jess asked again.

Between bouts of laughter so fierce that both Ally and Isabel's coke covered boobs jiggled as they held their bellies, Ally managed, "N-Nothing."

Jess kicked her shins up and down.

"Wait, why is my vagina numb?" she asked in a tone that was not laden with fear.

The question only renewed Ally and Isabel's laughter.

"Don't move," Isabel instructed.

Isabel laid flat on her stomach and started licking all of the cocaine off of Jess's butt, thighs, backside, and pussy. Seeing this, Ally quickly followed suit.

"What the fuck is going on?" Jess was more so confused rather than angry, but complied all the same.

"Well, Jess, don't be mad, but I accidentally spilt cocaine all over your ass. And, like, everywhere else," Isabel explained while Ally continued to lick coke off of Jess's butt cheeks.

"Am I going to be okay? Will I overdose?" as scared as Jess sounded, she did not attempt to get up. She did not want to leave the comfort of her frilly lace pillow.

Isabel giggled, "Oh, I'm not laughing at you, yes, hon, you're going to be just fine. Don't worry, Ally and I will get you all cleaned up. Promise," Isabel said, then went back to lapping up the white powder off of Jess's thighs.

"Will I ever regain the feeling in my pussy again?" Jess sounded like she was on the verge of tears.

Isabel was having too much fun, erupting into yet another fit of laughter.

"Yes, Jess. Yes it will, but only if you do exactly what I say."

"O-Okay."

Jess was very worried. What if her vagina was numb for the rest of her life? What would she do? Would Josh still be interested in a relationship with someone who had a broken pussy? Would she have to get handicap plates on her car so she could park in handicap spots because of her disability?

"Jess, spread your knees as far apart as they will go," Isabel instructed.

Even though Ally was just as naïve when it came to cocaine as Jess, she was well aware that Isabel was just fucking with Jess and silently cracking up next to Isabel all the while, with her hand covering her mouth as she choked back laughter.

"Okay. Okay," Jess complied, "Please hurry, I don't want to be stuck like this forever."

Ally half expected her friend to start bawling at any moment, and it was hilarious.

Both Isabel and Ally were very surprised at how far Jess could actually spread her legs apart, nearly to the point where she was doing the splits. Ally forgot just how flexible her friend really was.

As soon as her legs were spread wide, Isabel saw that there actually was a considerable amount of cocaine that had found its way into the folds of Jess's pussy. As soon as Isabel got her face in between Jess's legs and saw how tight her pussy still was, even after spreading her legs nearly horizontally, she looked Ally in the face and with a look of amazement on her face, mouthed the words in between little licks.

"Wow!"

"Oh my God!"

"So tight!"

In turn Ally took a quick glance at her friend's vagina, which she was becoming close friends with these last few days, and silently mouthed the words, "I know, right?"

Then Isabel said aloud to Jess,

"Jess, you have a beautiful looking pussy."

Jess groaned, "I know. Can you save it or will I be stuck like this forever?" clearly still worried.

Isabel sighed a deep, breathy sigh. "Well, I'll try my best."

"Hurry!" Jess groaned a very uncomfortable moan of anguish, the sound of someone who believed that they might lose the function of their genitals at any moment.

Isabel laid on her stomach facing Jess's pussy, her breasts pushed up underneath her, and started casually licking between her legs. "Can you feel that?"

"Mmm, a little, but it's still numb," she complained.

Isabel's mouth was near ground level with Jess's pussy, making access to it more difficult. Plus, Ally wanted some of it for herself, after all she promised Jess to make her cum.

Ally tapped Isabel on the shoulder to get her attention. When Isabel looked up, her tongue frozen in mid lick, Ally gave Isabel a series of silent hand movements and gestures, instructing her to tell Jess to sit up on her knees. Ally demonstrated the pose that she wanted Isabel to tell her to get into so that they could both play with her - basically a doggy-style position. Isabel smirked with understanding.

"Jess, honey, I've got bad news for you."

"Wha-ha-ha-at?" she whined.

"This isn't working, we're going to have to try something else."

"What else is there?" then she added, "Isabel, I swear to God if you broke my pussy I'm going to be pissed!" Her endless forlornness turned to anger.

"Don't worry, I'm pretty sure this will work. I just need you to sit up on your hands and knees! You know the doggy style position? Just like that, but with your knees wider apart. Like that, yes, perfect!"

It seemed like at this point, Jess was so desperate that she would rob a bank if Isabel told her it was the only way to get her pussy working again. Jess did exactly as instructed the moment Isabel commanded. With each passing second, her anxiety over losing feeling in her pussy heightened. Although Ally and Isabel felt a little bit bad about leading her on, they ultimately knew that they would make it up to her as best they could.

Once they had Jess on her hands and knees, Ally slipped underneath her, between her legs to lick her clit while Isabel positioned herself directly behind Jess's ass so she could tongue punch her vagina.

All things considered, the two were able to lap up all of the coke spilt on Jess's ass and pussy relatively quickly. Because both their mouths were so numb by then, they may have actually made Jess's pussy more numb by continually licking between her legs. Especially Jess's clitorus, which did not have any coke spilt on it to begin with, but by Ally sucking and licking on her clit, it quickly started numbing it.

But Jess did not seem to mind.

"Uh... I can feel my pussy again, Isabel? Did you hear me? Oh fuck. You guys, that feels really good. Oh my God, keep doing that. Hmmmm... Oh, wow. Oh fuck. Don't stop. Yes. Oh fuck. Yes. Oh. Oh!"

Jess twisted her grip on the pillow in her hands and collapsed forward, laying on her stomach again, breathing heavily. "My pussy still works," she said at last.

"I want to cum like that," Isabel said zealously.

"Come here, honey," Jess said as she flipped around on her back, still clutching her pillow, "you deserve it."

Isabel laid in next to Jess with Ally laying on her other side. Immediately, Jess started making out with Isabel, and her kiss was just as good as the last one she remembered. Jess brought her hand down, reaching in between Isabel's legs, and she eagerly spread them for her. Smooth, tight, and dripping wet, Jess used Isabel's natural lubricant to play with her clit.

Isabel's little moans she made into Jess's mouth as their tongues intertwined started to turn Jess on all over again.

She switched from massaging Isabel's wet pussy to slipping two fingers into her vagina. They were a tight fit, even for Jess's tiny hands, but before long she was able to fit in a third.

Isabel, with her eyes closed, raked her fingers through the back of Jess's head, pulling her face into her own for another hot, wet kiss. Isabel's other hand, stretching down to her right, crawling its way between Ally's legs.

Meanwhile, Ally was content playing with Isabel's bulbous fake breasts.

There was still a good deal of coke stuck to the perspiration on Isabel's chest, which was just a bonus for Ally, whose obsession with other women's boobs - especially huge tits like Isabel's - meant that she could occupy herself licking and sucking on her nipples pretty much all night.

And while Isabel proved that she wasn't particularly skilled at licking another woman's pussy, she certainly knew how to massage Ally's in a way that made her cry out in ecstasy with one long moan of satisfaction after another.

She was also an excellent kisser, Jess noticed, with a tongue that was more agile than most, while Jess was by no means a highly experienced pussy eater.

She wondered how Isabel could be so terrible at licking a vagina yet such an inspired make-out artist. But Jess enjoyed the breathy little panting groans that punctuated her wet kiss with Isabel. She particularly liked how rubbing and pressing on Isabel's clitorus gave her control of the frequency and intensity of those pleasurable reactions.

Jess had been fingered more times than she could count, but rarely had she ever been the one to finger another woman. As she accepted her small fingers on Isabel's G-spot, she paid close attention to the increase of her heart rate and her breathing.

She couldn't help but think to herself that this must be what guys feel like when they finger a woman, only Jess had one huge advantage over them - she was very good at making a woman cum using just her fingers, namely, one woman - herself. But she had been doing it for nearly half her life and had gotten very, very good at it.

So when Jess finally decided it was time to make Isabel cum she did the same thing that she had done to herself countless times.

She hit all the right spots, putting her fingers on her G-spot and clit simultaneously until finally the intensity was so much that she couldn't kiss Jess back anymore, all Isabel could do was throw her head back and announce the arrival of an orgasm that she made look so insanely good that both Ally and even Jess were jealous when Isabel screamed.

"Oh, fuck... Oh, fuck... Oh, I'm cumming, oh fuck I'm cumming. So. fucking. hard! Fuck! Fuck! Fuck!!!"

This was the orgasm that her husband denied her, and Jess felt dirty claiming it for herself. And yet, she also felt like only she could have given it to her, even as over the top dramatic as it may have been.

If any of their neighbors in nearby camps were asleep, they were certainly all awake by now.

"Hmmm, oh my god, that was nice," Isabel whispered, sweetly to Jess, who withdrew her fingers from Isabel's pussy and wiped her own juices on her thighs as discretely as possible.

"Will the two of you just lay with me here and cuddle? Please? Don't leave me." Isabel pleaded.

They were the requests a woman made of a man. Jess had made similar requests to men on several occasions, so she understood perfectly what Isabel was feeling. And what she wanted to feel.

No one wanted to feel abandoned after sex. Jess knew that first hand, and she wouldn't wish that feeling on anyone, not even her worst enemies.

"Yeah," Jess replied.

"Of course," said Ally.

The three women lay there naked on top of the pile of pillows in a cuddle puddle of their own design.

They lay there kissing, licking, and cuddling well into the night until all three of them fell asleep.

Chapter 10: Rude Awakening

Jess's coke nap was interrupted when she felt someone shaking her back.

It was not an urgent shaking, not a panicked hand demanding she get up, but a subtle and very gentle, if not incessant, rocking back and forth.

She opened her eyes to see Ally's beautiful sleeping face smiling in front of her, her arms still wrapped around her best friend's back. The two fell asleep still cuddling, embraced in one another's arms.

Jess yawned the wakening yawn of a lioness, stretching her arms over her head. She was hearing some distant squishing wet sound that didn't register to her.

Then she realized that someone was still shaking her back.

Jess looked over her shoulder to see Isabel there, awake, her back pressed to Jess's. Next to Isabel, she saw Jon, completely naked. He had Isabel's leg lifted high in the air and he was fucking the shit out of her.

"Oh, good. You're awake." It was Jon's voice.

She had to blink to make sure she knew what she was seeing was real.

"We were trying to be quiet until at least one of you woke up," Isabel's voice was bouncing up and down with her whole body as Jon mercilessly plunged his big dick into Isabel.

Jess's eyes fell upon their cock and pussy penetration show for just a few seconds and she froze like a deer in headlights. All of this was happening just inches from her, as if they intentionally wanted to be rubbing up against her as they started fucking.

"You can join us if you want," Isabel locked eyes with Jess while Jon held her thigh high into the air, plunging his fat cock into Isabel's tight pussy.

How he managed to get it inside of her in the first place, Jess couldn't imagine. Isabel's tits bounced up and down to the ruthless rhythm of Jon fucking her.

"I really enjoyed eating your pussy last night, Jess," Isabel's voice reverberated as she was getting fucked.

Jess could feel her whole face go tomato red. She stood up and started looking for her things. Her vision suddenly went black - she stood up too fast, forcing her to crouch down again.

"Ally. Ally, love, wake up." Jess gently shook Ally on the shoulder.

She opened her eyes, smiling wide as soon as she saw Jess's face right in front of her.

"We've got to go, Ally." Jess helped Ally to her feet, then Jess grabbed her and her friends' clothes that were scattered all across the tent in every direction and under pillows.

"Are you sure you ladies don't want to stay and play with us?" Jon asked in a grating voice that creeped Jess out.

"Hard pass," was all Jess said before the two girls walked out of the tent butt naked with a handful of clothing.

Jess wanted more than anything to grab that special pillow that she developed a personal bond with last night, but it was presently laying under Jon's ass.

"Traitor," Jess whispered to the pillow on her way out.

Chapter 11: The Lake

The daylight was blinding.

The festival was once again alive on the third day and small groups were already up and about and walking past their camp. Most festival goers smiled at the two naked, beautiful young women crawling out of the tent and into the daylight.

Ally wasn't fully awake yet. Neither was Jess, but she led her friend across the camping commons area, past the small single person tent that Ally brought but hadn't used once, and into the large tent that belonged to Jess and Josh.

"Josh? Baby, are you here?" Jess called out as the two girls ducked under the massive tent flap and into the shelter of the tent.

"There are two sexy nude girls looking for you!" Ally added, making Jess giggle.

But her laughter stopped abruptly when she saw that Josh was not in the tent. Their massive air mattress was still the unmade mess that it was in when they left it yesterday.

"He's not here." Jess pointed out the obvious.

"Now what?" Ally turned to Jess with a sullen look. Jess threw their clothes on the bed.

"Breakfast, that's what. Josh can take care of himself and I'm hungry as fuck. Ally, what's that in your hand?"

Ally held up a metal container of some sort, as if just noticing it was in her hand for the first time. "Oh, I swiped that tin of coke from Isabel's tent on the way out."

The two burst into laughter.

Then Jess handed Ally her clothes and the two women dressed in the steampunk outfits they had swiped the night before.

"We brought a camping stove and some food, help me find it," Jess instructed.

After digging through their packs, the two found the stove and were able to get it set up outside.

Before long, they had a pot of coffee heating up alongside bacon frying in a cast iron skillet and pancakes. The two girls set up reclining folding chairs underneath the canopy as they cooked up breakfast.

While they were both searching for the food in their packs, Jess uncovered another bottle of Irish whiskey.

The folding table that sat in between both girls in their reclining chairs contained two mugs of hot coffee, half full of whiskey, a plate with crispy bacon, another plate full of fluffy pancakes piled on to the sky, a coffee mug full of maple syrup that they used to dunk said pancakes before eating them, and last but not least, the cookie tin that was overflowing with cocaine.

As the two watched the world pass them by as they watched all of the ravers who were burnt out by the third day dragging ass to get to where they were going, Jess and Ally sipped Irish coffee, munched on crispy bacon, and were doing bumps of coke pretty much non stop.

All of this made for significantly more entertainment than anything else that could possibly be doing inside the music festival.

Their new favorite thing to do was to mercilessly persecute people as they innocently walked about the festival, minding their own business.

"This is not a walkway for ravers," Jess yelled at no one in particular as scores of people poured in and out of the festival in front of their camp. "If you are a raver, you are not permitted to use this road, and you will be cited according to law." Some of the people on the road scuttled along, not wanting to receive a citation.

"This is a public service announcement," Allison cried. "To any women who are caught walking the streets after dark without a man to chaperone them, I will personally put a baby inside you and sew your vagina up so it keeps growing, and growing, and growing, and explodes inside of you."

People looked at Ally like she had lost her mind.

Maybe she did.

Both women were absolutely snowblind when Josh finally walked up that they didn't recognize him at first.

"There you two are," Jess and Ally jumped at hearing his voice. "I'm so relieved to find you here." The tone of relief in his words was palpable.

"Josh?" Jess's heart skipped a beat. "Oh, Josh, baby, I've missed you so much. I'm glad you're here."

She led him by the hand and urged him to sit in the chair she had been sitting in, next to the folding table full of treats, which by now were half gone.

Josh hesitantly took a seat with an apprehensive look in his eye that said he sensed something was wrong.

But as soon as he was seated, Jess jumped on his knee, with an arm around Josh in a half hug, she sat on his knee. He gave her a suspicious look when he saw that she couldn't sit still.

Jess kept bouncing up and down on his lap like a child excited to meet Santa Clause for the first time.

"I've been looking all over for you girls. Where have you been?"

"Here, where you found us." Jess's lips curled in a smile, happy to be reunited with Josh at last.

"Where have you been?" Ally asked him.

"Out looking for you," he said as if the answer was obvious. Then he looked over at the table full of food, drugs, and alcohol. "You know what? It doesn't matter. What's important is that you're both safe. And I see you girls have been busy this morning."

"That's one way of putting it," Ally mumbled to herself.

Jess followed his gaze and realized what he was referring to.

"Oh, uh, I made you breakfast, babe." Jess smiled her toothy mischievous smile.

He chuckled, "So all of this is for me, is it? That's so sweet of you girls." He reached over to grab a piece of bacon.

"Oh, you remembered to make my bacon just the way I like it. Cold."

He set it back down and instead picked up a pancake and dipped it in syrup. He brought it to his face to take a bite, but stopped halfway, the drippy folded pancake suspended midair.

"You know what I've always liked on my pancakes? Powdered sugar."

As Josh moved his syrup covered pancake toward the pile of coke, both Ally and Jess at the same time screamed, "No!!!"

Josh froze. Smirked then popped the folded pancake in his mouth. "I'm just fucking with you." He said through a mouthful of confections. "But where did you get the blow?"

Ally and Jess shared a look. "It's Isabel's," Jess said at last.

Ally seemed to have a look of tension on her face. Her last boyfriend would have flipped out if he found her doing coke all night, even if it was just with her girlfriend.

She was genuinely worried that Josh would freak out at any moment.

But Jess knew him better than that. She knew that with his laid back personality and cavalier attitude, he would much rather choose to be happy and fun loving rather than get angry over something so inconsequential.

Given the choice, Josh would always pick having a good time over starting a fight. Jess was exactly the same way - they both preferred adventure over drama, and both of them had a hard time understanding why anyone would ever choose to be angry over choosing to be happy. Starting a scene over having a laugh. It was a rare quality that seemed to be in short supply nowadays - especially in the men that Ally dated.

"Cool. Can you rack up a line for me, babe?" Josh said with a nonchalant smile.

Jess eagerly returned the smile. "Of course, baby,"

As Jess broke down one of the bigger boulders of cocaine and went to work making an outrageously long, thick line for Josh, he continued with his story.

"You wouldn't believe the crazy shit I saw while I was walking around looking for you girls. First, do you remember that girl we ran into when we arrived? The one who peed on herself?"

"Yes," Both girls said in unison.

"Well, not only did she recognize me, she came up to me and thanked me for helping her out that day."

"She did?" Jess raised an eyebrow.

Josh nodded. "She asked about you. I told her we got separated."

"Did you, now?" Jess handed him the coke straw. Josh sucked up the massive line of white powder like it was nothing, then continued with his story.

"Relax. She was with her boyfriend." Josh sniffed. "Anyway, it turns out she works for the stage production. She hooked me up with a backstage pass."

Josh held up his left hand. Around his wrist there was a bracelet like one the ones they all got when they first entered the festival, however, the wristband Josh wore had a silver holographic pattern on it that said "production." Ally and Jess stared in awe.

"She said that if I ran into her again and you're with me she'll get you two wristbands, too."

"You went backstage without us?" Jess pouted.

Josh nodded. "Just for a second. Like I said, I was mostly looking for the two of you. Not gonna lie, though, it's lit." He smiled as he thought about it, "They have free beer!"

Something just occurred to Jess.

"Wait, Josh, have you slept at all?" She frowned at the bags under his eyes.

She already knew the answer.

"I was out all night looking for you." He shook his head. "I came back to camp twice but didn't see either of you here. So then I went to the Lake - "

"Lake?" Ally repeated, incredulous. "There's a *lake*?"

"Uh... yeah, there is a lake." Josh started hesitantly. He clearly had Ally's undivided attention.

"Then why aren't we at the lake right now?" she asked with the excitement of a kid going to Disneyland.

"Well, I see no reason why we can't all go to the lake today."

Jess stood up immediately, "Well, what are we waiting for?"

Jess and Josh exchanged a look.

"Baby, are you going to be all right today? You look tired." Jess rubbed Josh's leg that she wasn't sitting on. He smiled a tired smile at her.

"Rack up one more line for me and I'll be back to one hundred percent. Promise," he gave Jess their special smile.

Jess searched his eyes. He was telling the truth, or what he believed to be the truth. Jess gave him another quick kiss then went to work fixing up one last and massive line of cocaine for her boyfriend.

"Yeah, I want another one, too!" Ally yelled from a few feet away. She was jogging in place.

"NO!" Josh and Jess yelled back at the same time.

Josh snorted more coke and then they were on their way.

"Are we just going to leave all of that stuff sitting there?" Ally asked and gestured to the table with an ample amount of bacon, pancakes, alcohol, and cocaine left out in the camping commons.

Jess shrugged. "I'm sure Isabel and Jon will see it there and... appreciate it."

Josh looked at her. "Oh, are they back in their tent? Maybe I'll say hi before we take off."

Josh took one step in the direction of their tent before both girls yelled out, "NO!" stopping Josh in his tracks. He looked at Jess with raised eyebrows.

"I, uh, think they might be asleep, or, uh..." Jess stammered.

"They're fucking," Ally explained plainly.

"Oh, okay." Josh blinked.

And then the three were off to the lake.

Several times during their walk, Jess and Josh had to reign in Ally as she started walking way wide of the other two. More than once they had to remind her to walk like a normal human being.

"Josh, what are you going to wear when we go swimming at the lake?" Ally asked.

Josh looked at her like she asked him why he was wearing his skin. "It's a pretty big lake, I'm just going to jump in naked," He shrugged.

All three of them were wearing the clothes they got at the steampunk clothing vendor the previous day. Underneath the assless chaps Josh wore, he still had on the Chippendales banana hammock that Cheetch gave him.

"Oh," Ally considered this. "Is everyone in the lake swimming nude?"

Again Josh shrugged. "Some are. Some aren't."

"Why are you trying to see some swinging dicks, Ally?" Jess teased.

"Ew, please, it's probably a bunch of shriveled up old man weiners," Allison cringed.

Josh laughed. "You'd be surprised."

Even before the lake came into view, they could hear the joyful cheers and the splash of people jumping in the water.

The thicket of trees densened around the dirt trail leading up to the mouth of the lake, where colossal weeping willows crowded the bank in some areas and flat dirt and rocks in the lower areas where some people walked up into the water or lounged halfway in between. The amount of people who had come to the lake was palpable, though not as much as the size of the lake.

It stretched shore to shore in a crescent shape around the nearby festival grounds, then opened up a bit. No one was swimming over the deep expanse of the lake. Everyone was content to stay in the crescent within the festival grounds.

The water, Jess thought, looked pretty clean and transparent as far as lakes go. There were floaty toys and inflatables of nearly every shape, size, and animal, mythical or otherwise, posted throughout. The types of people enjoying the lake varied almost as much as the inflatables did.

Right on the path they were on leading up to the lake entrance, Jess saw a group of young women and a man lounging nude on the rocks beside a weeping willow. They were talking animatedly and laughing, clearly having a good time.

To the other side, Jess saw a group of guys wearing swim trunks sharing a joint and drinking beer.

Not too far off in the lake, she saw a guy and girl submerged up to their waist shooting each other with squirt guns.

Much farther off into the lake there were two topless women hiding on the back of a massive blow-up white unicorn.

"So, where should we put our stuff?" Josh asked as soon as the lake came into view.

Jess continued to survey the area around the lake when she at last spotted a weeping willow with a borough underneath it. It looked like it was just small enough to hold all of their clothes while still secluded enough so that no one would swipe them.

"There!" She pointed the spot out to them and they went to go check it out.

"Are you getting naked, too, Jess?" Ally asked, apprehensively.

"Bitch, please. You know that I'm always down for any opportunity where I can walk around butt-ass naked," Jess said, striking a pose.

Ally laughed nervously.

"But you don't have to if you don't want to, Ally," Jess continued. "In fact, now that I think about it, I'd prefer to not get a bunch of dirt and sand all up in my pussy. I think I'll just go topless," She smiled at her friend.

Ally looked relieved. "That's what I was thinking too," she returned the smile.

"Good point. Maybe I'll leave on the banana hammock. No one who comes to the lake wants to see dudes hanging dick, anyway," Josh already had his leather chaps off and neatly folded.

"Uh, yes the fuck they do," Jess said, poking a finger into his chest.

Josh looked at Ally for confirmation. She nodded her head silently.

Josh shrugged. "I'm still going to keep them on, all the same."

"You'd better!" Jess yelled at him.

"Mixed messages!" He yelled back in good humor.

Then, "Alright ladies, tops off." He laid his palms flat as if waiting for an offering.

Jess was the first to get her black leather top untied. "Woo!" She shouted gleefully as she jumped up and down, shaking her tits. She handed her top to Josh.

Both Ally and Josh couldn't seem to pry their eyes away from Jess's glorious, bouncing breasts.

"Girls Gone Wild, woo!" Ally screamed lasciviously after untying her brown leather top and shaking her boobs just like Jess did.

Josh delicately folded all of the clothes and stuffed them under the tree borough.

The three of them started for the shallow entrance to the lake when Ally stopped with an abrupt gasp.

"I wish I knew about the lake earlier! I would have brought Connell St. Picklebottom!"

A spark of delight lit up Jess's face. "Oh, Connell St. Picklebottom! I haven't seen him in years! How is he?"

"A little worse for wear last I saw him, but after my dad got him through that puncture wound a few years back, he's been holding up pretty well, I hear."

"I miss him so much," Jess lamented.

"I know. Me too," Allison added sympathetically.

As Ally and Jess began to commiserate, Josh butt in, "Okay, who is this Connell St. Picklebottom, and should I be jealous?"

Ally gave him a very serious look, "Oh, you should be very jealous."

Jess giggled and squeezed Josh's arm. "Connell St. Picklebottom is a giant inflatable hot dog that Ally and I used to play with all the time in her parents' pool. God, how many years ago was that now?"

Ally sighed a pleasant sigh, as if she were reminiscing. "It seems like it was only yesterday."

"A giant hot dog? I've got to be honest, now I am a little jealous. I wish my weiner were big enough for two beautiful women to ride on it at the same time."

"Flattery will get you everywhere!" Jess said as she pushed herself against Josh and stood on her toes to kiss him.

"Maybe we can put that big weiner of yours to the test later," Ally said with a devilish smile on her face.

Then a big splash drew her attention back to the lake. "What? Is that a tire swing? No way!"

Ally ran off in the direction of the tire swing.

Jess and Josh, still in each other's arms, could only stare at her as she went. With mouths agape, they weren't sure if they had really heard her say what they thought they heard her say.

Together they stood, his arms around her waist, her hands on his shoulders, both completely speechless. Finally, their gaze shifted to each other at the same time.

"Did... Did she just hit on you in front of me?" Jess couldn't get the shocked look off her face.

"Jess, I think you need to have a talk with your friend about boundaries."

Jess looked away, unable to maintain eye contact. "Look, she just needs a man in her life. It's been a very long time for her and

I wanted you to kind of help her get back in the saddle. Plus, we were all rolling hard on molly, and things kind of got out of hand really quickly."

"Well, I think she has this idea in her head that you and me and her are a thruple."

Jess paused to seriously think about the implications of entering into a thruple relationship with her boyfriend, whom she loved with all her heart, and her best friend, whom she also loved with all her heart.

She could not deny that having sex with her best friend the past two nights was a little... weird. For starters, Jess was sure that it never would have happened if she wasn't fucked up both times.

And, second, she and Ally never exclusively had sex. In both scenarios, the two friends were in a three-way.

But Ally had been Jess's best friend for 15 years.

This is the same girl who taught Jess how to slow dance when she and Ally were in junior high.

The same girl whom Jess taught how to put on makeup.

The one Jess used to cheat off in math class, even though both she and Ally got an F in math every year.

The girl that Jess got suspended for when she beat up Jimmy Sosa in 9th grade because he called Ally flat-chested and made her cry.

The girl Jess practiced making out with before we played spin the bottle for the first time at Brittany Howell's 12th birthday party.

And the girl Jess got a secret tingle of excitement for when it was her turn to spin the bottle, and it landed on Ally...

Jess was so relieved she didn't have to make out with anyone else, because Ally was the only one there that she had already kissed.

But it was more than just a kiss. Jess had always known that, but never admitted it to anyone - least of all herself.

Christ, this was the same girl Jess went with to get their pussies waxed every month since they were 19.

She held Ally in her arms and listened to her cry about boys countless times.

And Ally would listen as Jess told her every intimate detail of her sex life. Even the things she didn't tell Josh.

Jess loved Ally.

She often had lustful feelings toward her lifelong best friend, but she always felt bad about feeling that way, knowing that she would never be able to act on those desires, let alone confess them to Allison openly.

And openly confessing your deepest desires was sort of a big part of being in a relationship with three people at the same time... Wasn't it?

"I mean... would that really be such a bad thing?" Jess said at last, her voice rising as she asked the question.

Josh's eyes grew wide. That was clearly not the answer he was expecting from his girlfriend. "You want to be in a thruple? with Ally?"

"Honestly, I've never even given any thought to it until right this second."

That seemed to calm Josh down considerably.

"I'm sorry, I didn't mean to react that way. It's just that I know you and her have been friends for years and I just couldn't live with myself if I was the reason you two stopped being friends."

Josh paused to look over in Ally's direction and smiled. She was screaming her face off swinging on the tire swing topless.

"Don't get me wrong, the other night was incredibly hot, and any guy would kill for the chance to be dating two ridiculously sexy, smart, and funny women at the same time. But I love *you*, Jess, and I would never do anything that would jeopardize losing that love."

Jess took a minute to process everything he said. Part of her wanted to be mad at him, though for what she wasn't sure. She was experiencing a mix of emotions in that moment and wasn't quite sure how to sort all of them out. There was one emotion she was feeling, though, that she knew how to make sense of.

"I love you, too," on her toes, she kissed his lips. "How did you learn to say all the right words to women?"

"Trust me, this is definitely a first-time thing for me," Josh chuckled.

She put her head on his chest. His heart was beating in sync with hers.

"Let's not jump to conclusions, we don't know if that's what Ally wants. But I'll have a talk with her."

"No, really. If it's going to hurt your friendship—"

"It won't." She wrapped her arms around him and kissed his neck. "But you're sweet to worry so much. Thank you, Josh." Then she said, "Just don't ever fuck her when I'm not around."

That caught Josh off guard. "Baby, you know I would never do anything to hurt you. I love you so much."

Jess looked into his eyes and saw the conviction in them. She saw the love. Josh cupped her face with his hands and pressed his lips to hers. Jess felt her lips part as he pushed his tongue into her mouth. She eagerly accepted it, sucking it with her full, pink lips. Opening her mouth wide on his own, she licked the side of his tongue.

When he closed his mouth around her lower lip in a sucking bite, she couldn't help but make a soft moaning noise.

"Hmmm... Mmm... Oh."

Their hands explored each other's bodies as their make-out session began to heat up. Josh squeezed one of her breasts, dancing his thumb around her nipple as it hardened under his light touch. She ran her hand down his chest, feeling the corded muscles on his abs. Her hand wandered down even more.

"Oh my God, Josh." She didn't pull away from the kiss, but whispered the words into his mouth. "Why are you so hard right now?" she asked musically, drawing out the last word.

She ran her hand over the stiff bulge underneath the stretchy black pouch he wore. "Mmmm. That banana hammock is going to snap if you get any harder."

Her stroking his cock over his underwear was certainly not helping.

"What can I say? You inspire me."

The four guys who were smoking the joint earlier on the bank of the lake all started to cheer them on when they saw Jess stroking his boner and Josh squeezing her tits. The two couldn't keep their tongues out of each other's mouths for more than a few seconds, and even then it was only so they could talk dirty to one another.

"I want to fuck that juicy little pussy of yours in front of everyone in the lake," Josh delivered with hot breath.

This got Jess's heart pounding, really revving her up. But then she pulled away from under his kiss.

"Mmm... Not in the lake."

Josh was already panting to catch his breath. "No?" He protested with kisses all down her neck. "Where, then? I need you right now."

Jess felt their lust snowballing to the point where it was unstoppable. And when lust takes over all mental faculties, inhibitions quickly evaporate.

"I don't care. Just not in the lake. I don't want a UTI." She drank him in, his mouthful kisses flooding her mind. "There, by the tree."

He followed her gaze to a weeping willow roughly 30 feet away. Although it was certainly not the most private spot they could have chosen, it was the closest, least occupied space. The lake was crowded, so privacy would have been impossible. Neither were willing to make the long march back to the tent just for a quickie.

As it was, there were already a few people watching them, so in essence anywhere else they could have gone around the lake, their eyes would have followed.

Plus, both of them were staring at the lake longingly. Jess resolved that it would feel really good to have a quickie, then go for a swim in the lake.

With one hand wrapped around his hard shaft, Jess led Josh over the rocks carefully and beside the weeping willow. At least here, they would have partial cover from the tree's droopy vines.

As soon as she made it all the way to the tree, they realized just how good it was for cover. The green branches fell in nearly every direction around them. Suddenly Jess felt as if she were in some far away forest.

Jess unzipped her high black leather booty shorts and started to shimmy out of them. It was not a quick and easy process, but instead took a little work and a whole lot of booty shaking on her part.

Josh simply flung his banana hammock off, draping it over one of the nearby tree branches for the time being. Then he helped Jess the rest of the way out of her shorts by tugging them down and off her ass.

After she stepped out of her bottoms, Josh picked them up and hung them from the same branch.

"For safekeeping," he smirked.

There the two stood completely naked underneath the weeping willow, surrounded by a lake packed with festival goers. Getting proper footing on the slippery rocks underneath the tree,

Jess spread her legs shoulder width apart and bent over at the waist, supporting herself with the bark of the tree. She moved her black hair to one side, careful it did not touch the ground, then moved a few loose strands of hair out of her face so she could see Josh.

She wanted to watch him fuck her from behind.

He wasted no time in doing so.

He playfully slapped her on the ass while firmly squeezing her butt cheek with his other hand. Rubbing the tip of his cock on her wet hole teasingly, Josh slowly inserted himself between her legs.

"Oh God," Jess said in a husky voice as soon as she felt the satisfying penetration. "Oh fuck me."

She wanted everything he had to offer, and he was giving it to her.

With one hand steadying her hips and the other squeezing her ass cheek to reveal her wet pussy and her tight asshole.

As Josh thrusted his rock hard cock deeper and deeper into her impossibly small vagina, her pussy lips wrapped around his dick, moving with him, squeezing around his cock as he penetrated her.

With a handful of Jess's big, bubbly ass, he parted her cheeks so that he could admire his handiwork. Josh could not simply stare at her perfectly pink, tight asshole winking at him as he pounded her pussy.

At first he tickled the outside of it with his thumb, caressing her tempting, teasing her ass.

Then he worked the very tip of his thumb into her ass, testing it while he continued to pump his hips at a consistent rhythm.

Josh wiggled his thumb around in little circles, pressing against the inside of her asshole, widening it. Then he slapped the rest of his thumb into his girlfriend's ass, all the way up to his palm.

He watched as her tight hole swallowed up his thumb greedily, wrapping tightly around the knuckle of that hand.

"Oh, fuck yes! Just like that! Oh god, right there," Jess reacted pleasantly to his thumb exploring her orifice.

Josh got excited when he felt both her pussy and her ass contract around him at the same time. That flash of excitement made his cock throb and spasm inside her, renewing his erection as he stabbed at Jess's G-spot.

He was moving his thumb up and down in time with each thrust. With his thumb up her ass, he pushed down and applied pressure toward her vagina as his thumb was headbanging inside of her butt.

The way she squealed when he did this told him how much she was enjoying it. The way her thighs began to tremble told him that she was close to orgasm. He quickened his thrusts so that they could cum at the exact same time, or as close to each other as possible.

"Oh my god! Oh yeah, oh fuck, fuck, fuck, yeah—AHHH... yes."

Her pulse, her breathe, and her words all told Josh how close she was to orgasm. The quickness, tone, and pitch of every word—every moan of passion—was enough to indicate how fast, hard, or deep he should be fucking her.

Because they listened to each other—not just verbally, but more important, listening to each other's bodies, they were always able to time their orgasms together.

Josh could feel the final, powerful contraction of her pussy. He had listened to the sharp rise in pitch of her voice, her moan, and that final "yes" uttered meekly as he continued to fuck her, even as she was in the throes of an orgasm.

Jess grabbed a hold of her dangling tits that bounced freely with every time he filled her with his warm, hard cock. She squeezed them as continued to fuck her pussy hard during her most sensitive time.

It felt so good, that it almost hurt—almost.

It felt too good. She could resist no longer.

With one hand still supporting her weight on the tree, she released her breasts with the other, letting them continue to bounce in rhythm with their passion.

Instead, she thrusted her hand between her legs and furiously started rubbing her clit in little circles.

Again, pleasure flooded her body—and so did Josh.

She felt his hard cock sputter and convulse as he came inside of her. She could feel the white hot fluid flush her pussy. She could feel his cock begin to soften inside of her.

Yet he still continued the mechanical action of fucking her in the pussy—even with a half-soft dick.

Jess savored the moment, knowing that they couldn't keep doing this in public, in front of dozens of people who undoubtedly heard her uninhibited cries of lust and passion.

Even though she liked Josh to keep fucking her after they had both came, she stood erect and, much to her chagrin, stepped forward to remove his dick and finger from her orifices.

With a satisfied sigh as if she had just finished assembling an Ikea desk that comes in a million little pieces, she turned to admire her butt-naked boyfriend.

Lifting one foot to her bottom, she leaned forward and kissed him with puckered pink lips.

"Mmmmuh," she kissed him, and he kissed her back.

"Ready for a swim, now?" he said as he picked his banana hammock off of the tree like he was picking fruit.

With her lustful desires satiated for the time being, Jess felt good. Her body still felt warm and tingly from their quick fuck in the forest.

Tiny as she might, Jess could not wipe the smug girlish smile from her face. Her face felt warm, her body a glow. She imagined at least one of these things was from the cocaine still in her system.

"I am so excited for this! I mean, maybe not as much as Ally is, but still."

"Yeah, what's with her, anyway? Why did she get so excited at the first mention of a lake?"

Jess was remiss that, only a few seconds after they finished having sex, they were talking about Ally again. Even if it was her fault for bringing it up in the first place.

Then as Jess went to go and put her leather shorts on, she found the perfect opportunity to change the subject.

"Shit!" She shouted loud enough to draw the attention of the entire lake, if the couple hadn't already.

Jess held her shorts up with a thumb and index finger on each side, like she was picking up road kill off the highway.

"What is it?" Josh's post-coital smirk was gone.

"Josh, I can't wear this in the lake. It's leather!" Jess exclaimed.

Josh blinked. "So?"

"So, water ruins leather, Josh. If I wear this in the lake, I can never wear it again."

She didn't blame him for not knowing. Jess was a clothing designer, after all, and Josh was a graphic designer. They were like Montagues and Capuletes.

"So, what are you going to do? You didn't pay for it, remember. Are you going to hang back or did you want to go back to camp and grab something else to wear?"

Jess could tell by the way he asked her that he was dreading the idea of going back to camp when the lake was right there and the camp was so far away. She felt the exact same way.

"Oh, fuck all that. I'm still going in the damn lake. I just didn't want to go butt ass naked."

Jess shrugged, then handed the shorts to Josh. "Babe, could you please stick these with the rest of our stuff?"

Josh took the shorts from her. "You don't care about getting a UTI, then?" he smirked.

Jess had a love/hate relationship with his stupid handsome smirk.

"We would have to have sex in the lake for me to get a U.T.I." She hoped. "I said I just didn't want to go swimming with no bottoms because I'd get sand in my pussy."

"We all have to make sacrifices," he laughed as he went back to the borough below the tree where they kept their clothes.

Jess ducked down to see underneath the weeping willow and get a better view of the lake.

She could see people swimming not far from the rock overhang where she stood from underneath the tree.

She could also see people staring at her. She had no doubt that she was going to attract the attention of creeps and pervs before she even took her clothes off. There was nothing she could control about how other people reacted to things.

Besides, it had been well worth it to fulfill her lustful needs. She was horny and had no lingering regrets.

Plus, the thought of other people getting turned on watching her fuck her boyfriend was itself a turn on for Jess.

"Hey, baby, why don't you come and sit on my face?" It was one of the young men who were sitting near by the lake, drinking.

His three friends exploded with laughter as soon as he said it.

"Keep dreaming, little boy. I will break your face,"

As soon as she said it the same three guys let loose a chorus of child-like "oooh's."

"Maybe I'd like you to break my face!" one of the guys replied, earning him chuckles from of his friends.

"Then your priorities are fucked up. You should be trying to get your balls to drop first. I'm with a real man."

His face went from snow to scarlet.

Jess stood up, not wanting to deal with the heckling boys any longer. She went to go see where Josh was.

The borough where they left their clothes was not far, and he should not have been taking this long.

The moment she poked her head around the tree to find him, he came walking up to her.

"Well, I'm afraid I have some bad news…" he started, palms facing upwards.

"Josh, that's not something you want to tell your girlfriend when she is standing in front of you completely naked."

"Well, you might as well get used to being naked because all of our clothes are gone."

Jess's knees felt wobbly. "You mean, in the time span of one quickie, someone snagged our clothes?"

Josh sighed. "That's exactly what happened. I'm sure it was some perv who saw you and Ally take your tops off and snagged them right away. I asked around, but no one saw who took them."

"Then what did you do with my shorts?"

"Well, you're going swimming nude, right? I found a different spot to stash them."

"Well, at least there is that." Jess pulled him into a hug, feeling his hard body press against her soft breasts. "Let's go for a swim, babe."

Jess led him to the deep spot in the lake and together they held hands and jumped in at the same time.

The lake water was not nearly as dirty or sandy as Jess originally thought, which was a relief. Together they played and splashed and froliced in the water like they were little kids.

In the water of the lake, they were in their own little world. They splashed each other by closing their fists, half submerged in water to shoot it like a water gun.

He filled their mouths with filthy lake water and spat it at each other playfully.

Jess showed off her underwater hand stands.

Josh disappeared under water and, when she wasn't looking, he would swim under her legs and bring her up on his shoulders, only to throw her back in the water.

They had swimming races between just the two of them, showing off different strokes.

And they kissed, both above water and below water, in each other's arms.

Finally, after playing in the lake all day, frolicking like two naked toddlers having the time of their life, at last they sat on the rocky shore sunbathing and holding hands.

Chapter 12: Betrayal

The two sat in silence for a long time before finally Josh burst out into laughter for seemingly no reason.

"What? What is it?" Jess asked after catching Josh's infectious smile.

"I just realized something funny. Ally's probably been swimming in the lake all day, too."

"So? Why is that funny?"

"Weren't her shorts made of leather, too?"

Jess chuckled at the thought. "They're probably ruined by now! Plus, she has no idea that someone stole her top!"

The two laughed at the mental image of poor topless Ally and her ruined, devastated shorts.

"By the way, you never told me the reason behind Ally's obsession with lakes?"

"You seem to be thinking an awful lot about my friend Ally, lately. You know, I'm starting to think that letting you fuck her was a mistake," the words tumbled out of Jess's mouth before she realized what she said.

"Whether it was or wasn't, that doesn't change the fact that I love you with all of my heart. I only did that because you wanted me to."

"Yeah, but you enjoyed it."

"And? You can't be mad at me for enjoying sex. Even if it is with your best friend."

"Excuse me, I can be mad at you for whatever I want. That's my prerogative as your girlfriend."

"What's wrong with the fact that I enjoyed fucking your friend. You were both good for different reasons."

"You're digging yourself a deeper hole."

"I just don't see what the big deal is."

"You fucked her in the pussy and you only fucked me in the ass!" Jess yelled this loud enough for several different groups of people surrounding them to stop their conversation and look over at the naked couple sitting on the rocks arguing.

Jess could feel tears welling up in her eyes. "Is that what this is about? We literally just had sex a few hours ago. If you already forgot about that, just ask any of the dozens of people here who watched it happen!"

"She hit on you and you didn't say anything!" Jess screamed.

"So what? I enjoyed fucking her, and I'd do it again!" Josh screamed back.

"All you talk about all day is fucking Ally. I see the way you look at her. You look at her tight pussy. You look at her huge ass.

And don't think I don't see you staring at her tits when you think I'm not looking. She's all you think about, and now your big dick is all *she* thinks about! Well I'm done, Josh. I hope you have good time fucking my best friend."

Jess got up and as quick as she could, just started running into the trees. She ran off the trail, past bushes and weeds and sharp little rocks, all of which felt like knives in her feet because her sandals were stolen along with her other clothes.

But that was nothing compared to the knives she felt in her heart after Josh betrayed her.

All day long she had been cool, she let the little things go. The little glances Josh and Ally shared. The little comments. The little touches when they thought she wasn't looking.

She should have walked away after the first red flag. She should have called it quits when she walked in on them fucking in their tent that morning.

And what was she going to do now? She and Josh lived together. They had the same phone plan. They... they did everything together.

But now Josh and Ally could do everything together.

Jess kept running past trees and sharp bushes and mud and rocks. She kept running until her lungs burned and her eyes stung, until finally she could run no more.

She squatted down next to a large cypress tree and started racking in choking sobs. Everything was ruined. She had nothing left. Not even the clothes on her back.

"Whoa! Check it out, dude!" a voice from the bushes on her far left startled her.

She couldn't stop the tears from flowing, but she stood up to see who it was.

Two guys, each no older than 20, pushed through the bushes towards the small clearing where Jess wept.

One wore a bucket hat, brown curly hair, a tie-dye T-shirt and bandana around his neck. The other had long straight brown hair that looked nearly a foot longer than her own. He wore a Grateful Dead T-shirt and an abundance of beaded jewelry both around his neck and all up and down his arms and wrists.

Jess was surprised to see that they both wore matching cargo shorts. She was quite taken aback when she saw how huge their pupils both were. Like a solar eclipse, they left no room for an iris.

These were no ordinary ravers.

These were hippies. And hardcore hippies by the smell of them.

The way that they regarded Jess gave her pause.

"Whoa, she looks like one of those wood Nymphs!"

"Go away. Leave me alone," she said between bouts of sobbing.

"Aren't nymphs supposed to give you three wishes, or something?" The one with the bucket hat turned to the other hippie for confirmation.

"Yeah, dude. I wish she would suck my dick. I mean, just look at her." The long-haired hippie took his gaze up and down Jess's body in a way that filled her with anxiety.

"Go away," she repeated as she reigned in her tears.

"Well, they're called nymphs because they're all nymphomaniacs, right?"

The two carried on as if she weren't making any protests. They seemed to ignore every part of her except for her flesh.

"Fuck off!" She couldn't have been more clear than that.

"Hold her down," said the long-haired hippie, making his intentions very clear to her.

"Stay away from me!" Jess backed up, but behind her lay a dense thicket of bushes and trees blocking her path.

The two ignored her pleas and pressed onward toward her with their hands raised. Jess saw the dirt underneath their fingernails from where she stood. She could envision their filthy hands groping and molesting her.

Fear settled into a lump in her throat and paralyzed her. She cowered away from their needy hands, their predatory fingers.

Jess couldn't move.

She couldn't scream.

All she could do was close her eyes. Hot tears squeezed from her eyes, streaming down her face.

Frozen by fear, she didn't know what to do. She didn't know what she could do. None of this seemed real to her.

She felt like if she closed her eyes tight, she would soon awaken from this strange nightmare.

Thud.

Thud.

Jess continued to shut her eyes. She felt like her assailants would have been upon her by now, but all she heard was the rustling of leaves and the distant music from the festival, which seemed so very far off now.

Cautiously, Jess tentatively opened one eye, then the other. This was not what she expected to see when she woke from her nightmare.

Josh was standing over her, wearing nothing but his black Chippendale banana hammock, with his hand extended open.

She looked behind him to see that the two hippies who thought she was a wood nymph, the ones who wanted to hold her down and do terrible things to her, were both lying unconscious on the ground.

Jess, slowly and apprehensively, took Josh's hand.

"You forgot your shorts," he said, holding up her black leather shorts in his other hand.

Jess took them and immediately started dressing.

"Thanks..." Then, after she finished zipping up the tight black leather shorts, "What happened to them?" She pointed with her chin to the two bodies on the ground.

"Oh, them?" Josh said, as if not noticing the two hippies who lay unconscious on the dirt for the first time.

Jess could smell them even from a few feet away.

"They tried to despoil the honor of my girlfriend, that's what!" Josh said with that stupidly handsome face of his.

Then he pulled her into his arms, into the warm safety of his bulky biceps wrapped around her, and in his embrace, all of her anxiety started to melt away.

And was replaced by despair.

Jess put her head against Josh's chest and started to weep uncontrollably.

"Shush, shush. They can't hurt you. You're safe now. You'll always be safe with me." Josh kissed her black matted hair as he whispered consoling words.

"It's not that." She looked up into his handsome face.

She was sure she looked a mess from all the crying. She was sure her nose must be red and runny, her eyes puffy. Her hair tangled. She wanted to die.

"Everything is ruined now," she said.

"Nonsense," he said, holding her in his strong arms as he gently rocked her back and forth. "This changes nothing. I love you from the very depths of my soul. You are the reason I wake up every morning. And no other woman besides you will ever turn my eye because you are the most beautiful creature on the face of this earth. I've been incredibly lucky to find you, Jess, and I would walk through the fiery gates of hell just to be next to you."

Jess sniffed hard. Her tears had stopped. She looked up at Josh with watery eyes.

"I feel the same way about you," her voice cracked.

She put her head back on his chest, finally embracing him in a hug.

"I don't want anything to change. I love you," she said.

He kissed the top of her head. "Then don't run off like that. You scared me."

"I guess I kind of overreacted, didn't I?"

"Well…" He treaded cautiously. "That's your prerogative. As my girlfriend."

She smiled for the first time since running off. "I like being your girlfriend."

Josh put his hand under her chin, tilting her head up so he could kiss her. "I like you being my girlfriend, too."

She buried her face in his chest. "I must look a mess right now. Like a silly girl crying."

He moved her face so that he could look her in the eye. Josh took in every detail of her face as if it would be the last time he ever saw her.

Jess wanted to pull her face away. She felt ugly. But he held her there, studying her. Analyzing her. She felt like he was about to point out all of the things that were wrong with her.

Then he said, "You are perfectly beautiful in ways I can't even begin to describe. Your beauty could move stars. Every time I look at you I still get butterflies in my stomach and my heart starts racing like the tempo of a Drum and Bass song."

Jess put her hand on his chest and could feel his heart pounding away. He wasn't lying about that. It was the type of sweet, romantic thing that she loved him for.

In his arms, with her bare breasts pushed up against his hard chest muscles, Jess had one hand flat against his chest. With the other hand up to Josh's face to caress the light stubble on his cheek.

Although he typically shaved every day, he did not bring any razors to the festival and allowed his stubble to grow in freely.

Jess liked the manly feel of his light stubble against her soft skin when she kissed in, and as she cupped his manly cheek in her hand.

Jess guided his face to hers as she stood on her tippy toes for a long, romantic kiss where she held her mouth on his for a whole minute. Jess wanted to taste him, to kiss him as if she would never get the chance to kiss him again.

At long last, she lowered herself to place her heels on her feet on the ground, and through the smile that she never shared with anyone else other than him, she said, "I love you, Josh."

He returned their special smile.

"And I love you, Jess," he replied. "Do you want to go back to the lake?" he asked.

Jess was wondering when he would ask.

"Yes," She took his hand in hers and started to walk in the direction she thought the lake was. "But what should we do with these guys? Do you need me to help you bury the bodies?" She said in earnest, a dead serious expression on her face.

Josh threw his head back and let out a sharp, hard laugh. "Well, they're not dead, but I love that you're willing to be an accomplice to murder for me."

Jess's whole disposition changed. She had really thought that Josh killed the two men from the beginning, though she saw no blood.

"Oh?" Is all she said, feeling embarrassed.

"One of them I knocked out," Josh pointed to the long-haired hippie in the Grateful Dead T-shirt. "The other I put to sleep by cutting off the blood to his brain. It's called a Blood Hold. He should be waking up any minute."

He pointed to the other guy wearing a colorful tie-dye T-shirt. He was wearing a bucket hat at one point, but it must have come off when Josh did whatever he did to him because it was nowhere in sight.

"Josh, where did you learn all of this?"

He shrugged. "Reddit," he said simply by way of explanation.

Jess shook a finger at him. "Let me find out that you're really a spy posing as a graphic designer and I'm going to be really mad. Especially if you don't bring me with you on your next spy mission."

Josh made a gun with his fingers. "You got me, babe. My moniker is Double-Oh Six-Nine."

He could see an idea spark to life on Jess's face. "I know what to do..."

Jess didn't know who the two smelly hippies were, but she did know that they both looked to be tripping on some sort of psychedelics.

And that they were both idiots.

She could have stolen their wallets.

She could have stolen all of their clothes and left them naked in the woods.

She could have realistically slit their throats and buried them so deep that only the wolves would find their bodies.

She could have done any of those things and she felt like she would have been justified in her revenge.

But Jess was a mischief maker, and she had something much better in mind.

First she had Josh remove the cargo shorts on both of them. Off into the distant bushes they were flung. Jess arranged the long-haired one with his face in the dirt, knees bent, and his ass pointed up in the air. It took a bit of juggling before they found a way to keep him propped up in that fashion.

The other one, the one wearing the tie-dye, Jess set him on his knees directly behind the long-haired hippie, with his hands and body all slumped up against his back.

When she was finished, Jess took a couple steps back.

"Voila!" She said with both arms raised, as if presenting her work.

Josh stepped back and placed a finger on his chin and cheek, admiring it the way an art critic might.

"It looks like they're butt fucking," He said at last.

Jess turned to him and laughed. "How funny is it going to be when they sober up from their memory of trying to rape me, then when they wake up they think that they were really butt fucking each other?"

"The naughty woodland nymph strikes again," Josh said, and the two walked hand in hand back to the lake.

Both were bare foot because their flip-flops were among the things stolen, along with Jess and Ally's bikini tops and Josh's assless chaps.

"We'd better find Ally and go back to camp before the sun goes down and it starts getting cold out." Jess suggested.

Josh looked very pleased with this recommendation.

"Yes, please. I am freezing my dick off in these things." Josh had been walking around practically naked all day. But then again, so had Jess.

When they returned to the lake, they found Ally right away. She was sitting on a rock by the tire swing, surrounded by three men wearing swim trunks. All three of them seemed to be absolutely captivated by whatever Ally was telling them, hanging on her every word.

As soon as Jess and Josh came into Ally's field of vision she left the rock and the swing where she was the center of attention and ran up to her friends. One of the three men followed closely behind her while the other two stayed seated on the rocks.

"Hey, you two." She ran up to them bearing a toothy smile of genuine happiness. This was a smile that Jess had not seen on her friend in quite some time.

"Hey! This is Rick," she turned to the guy trailing in behind her. Jess thought he looked like a stereotypical surfer guy, complete with 90210 hairstyle, a pooka shell necklace, and gold and black swim trunks. He had a lean frame. Not nearly as big or muscular as Josh, though because he was so lean his muscles were all very pronounced. His eyes were as blue as the ocean and his teeth as white as clouds. Jess could easily see why Ally was charmed by Rick.

"Rick, these are my friends I was telling you about, Jess and her boyfriend, Josh." Ally looked very excited to make this introduction.

"Hey. I've heard a lot about you," Rick said, as he shook Josh's hand. When he went to shake Jess's hand, she pulled him in close and whispered loud enough for everyone to hear, "If you hurt my friend they will never find the body."

When he went to shake Josh's hand, he said, "If you even think about looking at my girlfriend's tits they will never find the body."

"Your friends are intense," he said to Ally, a grim expression replaced his handsome smile.

"Stop it! You'll scare him away," Ally laughed.

Rick did not.

"Ally, I'm afraid we have some bad news," Jess said, her eyes going back and forth between Rick and Ally.

"What happened?" she asked soberly.

"Someone stole all our clothes."

Ally didn't say anything. She continued to stare at Jess as if she was waiting for more bad news.

"Oh. That's too bad. You mean my top is gone?"

Jess saw the faintest smirk on Rick's lips. He did not appear displeased by this information one bit.

"Yeah... we're going to head back to camp before the sun goes down," Jess pointed vaguely in the direction of where their camp might be. Ally made a funny face.

"Um... actually, I think I'm going to go back to Rick's camp and hang out for a little bit."

Jess had to fight hard not to smile. She knew this was coming from the moment she saw her sitting on the rocks surrounded by all those boys. She also knew very well what "hang out" entailed.

"Okay, Ally. Well, I love you, and you two stay safe."

"Thanks, we will."

Jess and Ally embraced in a hug. Jess was happy that her friend had found someone. That was the main reason for her coming. Jess just hoped that she made the correct choice.

"Remember, Rick, there are a lot of woods out here for cadaver dogs to cover and hydrochloric acid dissolves very quickly," Jess said as sweet as honey.

Rick gave a very nervous laugh and then the two were off. As Ally and Rick were walking away, Jess heard him say, "I like your friends."

As Jess and Josh turned to walk back to camp basically half naked and barefoot, Josh said, "Good for her."

Chapter 13: Allison's Obsession

Jess and Josh started back to camp as the sun hung low in the sky. The number of people walking the plain dirt trail back into the festival dwindled. They could still hear the distant music pulsing from the powerful stacks of speakers. Jess listened intently.

She didn't know who was performing, but it sounded like one stage was playing a Marshmello song while the other was Boogie T. Jess wanted to dance-walk, but it was a long way and she was tired.

Jess felt Josh give her hand a squeeze.

"Are you really going to make me ask you again about Ally and the lakes?"

Jess smiled but inwardly sighed. "You can't let that go, can you?"

Josh shrugged. "I know there is a story there."

"There is," Jess began. "A long time ago, when Jess and I were in middle school, our parents sent us to the same summer camp one year. It was not a very nice or expensive summer camp. It was pretty much just a place our parents sent us so they didn't have to see us over the summer. Come to think of it, it was a lot more like a prison than a summer camp for kids. Even at that age, it was very clear to us that they were pretty much just babysitting us.

"But it looked like it was a proper camp, like, in the mountains and all of that. All of the buildings were made out of logs, like those old-timey cabins. So, it gave the whole experience a very unique feel. We just didn't do anything the whole time we were there.

"One of the few activities they did have was swimming at a lake. There wasn't much else, no kayaks or anything like that, but they did have a tire swing."

"Ahh..." Josh was captivated by her story.

"So there were two cabins where we slept, one for boys and one for girls. Everyone loved going from the tire swing and jumping into the lake. Come to think of it, it was very dangerous, and I'm surprised they even let us do that, but like I said, it wasn't a very nice or expensive camp.

"All of the kids lined up for their turn to jump into the lake from the tire swing. Ally and I were in line. I went first and made it in the lake. I was a bit of a cannonball freak, come to think of it."

"Oh, really?" asked Josh.

"Yeah, so, I go. Then, when it's Ally's turn, she freezes up. And mind you, there is a huge line of kids behind her waiting for their turn. So, I'm in the lake and I see Ally up there clinging to the tire for dear life. She looked scared out of her mind, and the other kids aren't making it any better. Ally is holding onto the tire with her eyes squeezed shut. Then, out of nowhere this boy steps up to her and starts telling her that everything is going to be okay. He calms her down, and together they fling themselves off of the tire swing, holding hands, into the lake. It was the most romantic thing that my 13 year old brain could imagine at the time."

"Aww... What was his name?"

"Billy Finnie. Don't ask me how I still remember that, but I do. So, Ally and Billy end up spending every minute of the rest of our time at summer camp with each other. Even though there was only, like, two weeks left. But for a teenage girl, a lot can happen in two weeks.

"Obviously she developed a huge crush on him. She even got in trouble for sneaking out of the girl's sleeping cabin and into the boy's cabin after 'lights out' just to be with him. It was so cute.

"But Billy was from Santa Barbara, and Ally's family lived in Pasadena, so when camp ended they said their goodbyes. Ally never wanted it to end, but after that summer they never saw each other again. I had to console her for weeks after that happened before she finally stopped crying."

"And that's why she has an affinity for lakes?" Josh asked.

"Well... that's part of it." Jess tried off,m as she gazed distantly out at the lake.

"There's more?"

Jess craned her neck around to the distant foothills on the horizon. The sun had begun to set. "When we were juniors in high school, Ally's family brought me on a vacation with them to celebrate our good grades. That year, they rented out a cabin at Lake Arrowhead."

Jess saw Josh's eyes roll. She felt that he could already tell where this story was going.

"And she met a boy up there, did she?" He raised one eyebrow.

Jess nodded.

"He was a local who lived in Lake Arrowhead. Ally fell for him hard. One day, when her parents were off skiing, they hooked up in the cabin they rented."

"And where were you during all of this?"

"In the living room, playing Guitar Hero."

Josh chuckled. That was so very much like her.

"Anyway, that guy was the first boy Ally has been with. Don't ask me his name because I don't remember. And please don't ask Ally either, because then she will know I told you this story.

"Anyway, as you can imagine, Ally was once again devastated that he had no intention of keeping in contact with her. And because he was the very first guy she had ever been with, it took her a while to recover from that one too."

"It seems like Ally has bad luck with lakes," Josh pointed out. "You'd think if anything she'd have some sort of aversion to lakes."

Jess gave him a look. "One would think." She breathed a deep sigh. "And you remember her last boyfriend?"

"Yeah. They were dating for a while. Don't tell me..."

A sad smile curled Jess's lips. "Guess where he lives?"

Josh shrugged.

"Silverlake."

"Is that the one with the swan paddle boats?"

"No, that's Echo Park, but we did that with him and Ally, too."

"Wow, okay. Now I'm seeing the association. From her perspective, at least."

"Ally once told me that her future husband has to be an Aquarius and that her wedding would be lakeside."

"I see." Jess could tell that Josh wanted to say more, but was withholding.

"Yeah," she said. "It's a bit of an obsession. She is like a dog with a bone sometimes. It's cute, though. How she is obsessed with my tits."

"Your tits?" Josh was surprised the conversation took this turn.

"Yeah!" Jess said as if it were self-evident. "Ally is a little self-conscious because she has small breasts. So she has always been obsessed with anyone who has big boobs. Josh, how have you not noticed this?"

Josh stared at Jess's breasts which hung free in the wind. Jess's tits were firm, supple, and perky D-cups. Josh frequently referred to them as "perfect", "every man's dream", and "proof of the existence of God."

Currently, the cold twilight breeze made her nipples feel like icicles. She wanted to cover them up to warm herself, perfect or not. Also, because they attracted the attention of every man they crossed paths with.

In a way, Jess was just happy that her body could put a smile on their faces.

"Ally doesn't have small titties," Josh said at last.

"Oh, you know what I mean," Jess replied.

Jess was being a little facetious when she said Ally had tiny tits. In reality, they were on the large side of a C-cup. But size is all about perspective.

"Oh," Jess added, as if she was just struck with urgent news. "I forgot to tell you. Isabel and I had sex last night."

Jess phrased it like that specifically to see what type of reaction she would get from him. But he didn't even flinch.

"Yeah? How was it?" Josh asked.

Jess made a sort of frown. "Not great. Isabel has no idea how to eat a pussy."

Josh raised one eyebrow. "But, she does have a vagina, doesn't she?"

"Yes!" Jess laughed and squeezed his hand. "I said pretty much the same thing." Jess ran her fingers up Josh's arm, caressing his biceps, running her finger along the outline of his tattoos. "We were just coked out and fooling around." She said softly, as if trying to ease him into the idea.

"By the way, that reminds me..." Josh began. "You're not about to tell me that you and Jon had sex last night, are you?"

"No, but he did ask me if we wanted to join them in a four-way."

Jess blinked. "So, he DID ask you if you wanted to have sex with him." She teased.

"No, well. Maybe." Josh put a thumb and index finger to his chin, thinking. His eyes narrowed as he looked at Jess. "Did he?"

She giggled and squeezed his hand. "I'm joking!"

A moment passed in which Jess and Josh both independently thought about it.

"Well," he said at last.

"Well, a foursome seems boring, doesn't it? I mean, I can honestly say that I really enjoyed all of the threesomes that you and me have had together."

"Just not the lesbian ones," Josh interjected.

"It was not a lesbian threesome! And anyway, that's why I said that I enjoyed all of the times that YOU and I have had a threesome with someone else. But what I'm trying to say is that a foursome just sounds boring. It's just two couples fucking right next to each other. What's the big deal? Even that one time with—what were their names? Crystal and Chong?"

"Crystal and Cheetch," Josh corrected. "But they also told us that those were just their rave names."

"Okay. Whatever. At least when we were in their bed I got to eat Crystal's ass. Wait. Did she squirt on your face?" Jess asked.

Josh laughed, "she did indeed."

"Right, well, the point I'm trying to make is that with three people, it's always a good time, with four people, it's just two couples having sex in proximity to each other. But with five people, well, even that was fun."

Jess wasn't sure if she was getting her point across. She wasn't sure why she was having a hard time articulating this.

Josh breathed a sigh and started slowly, "so, essentially, you're saying that it's only fun to have sex when the number of people involved is a prime number?"

"A prime number!" She swatted his arm. "Stop making fun of me! I'm trying to have a serious conversation."

"I'm not making fun of you, I'm trying to understand. And for the record, I agree with you. What are prime numbers? One, two, three, five, seven, eleven, and so forth. It seems like if there are an even number of people who agree to have consensual sex, they would simply break off into pairs. I mean, isn't that the definition of coupling, after all?"

"You do get it." Jess smiled.

He squeezed her hand again. "That's because we're so in sync."

Chapter 14: Ferris Wheel

As they walked closer to camp, they passed the entrance to the main festival grounds. Jess was at ease to at last see that she was not the only one walking around topless.

While the ravers who attended smaller festivals such as this had a tendency to dress as scantily clad as possible, the women especially enjoyed dressing provocatively.

Being a nudist, women confident in her own skin, being among peers, her sisters in sensual fashion, put her at ease.

In addition to several knots of naked people who had just come from the Shower Stage, Jess smiled and nodded at a group of girls all clad in different colored tutu's all wearing elaborate pasties on their nipples. Each one was the same color that corresponded to their tutus.

Just at a glance, Jess saw pasties that were shaped as cup cakes, middle fingers, unicorns, Rick and Morty Portal Pasties, and Excision X pasties, just to name a few.

Inside the festival grounds, the din of the festival grew to a clamor that now required Jess and Josh to scream at each other just so they could hear themselves.

Jess looked at Josh as he mouthed something to her. He was pointing into the festival.

"What?" Jess yelled.

"Ferris Wheel." He repeated, squeezed her hand, and then pulled her underneath the decorative arch connected to the fence that separated the festival from the campgrounds.

Jess didn't understand what was happening or why Josh was suddenly leading her through the thick crowd of festival goers like a man possessed. It was so loud with the music, being that close to the stages, as well as the throngs of people all shouting at each other, so they could hear themselves over the music.

It was impossible to hear anything any one person said, Jess thought, and it was impossible for her to see where they were going. All she could do is hold on to Josh's hand for dear life and cover up her boobs as best she could with her other hand.

An amazing thing happened to men when you put them in a compact cluster with other men when they had to stand elbow to elbow. You could take the most honest, hardworking, educated, and handsome gentleman and put them in a group of 100 other equally nice and decent guys. Then you add one topless female in the middle of all of them and suddenly everyone will try their hardest to touch, grab, fondle, grope, and molest her breasts because they think that in the anonymity of the crowd they can get away with sexual assault.

So as they walked past a crowd of people, Jess did her best to use her free hand to hold her bare breasts in place, and protect them from anonymous sexual offenders in training.

Because she was looking around at all of the other people, not only trying to protect herself from assault but also admiring other peoples' rave costumes, Jess didn't realize exactly where they were when Josh stopped.

He pulled her along and out of the thicket of ravers, leading her between two metal barricades, the kind they use to fence off the very front of the stages. When she looked up, she realized that she was in line for the Ferris Wheel.

"Josh, what are we doing here? I thought we were going back to camp?"

"Jess, this is a rare opportunity. Did you see the line for the Ferris Wheel the day we got here?"

Jess shook her head. The only thing she could remember about their first day at the festival was rolling hard on molly and the ensuing threesome with Ally.

When Josh spoke, she only heard part of what he said to her. "Lile Splash Mountain. I imagine they were there for hours. It was nothing short of divine intervention. Especially considering the time of day."

Jess had no idea what he was talking about, but he suddenly seemed very adamant that they ride the Ferris Wheel, and Jess wasn't about to get in the way of that or try and convince him otherwise.

She realized that she had her arms folded over her chest and was tapping her foot impatiently.

"Okay, Josh. One time around. Then we go back," she said quietly.

The smile on his face told her that he was very content with this decision.

The couple in front of them boarded one of the carriages on the Ferris Wheel, then it spun just a little so that Jess and Josh could get in the next empty one.

The cart only seated two people. They were surprisingly in excellent shape for a carnival ride. Every carriage was painted bright red with a golden pinstripe going around the outer edge. The white safety bar against the bright red of each carriage reminded Jess of Christmas.

The ride operator said something when their empty carriage arrived, but Jess could not hear a word of it over the loud music. Josh got up into the cart first, then turned around to offer Jess his hand.

How very chivalrous, thought Jess.

She took his hand and he helped her up the large metallic step and into the carriage. Jess barely had time to sit down before the ride operator clicked the white safety bar down to rest just above their laps.

In an instant, they were off. Jess's back slammed against the fiberglass cart as soon as the ride jumped to life. She was surprised that it had such a kick to it, as far as Ferris Wheels go.

As soon as their carriage crested the top of the wheel, Jess immediately realized why Josh wanted to ride the Ferris Wheel so badly.

Jess sighed at the breathtaking view, "Wow, Josh. It's beautiful."

She couldn't look away. At that very moment, the sun was setting over the trees and distant foothills off in the horizon. The entire sky, as far as Jess could see, was lit up with stunning pink, orange, and yellow clouds all melting to gather like cotton candy that stretched out and fell beneath the hills. It was by far the most beautiful, exquisite sunset that Jess had ever experienced.

"This is nothing compared to the beauty you bring into my life." Josh slid his arm behind Jess's neck. She laid her head on his chest.

"Thank you for bringing me up here, Josh. I love you." She squeezed him tight from where she was sitting.

"I love you, too, Jess, I love you, too."

In that moment, she could feel his love fill her up. She could feel her own love for herself. His love completed her—fulfilled her. In that moment she felt like every action, every decision she had ever made in life was the correct one, because they all brought her here, to this moment.

Watching the sunset on a Ferris Wheel with the man she loved, knowing that he loved her back. Completely, wholly, fully loved.

Jess gently tilted his chin so that her lips could touch his. Never before had such a kiss sent tingles all up and down her body. Never before had she felt so completely happy on the inside that she thought she might burst like a bottle of champagne.

"You make me so very happy." Her voice broke as she said it, so content that she was moved to tears.

"That's been my greatest aspiration in life."

There was no sarcasm in his voice, for she knew that this was how he felt; Josh was so deeply in love with her that he took great satisfaction from her happiness, from putting her needs before his. He happily sacrificed for her love, and she would do the same.

Josh took her in his arms and she took his face in her hands and all of a sudden they forgot about the sunset.

As they spun around once more down the Ferris Wheel and then back up again, their lips wrapped around together, their tongues just as intertwined as their souls. All Jess could think about while they shared that intimate kiss on the ride was how much she loved him. How she would do anything for him. How her lust for him was insatiable, like a bottomless well.

Their carriage crested the top of the Ferris Wheel once again, pausing there so that others below could get on. Behind them, they could see the entire festival laid out before them.

They were at the highest part of the entire music festival and could see everything from their romantic vantage point.

They could see the stages with their flashing lights and wall of speakers.

They could see the ocean of people in front of those stages.

They could see the pockets of clearings in the middle of that ocean of people where mosh pits were going on.

They could see the lake far to the northeast and just how big it really was.

They saw the long trail they walked from the lake to the festival entrance.

They saw the camp grounds that seemed to stretch out and blanket the land like the ocean of people.

They saw into each other's eyes and the infinite love they had for each other.

And then the sun had set, and they saw nothing but darkness as tiny lights flickered on from everywhere, all over the festival.

And then their carriage began to sink backwards and the next thing they saw was the ride operator telling them that the exit was on the right.

Even though they were no longer on the ride, they were both mentally in another world, still wrapped up in the high of seeing the world from way up there. From seeing the height of their love for each other.

On the corner by the metal barricades, next to the Ferris Wheel exit, they stood just holding each other in their arms. Jess lay her head on Josh's chest. Neither wanted to break off from the embrace.

Unfortunately, the many assholes who were getting off of the Ferris Wheel who kept bumping into them on their way out did.

"Baby?" Jess said loud enough for only him to hear her.

"Yes, love?" She could hear and feel his entire body vibrate when he spoke.

She placed the bottom of her chin directly in the middle of his chest so she could take up at his beautiful blue-gray eyes.

"I think I'd like to have a foursome with your friend and his wife." She thought that if she had to say their names, she might back out.

"I see," he said in a completely non-judgemental way.

"And how did you come to that conclusion?"

"Walk with me and I'll tell you." It was a question, of course, "my love."

Josh smiled down on her.

Josh only took one step before Jess pulled him back.

"Baby?"

He looked at her as if there were a problem. He was eager to solve it. "Yes, Love? What's wrong?"

She smiled a shy smile. "Will you carry me?"

He smiled warmly at her. It was as if the sun had set all over again. Without another word, Josh turned around and crouched down so that she could mount him.

Jess climbed up his back and, using the hair on his head to balance herself, put one leg on either side of his head so that her things dangled down across his shoulders, her feet came down to his chest. Josh was already tall. When he stood up, Jess towered over everyone else.

She couldn't help but think to herself, *try and grab my tits now, motherfuckers.*

Chapter 15: Loud Dirty Talk

Jess loved riding on Josh's shoulders. It made her feel big and powerful while at the same time reminded her of when she was a child. Because Josh held on to the sides of her upper thighs for balance and support, Jess did not need to hang on to anything to remain upright. This freed up her hands for important things like flipping people off and squeezing her boobs when people gave her a dirty look.

"You okay up there?" Josh asked as he pushed his way through the crowd. "You're going to have to tell me where to go. Be my navigator. It was much easier to hear him when he was talking to her without yelling now.

"I love this so much!" she giggled like a child. "Keep going straight. You're on the right path."

"So, why the sudden change of heart?" She knew what he was talking about.

"Well, when we were riding the Ferris Wheel, I realized something."

"What's that?"

"That our love runs so deep and is so complete that I trust you fully, with every bit of my heart."

"Aw, that's sweet. I feel the same way."

"I know you do. And that's why I'm okay if you fuck other people, like Isabel, as long as I get to watch."

"I guess I'm all right about you fucking my friend, Jon, but only if you really want to."

Jess hesitated. She knew that by not saying anything, it was making Josh nervous. She didn't want him feeling nervous, but she was unsure if she should divulge what she knew about Jon.

"I saw his dick."

Josh missed a step.

"You WHAT?"

"When Isabel and Ally and I were all fooling around, we fell asleep for a minute and when I woke up Jon was fucking Isabel. I saw his dick."

"He was having sex with his wife in front of you and Ally?"

"Well, we were asleep at the time. Anyway…" Jess wanted to quickly get off this subject. She still felt bad that while he was combing the festival looking for her, she was having sex with the girls in the tent right next to their own.

"Anyway, the point is, I don't want that thing inside me."

Josh didn't say anything for a few seconds. It made Jess incredibly anxious.

"Why? What's wrong with his dick?"

"Babe. It's HUGE."

Jess thought Josh's knees were going to buckle.

"Are you serious?" And then he asked the one question Jess knew he would ask. "Bigger than mine?"

"I don't know, and I don't want to find out. You can tell him that I'll suck his dick if he wants but under no circumstance is he to put that thing anywhere in the proximity of my vaginal area. You tell him that."

"Okay."

"Or anal area. I don't want him to try and find a loop hole in my loop hole."

"Got it. And you don't mind if I fuck his wife?"

"No, baby, I want you to. I like doing stuff like this with you. Besides, I already made her cum once."

"You made her cum?"

"Why do you sound surprised?"

"Because you said she was bad at eating pussy."

"That doesn't mean I'm not! Besides, I'm pretty sure that Ally and I taught her a few things."

"You're going to have to tell me all about that one later."

"Oh, I will,"

"Babe, you can have sex with as many women as you please as long as I get to hear about it at the end of the day."

Jess giggled. "How generous. And you can have sex with as many women as you want, as long as I get to watch. I think I am okay with that."

"See, baby? Our love is stronger than all that, because no matter who we invite into our bed, it's still going to be just you and me who make the bed in the morning, forever and ever."

Jess patted his head lovingly. By now, they were on the dark and sparsely populated trails leading into the camps.

"Stuff like this is good for us, baby."

"As long as we set the ground rules ahead of time," Josh added.

"Yay! Now I'm excited for this four-some! And she really was.

Their exuberant, zealous conversation was attracting the attention of bystanders as the practically naked couple walked the dirt trail back to camp—with no shoes.

"Babe, I think you'll really like fucking Isabel's pussy. I was surprised that it was so tight!" Jess started talking louder just so she could try to get a reaction from the people around them who she was certain were listening.

When she stopped to actually consider the words coming out of her mouth, Jess thought to herself what a fucking crazy life I live. "You mean, because Jon's dick is so big?" Josh matched her volume level. He knew how to play the game as well.

"Uh-huh. When I was watching him fuck his wife, I couldn't believe he could fit such a huge cock in her itty bitty vagina hole!"

"Well, we thought the same thing the first time I tried fitting my massive cock in your unrealistically tight pussy, but we solved that crisis pretty quickly, did we? And plus your vagina somehow got even smaller after taking that pounding, didn't it?"

"Baby, you're forgetting that I have a magical pussy, you know they don't make them like mine."

"Yes, you certainly have a one-of-a-kind pussy. That's for sure. So, how many fingers did you fit into Jon's wife's vagina?"

"Three fingers. But I have tiny fingers."

"Hmm... Babe, please tell me she doesn't have an 80's hairy pussy like that girl we saw when we got to the festival."

"Oh, no, it's actually a freshly waxed vagina. When my friend and I were licking her pussy at the same time, I noticed it didn't even have any stubble on it. No razor burn, either. So she must have just had her snatch waxed for the festival."

"That's good. Does she have a tight asshole? I might want to fuck Jon's wife in the ass while you suck his cock."

"Oh, babe, that sounds so nice, I would really like that. But I want you to fuck her in the pussy, too. So you can tell me how tight it is, okay? Can you do that for me, love?"

Jess saw that the two guys who had been walking in the same direction next to them had to adjust their pants to hide their erections. Even in the dark, that was obvious to Jess. In fact, that was kind of the whole fun about having these conversations in public and as loud as possible.

"Fuck, babe, this is getting me so wet and horny. Are we almost there? If not, we're going to have to pop into one of these strangers' tents so you can fuck me. And maybe see if anyone wants to join in." She added that last part to see what the guys walking beside them would do, other than that, every word of it was true.

"I think we're almost there, babe. Honestly, it's hard to tell in the dark. Tell me more about how you want to get fucked when we get back to camp."

This picked up her spirits.

"Well...." she said loudly, in her best phone sex operator voice. "I'm having trouble deciding whether I want you to fuck me in my pussy or fuck me in my ass. But I know that I definitely want to have your friends' dick in my mouth, while your fucking me from behind. Baby, I'm just not sure. Why don't you surprise me and stick your big cock in any hole you want."

"Well, if I'm going to fuck his wife's freshly waxed pussy like you asked, then I might as well fuck you in the ass tonight, babe."

"Hey! I said I wanted you to surprise me with which of my tiny holes you stick your dick in tonight! But since you already came in my pussy a few hours ago, I guess it's only right that you fill my ass full of cum tonight. You know how much I love it when you cum in my ass."

This was a game that they called "Loud Dirty Talk" and not only were they good at it, it could go on for a very long time until they eventually made everyone else around them uncomfortable.

Sometimes they talked about made up scenarios that were just outlandishly obscene. Sometimes they really did talk about the things that they wanted to do to each other as loud as possible in public. Either way, the game never failed to turn them on and get them worked up.

This one was the latter.

Although Jess wasn't lying when she said she was growing increasingly wet and horny, in reality, all she really wished for was to be held in the safety of Josh's arms and cuddle all night.

But if everything went according to plan, she would have all of her wishes fulfilled tonight.

Chapter 16: Foursome Friends

They finally arrived at their camp after getting lost for a bit, having been distracted by their game of Loud Dirty Talk. Josh set Jess down and she proceeded to rub her sore vagina, having been rubbed raw against the back of Josh's head for the better part of an hour.

They found Jon and Isabel making s'mores on the camp Coleman grill. Jess was a bit nervous at the sight of them after their game of L.D.T.

"You did all my cocaine," Jon said by way of greeting before he sunk his teeth into a freshly constructed s'more.

"I thought it was Isabel's?" Josh said, as if that made it any better.

Jess interjected, "Jon, you wouldn't have wanted all that coke anyway. It definitely had a weird smell to it. Trust me, I checked many times and it smelt funny."

Isabel was the only one who laughed at Jess's joke.

"Jonny," Josh wanted to get his attention, "Jess and I are in."

Jon's entire demeanor changed after he said that. Jess saw him silently celebrating, mouthing the word, "Yes!"

Even Isabel broke into a big smile.

"But—" Josh continued and Jon's smile faded.

"But what?" Jon asked with eager anticipation.

"BUT" Josh went on, "I the only ground rules are that Jess wants to suck your dick, but she doesn't want it anywhere near her ass or pussy. She is afraid of your hideous monster cock and is scared to have it inside of her."

Isabel and Josh burst into laughter.

"It's not all that bad, Jess, really," Isabel said between fits of laughter.

"No, no, that's fine. I totally understand. Jess looks like a very nice, petite woman and I would hate to hurt her or ruin her for you, Josh." Jon erupted into another fit of laughter.

When he finally got his laughter under control, Jon added, "And I've got a rule for you, Josh!" The way he was snickering, Jess was sure he was about to make another stupid joke. "I don't play that gay shit. I know it'll be hard for you, Josh, but try and keep your hands off my dick."

Josh shrugged and deadpanned, "I'll do my best."

There was a pregnant pause that followed where no one knew what to say next, but everyone was smiling and looked like they were going to burst into nervous laughter at any moment. In that silence, Jess fully expected the next words out of Jon's mouth to be, "Let's fuck!"

But they weren't.

He surprised Jess when he said, "S'more?" and handed her a freshly constructed tasty treat.

Then he offered one to Josh, who cautiously took it and tried a bite. Jess was trying hard not to get the melty marshmallow and chocolate on her fingers, so instead she just tried to eat it all as fast as she could. It did not taste very good at all and was quite bitter.

"Jon, I appreciate you taking the time to make these for us, but I've got to be honest with you, these are fucking terrible." Josh took another bite. Then spit it on the dirt.

"I've had three of them!" Isabel said excitedly.

A sly smile appeared on Jon's face. "Did you not like that one? Here, try this one. I used a different type of chocolate in this," he handed Jess another complete s'more that looked identical to the last one. When she bit into it, she immediately noticed a difference, but there was still a bitter aftertaste.

"Did you use, like, 90% dark chocolate in these, Jon?"

Jess, again trying to balance the gooey, drippy s'more in her hand without making a mess, simply popped the entire thing into her mouth. She would have just thrown it in the dirt, because even the second one wasn't particularly good, but she didn't want to be rude. She knew she would have this man's massive cock in her mouth within the hour, and maybe the chocolate would mask the taste.

"I don't think so. To be honest, I'm not sure. I got it off the dark net," Jon answered before taking another bite.

Jess froze. "Excuse me?"

"You know, The Dark Net. The same place I got the coke and molly."

"Molly?" She turned to Isabel. "What molly?"

"The molly I put in the marshmallow fluff. The chocolate in the first s'more I gave you was THC chocolate. The second chocolate had psilocybin in it."

Jess was speechless. She looked at Josh.

As soon as Jon finished explaining what was in the s'mores, Josh popped the rest of his in his mouth. "They taste like chemicals," he said simply, licking his fingers.

Josh appeared to have no problem being slipped drugs unknowingly by his friend. As if he was reading Jess's mind, he turned to her and said, "Baby, it's our last night here at Electric Love. Let's just enjoy ourselves and make some memories, okay?"

She smiled at him, "Okay, babe." Although she didn't like being slipped drugs, and the last guy to try to do that had his teeth knocked out, Josh was right. There was no harm in getting high on their last night. Especially if they planned on having sex all night long.

"I like them." Jon pointed to Isabel. "She likes them. Have as many as you want."

"I'm good," Josh and Jess said at the same time.

"Jess." Jon looked directly at her. Jess's heart beat nervously. "I want to apologize to you for my behavior this morning. If I offended you or made you uncomfortable in any way, I am sorry."

This was just about the last thing that she expected to hear come out of Jon's mouth. The apology sounded a bit forced and rehearsed, but that didn't make it any less amicable. Jess had a hunch that the apology was Isabel's idea. Even so, it was nice to hear him say it.

The truth was that she was a bit uncomfortable around him and over the course of the weekend, she formed a strong opinion of him. Whether he meant it or not, the apology was nice to hear and it did soften the picture of him that Jess had created in her head.

"Thank you, Jon. That means a lot."

Isabel shot him a look after that, as if to say, "See?"

"And, Jess." Isabel started in an atypically polite and formal tone. "I want to thank you and Ally for last night. I've never gone down on another girl before, but I really enjoyed doing it with you." She cleared her throat nervously and moved her gaze to the ground. "I was hoping that maybe you might let me... do it again?"

Jess had never seen this nervous side of Isabel before. In fact, she was surprised that someone as aloof as her could even get anxious.

Jess opened her mouth to answer, but before she could say anything, Jon asked, "Where is Ally, anyway? Will she be joining us this evening?"

"She found herself a man," Josh answered before Jess could. "I believe they are having a slumber party of their own tonight."

Both Jon and Isabel looked very disappointed at this news. "Well, that's too bad." Jon gazed off into the distance. He was staring into the darkness beyond camp, deep in thought. "Too bad for her. She'll be sorry she missed out, I'm sure." A forced smile returned to his face.

"She found herself a guy she likes, I'm sure she will be just fine." Jess turned from Jon to Isabel. "A cute surfer hunk she met at the lake." Jess folded her arms defiantly over her breasts.

Isabel smiled. "I'm happy for her. She deserves a good man in her life."

The sincerity of her comment put a smile on Jess's face. Isabel must have noticed her change in posture after Jon's comment and thought that she was trying to cover up.

"Jess, have you been walking around topless all day? What happened to your cute matching black leather top?" Isabel added.

Jess did not move her arms, keeping them folded over her breasts, doing her best to cover them up. "I took it off to go swimming in the lake, and then someone stole it. Ally's top and Josh's pants as well."

"Oh, no! I'm sorry..."

"I was wondering why you've been walking around with nothing but that ridiculous banana hammock, bro!" Jon nodded toward Josh's crotch jokingly.

"That is a whole other story for another time," Josh said, looking down at what was basically just a black pouch around his package.

"Jess, that reminds me, you design clothes, right?" Isabel asked.

"Uh, yeah. I guess I do." Jess shrugged. Her body language was becoming increasingly indifferent, but that was only because she was becoming increasingly anxious.

Isabel stood. Jess could see that she was wearing a tie-dye bikini top and bottom set that was tied on with string. "I have a bodysuit I want to give you. I think you'll really like it, and I have two of them."

Isabel froze for a second. Jess could see the gears of thought turning in her head. It looked painful.

"Actually, just follow me," Isabel walked to the entrance of the tent she shared with Jon.

She turned around and saw that Jess hadn't moved a muscle.

"Come on. Don't make me drag you, now," Isabel stomped her foot like a child throwing a tantrum.

Jon chuckled. "I'd go with her if I were you, she *will* drag you."

Jess didn't doubt it for a second.

With a small sigh to show her disinterest, she reluctantly followed Isabel into the tent, not knowing what would really happen once they had her in the tent. She knew that the bodysuit was just a pretext, but she was genuinely interested, even if she didn't outwardly show it.

As a fashion designer of women's clothing, the bodysuit was a style of clothing that she thought was the most interesting, versatile, and often underutilized in modern women's fashion. But there was no way for Isabel to know all that.

Not even Josh knew that.

When she entered the tent with Isabel, it was already illuminated by the same array of multicolored lights that she remembered from the last time she was there. Isabel was already in the far corner, adjacent to the pillow pile, digging through a trunk of luggage. She tore through it, separating clothes into a pile as she furiously rummaged through it, searching for something.

At last, Isabel let out a long gasp as soon as she stopped digging, a look of pure delight on her face.

She had found it.

"Here it is!" Her pitch sharply increased on her last word.

Still on wire hangers, Isabel held up one in each hand. The bodysuits had a deep-V cut on the chest, were both strapless, and tapered at the crotch to reveal the hips.

Jess recognized them immediately for what they were. Her jaw fell open when she saw what Isabel was holding.

"Isabel, are these real?" Jess had to get a closer look. She wanted to run her hand along the fabric, but at the same time she didn't want to damage it.

"Yep!" she said proudly. "My girlfriend did some work with Playboy and she stole these two Bunny bodysuits while she was at the Mansion. But then she got bigger boobs and couldn't fit into these any more. And now they are mine." Isabel smiled wide, showing off one of her prized possessions. "And now this one is yours!"

Isabel held up two Playboy Bunny bodysuits. These were the classic Playboy outfits that everyone thinks of when the word "Playboy Bunny" comes to mind. Jess checked the back of the outfits. They even had a plush little bunny tail in the back that felt like it was made of real rabbit fur. The only thing missing was the ears and the classy white collar.

Jess imagined what she would look like wearing the whole Playboy Bunny costume and she could hardly contain her excitement.

Isabel held up two identical bodysuits, only one was yellow and the other was pink. She held out the pink one to Jess.

"Isabel... I can't accept this. I mean... Do you have any idea how rare a real Playboy Bunny outfit is?"

"I do. And I have two. But I only need one. And since I'm a Filipina, I like wearing the yellow one. And since your clothes were stolen today, I would really appreciate it if you accepted this one as a gift from me."

Isabel's dazzling smile returned.

Jess eyed the outfit up and down lengthily.

"I... will it even fit me?"

"My friend was a 34D."

"And she wore it?" Jess's eyes opened as wide as possible.

Isabel nodded. "Now she's one of those models for enormous tits websites. I don't even think there is a name for the cup size she wears now. Her work gives her custom bras made from recycled military duffle bags."

Jess was shocked that anyone would do such a thing.

She thought that 34D was the perfect breast size. Not just according to her, but pretty much every guy she had ever dated. Although she was under no illusion that her ex-boyfriends probably told all of the women that they were with that they had perfect boobs, and other sweet little lies.

Jess tried to imagine what a nightmare it would be to have beach balls attached to her chest and how they must interfere with normal, day-to-day activities. Not to mention, any man who lusted after a woman whose boobs were so big that she could not drive a car was probably in great need of some therapy.

But Isabel's fake boobs were almost the same size as Jess's own natural breasts. And here she was offering Jess a one-of-a-kind, priceless bodysuit that was practically the perfect size for her.

"I'll bet Jon can't get enough of you wearing this thing, right?" Jess said distantly. She couldn't take her eyes off the pink Bunny outfit. She was captivated.

"Actually, he's never seen me in it." Those words jerked Jess out of her trance.

"What did you say?"

"I've never worn it in front of him before. I brought it because I wanted the first time to be at the festival!"

A mischievous smile began to spread across Jess's face.

"Could you imagine the look on the boys' faces if we walked out of the tent in these?"

"Correction: *when* we walk out of here wearing these," Isabel said, holding both bodysuits higher.

An equally sly grin appeared on Isabel's face as she handed the pink Playboy Bunny outfit to Jess. She took it gingerly, as if she were handling a national treasure. She ran her hand down the length of it, feeling the softness of the fabric.

When Jess looked up from ogling the bodysuit, she saw that Isabel had already taken off her bikini and stepped into her yellow Bunny bodysuit.

Isabel fit her legs through the bottom but was having a hard time pulling the top of the strapless bodysuit up over her big boobs.

"Could you pull this up for me?"

Jess gave her a hand. She literally had to stuff Isabel's tits into the bodysuit so that it would cover her nipples but still push her boobs up with the built-in underwire, the way they were supposed to.

When Jess had pulled it up as far as it would go, the bodysuit still covered Isabel's breasts, but it looked like they were spilling out. Jess figured this was because the bodysuit was still technically one size too small for her.

"Well? How does it look?"

Isabel spun around, excitedly, eagerly awaiting Jess's appraisal. If she had the white and black collar around her neck, she would have looked like a centerfold-worthy Playboy Bunny.

"It looks... fucking hot!"

Isabel squealed with glee.

"Really? Honestly?" Isabel said, jumping up in approval. While nearly popping out of the bodysuit.

"Yeah. I mean, you look like a legit Bunny. No cap," Jess nodded her approval.

Isabel let out a long full of air. "Good, because this is really fucking uncomfortable."

Both girls laughed.

"I don't know how they do this," Isabel started, unzipping Jess's shorts for her. "Okay. Now you."

Jess was grateful for the help taking off her shorts considering how tight they were. She shimmied her hips while Isabel tugged her shorts down. As soon as Isabel had them around her ankles, she just sat there staring at Jess's vagina.

Jess wasn't sure what she was staring at, but was embarrassed all the same. She quickly threaded her feet through the pink bodysuit and pulled it on.

"Jess? Can I ask you something?"

"Of course."

"Does Josh have a big dick? Like, will I even feel it, or will it hurt me?"

That was not the question Jess was expecting.

"Let's just say I think you'll be pleasantly surprised. Help me get my boobs in."

Jess had the same problem. The bodysuit hardly covered her nipples but pushed her breasts up like a Duchess at a Debutant Ball.

When she finally was able to pull the bodysuit up all the way, she could feel what Isabel was referring to. With every step, it felt like her boobs were about to spill out. But she also felt like she looked good.

And judging from Isabel's reaction, she was very confident with the way she wore it.

"One more thing," Isabel started digging through the pile of clothes in her luggage once more. "I know I put it in here... Come on!"

"Are you girls coming out or should we come in?" Josh called from outside.

"No!" Isabel screamed.

"Wait!" Yelled Jess.

Both of the girls shrieked at the top of their lungs, in a way that would have kept a bear away from honey.

"Okay, okay. But if you don't come out soon I'm going to get Jon pregnant." Jess could hear Jon laughing from outside.

"The boys are fine," Jess said to Isabel, "They can wait."

"Have a seat, boys. We will be out in 2 minutes, promise!" Isabel called, then looked at Jess, as if reading her mind. "They'll be fine without us for a bit. But we should still hurry."

"What do you think they're doing out there?" Jess asked.

Without looking up from the luggageIsabel said, "knowing Jon? Lots of drugs. Oh, fuck yeah, here it is!"

Isabel stood up holding the vertical strips of plastic over her head triumphantly. She started furiously unwrapping them, then handed one to Jess. They were the white and black collars and bowties. The ones that every Playboy Bunny wears when they put on outfits like these.

The ones needed to complete the costume.

As if reading Jess's mind, Isabel said, "These will totally complete the costume."

And when the girls finally put the bowties on, it did indeed complete the costume. Isabel in her yellow Bunny outfit and Jess in her bubblegum pink one, the two unmistakably looked like Playboy Bunnies.

"The guys are going to freak when they see this," Isabel whispered excitedly.

Eavesdropping from outside, Jon took a step into the tent, then immediately screamed.

"OH MY GOD... JOSH! GET IN HERE!"

Jon was positively paralyzed. He stood just inside of the tent with his jaw hung slack, unable to move a muscle.

"Why? What happened?"

Josh entered the tent and he, too, was completely stunned by the remarkably sexy and beautiful women before them. "Oh my God..." were the only words to come out of Josh's mouth. Although he worked his jaw, no more words followed.

Now Jess and Isabel were striking different poses for the boys. Given what they were wearing, it was not difficult for them to turn on Josh and Jon.

"What... How... Is that my wife?" Josh stammered.

In response, Isabel took hold of each of Jess's hands and pulled the pink Bunny to the arms of the yellow Bunny. Isabel wrapped her arms around Jess's waist, then wasted no time sliding them down to her perky ass so she could give her butt a squeeze.

Isabel and Jess's breasts nearly fell out of the top of their bodysuits as they pushed their bodies up against one another. Isabel was the first one to instigate a kiss. Jess remembered what a great kisser Isabel was, but wasn't sure if that was because she was on drugs the last time they kissed.

Well, Jess thought to herself, *I'm on drugs now too, I guess. I just can't feel them yet. I don't think. Or maybe Jon was just fucking with us—I have no idea.*

Jess closed her eyes and kissed Isabel back. It wasn't the passionate kiss that she remembered from before. This one was wet and sloppy. Jess did her best to receive Isabel's tongue and guide it with little playful licks, bites, and sucking it with her lips every now and again, but Jess couldn't help but wonder what happened to the sweet, intimate kisser from last night.

And then Jess remembered that Isabel said she already ate three of the Molly and TFIC smokes after her and Josh arrived at the camp. Jess noticed that Isabel's skin was becoming all warm and sweaty. That must be it. Isabel was really high, but it just didn't kick in yet for Jess.

"Ladies," Josh called to them. Jess was thankful that he interrupted her kiss with Isabel, although she still had two handfuls of Jess's ass. "We've decided that it would be best if we retire to the tent with the air mattress this evening." He said in a very formal and commanding voice.

Jess and Isabel stared at him. Jess wanted to go to him, but Isabel had a firm grasp on both her butt cheeks and until she relinquished those, she wasn't going anywhere.

"Is that right? Did you decide that?" Isabel said defiantly, slurring every other word.

All Jess could think was, *oh, please don't tell me she is THAT fucked up...*

"Well, what if we wanna stay here?" Isabel said as she sauntered up to Josh.

Jess held her breath. She could see this whole night unraveling because of Isabel's stoned defiance. She had to do something.

"This is going to be so fun, Isabel! Let's bring your guys' pillows over into our tent and you and I can be Playboy models on the bed together."

"But, I like it here..." Isabel said in the weak voice of a child.

Jess knew she needed to seal the deal. She could feel that they were on the cusp of a drama bomb.

"But, I want you to go down on me in bed." Jess cupped Isabel's face and matched her tone of voice.

Isabel's face brightened immediately at the mention of eating Jess out. "Okay."

"Are we in heaven?" Jon asked Josh.

"No. But we are about to be," he replied.

"I'm going to have all three of you screaming for God," Jess said and both of the guys started laughing.

It took a bit of convincing, but Jess made the guys take all of the pillows they could carry and bring them over to the air mattress in Jess and Josh's tent.

At that moment, Jess felt so powerful in her Playboy Bunny costume that she felt like she could get Josh to do anything. She said, "It was time to put this theory to the test."

Jess jumped backward onto the center of the bed when all of the pillows had finally been scattered around. Not all of them fit on the bed, so the floor was also swimming with lacey, frilly pillows of every sort.

Jess had all eyes on her as she lay on her back in the dead center of the mattress. Then she looked down and realized it was because her boobs finally popped out of the top of the Bunny costume and spilled over the top. "Even better," Jess thought, "I'll use this to my advantage while they're all captivated by my tits. She knew she had everyone under her command.

She knew that she was in control.

"You," She pointed at Isabel. "Lick my pussy!"

Isabel got on her knees before the bed, preparing to hunch over to where Jess lay and do as she commanded.

"No," Isabel looked up, a dejected look on her face that she was doing it wrong.

"Lay exactly where I am," Jess moved from her position to the side of the bed, sitting up on her haunches. Jess snapped her finger impatiently and pointed to the spot where she was just laying in the center of the bed as if she were commanding a disobedient dog.

When Isabel laid in the center of the bed, she gave Jess a look as if she were seeking her approval that she had done it correctly. Jess had to push her knees down so her legs were flat on the bed and her feet barely dangling off the edge.

"Good. Good." The guys just looked at her as if they were waiting to be commanded.

Jess got on her hands and knees, hovering above Isabel, facing the opposite way. Jess's butt was pointed at Isabel's face and Isabel's ass was directly under Jess's head. The two girls were aligned in perfect sixty-nine position.

"Now, you," She pointed to Josh. He stepped up, excited he was being called into duty. "I want you to fuck me in my ass, okay? And don't stop until you fill my ass full of cum. And even then, I don't want you taking your dick out of my ass without my permission. Do you understand?"

Josh looked hesitant. Scared, even. "The Bunny suit covers your entire bottom. How am I supposed to fuck you in the ass with this thing on?"

Jess's eyes suddenly flashed with rage. "DO I HAVE TO SPELL OUT EVERYTHING FOR YOU?! Fucking rip it off of me! And you!" she screamed, pointing at Jon, who looked legitimately frightened. "Why isn't your cock in my mouth right now? In fact, why are you wearing clothes?!"

Jon was the only one still wearing normal clothes. He still had on a pair of jeans and a tank top. Jess had never seen a man so terrified to be wearing clothes in her life. He tore them off his body in record time.

Jess didn't know what suddenly overcame her. Maybe it was the Bunny suit that gave her the confidence of a badass dominatrix, but part of her was also irate that they had planned this whole thing out, set the ground rules, and then everyone was pussyfooting around, as if they were scared to pull the trigger. So she decided to take control. And to her surprise, she very much liked that control.

She was worried, however, that as soon as Josh undressed her, she would lose all of that confidence if she were no longer wearing the Playboy Bunny outfit.

To his credit, Josh was able to find the hidden zipper on the bodysuit. He began undressing her the way the outfit was designed to be removed instead of literally ripping it off of her, which Jess thought would be a sexy thing to say, but didn't actually want to happen.

Josh almost had the bodysuit off of her and was helping her legs out of it. Jess tried to get one more squeeze out of the confidence that her Bunny outfit afforded to her before it was lost forever.

"Jon, after I swallow your cum, I want to watch you fuck your wife in her tight little asshole while I eat her pussy. Now, what the fuck is the hold up, you little bitch, why isn't your cock in my mouth already?!"

After calling him a little bitch, she practically screamed the last part as loud as she could. There was no doubt that all of the campers in a mile radius heard her. This thought made her smile.

Until Jon's flaccid cock parted that smile. Jess guessed that calling him a little bitch didn't exactly get him hard.

But she knew how to fix that with some expert tongue work. Meanwhile, she could feel Isabel's mouth on her pussy, but she was still fishing around for her clitoris. She heard Josh rifling through their things, no doubt trying to find something he could use as lube. She was grateful for at least that much. Jess did not like getting fucked in the ass without lube. She didn't know anyone who did.

When she finally felt big manly hands squeeze her ass and spread her butt cheeks, she reckoned that Josh must have found the lube. She could feel him push his slick tip up against her tiny asshole. He wasted no time quickly working in the end of his cock, and then the rest quickly followed. Jess let out a big grunting moan that was muffled on Jon's dick.

While she hadn't realized it at the time, the way that Jess had masterminded this foursome to revolve around her was effortless on her part. When she started giving orders to people, she was really just trying to get things rolling while giving everyone what she knew they wanted.

Isabel had asked to eat Jess's pussy a number of times, and now she not only had a mouthful of her pussy, the way Jess laid on top of her she was able to direct Isabel's surprisingly nimble tongue to her clit. As soon as she found the sensitive place, Isabel knew what to do and apparently had taught her well.

Jon knew that she would only suck his dick, and after fondling her tits he became rock hard. Soon after that, Jon took matters into his own hands and decided he wanted would rather fuck Jess's face than have her put effort into sucking his cock. All she had to do was keep her mouth and throat open as she breathed through her nose and Jon was content to thrust his massive cock all the way down her throat.

Of course, he was a gentleman and held her hair to the side while he fucked her throat. Jess was happy because not only did she find this very hot, more importantly she didn't have to do anything.

And of course Josh was very familiar with fucking Jess in the ass. He knew her likes and dislikes when it came to anal sex, and even in a foursome he was very respectful to fuck her in the ass the way that she liked to get fucked in the ass.

They had discussed this earlier during their game of "Loud Dirty Talk," and had already agreed that since Josh already came inside of Jess's pussy just a few hours ago, at the lake, that they both thought it advantageous if he came in her ass this time around.

When Jess gave everyone their pre-decided designations, she didn't even realize that she would be the object of everyone's attention. Also, the fact that she didn't really even have to do anything was even better. Jess felt the molly and other drugs she had been unknowingly slipped start to kick in just at the apex of pleasure.

Jess closed her eyes and gave herself over to rapture. She focused on Isabel's soft wet tongue now rapidly licking her clit, flicking her tongue back and forth, licking between her lips and sucking on it. Oh how sensitive her pussy is. On how good her mouth felt between her legs.

She focused on Josh's hard cock sliding in and out of her tight little ass. On her ass wrapped around his dick as he penetrated deep into her ass, squeezing and spanking her cheeks.

She focused on Jon's big dick in her mouth, on how he held the back of her head as he forced his thick and juicy cock down the back of her throat. On how it tasted like pussy. On how she must be tasting Isabel's pussy on his dick.

She focused on the molly kicking in, on how warm her skin felt, how her eyes rolled to the back of her head, and every single tactile sensation was pure ecstasy, pure rapture.

She focused on the love she felt for everyone who was so dedicated to giving her pleasure. And how hot it was that they were using her for their pleasure.

She screamed and moaned but it was all muffled by the dick in her mouth. Her words were absorbed by the cock sliding down to the back of her throat.

And then she had the hardest, most satisfying orgasm that she could remember. Almost as soon as it started. She came after only a few minutes. She tried to fight it. She tried to push it back. She wanted this to keep going, to feel this way just a bit longer, but it over took her. Jess came hard and just like every time she came while getting fucked in the ass, she started squirting.

Jess squirted right in Isabel's face and all over her tits, which had long since spilled out of her yellow Playboy Bunny bodysuit.

To her credit, Isabel did not stop or slow down. She didn't even seem to notice that Jess just squirted all over her tits. She just kept licking away at Jess's super sensitive pussy. Jess could feel the vibrations from Isabel's mouth that she, too, was moaning into Jess's pussy.

With her hands free, Jess pictured Isabel either fingering herself or playing with her own huge fake tits, as she was prone to doing.

"I'm going to cum. I'm going to cum," Jon announced the arrival of his orgasm next, but by that time Jess already knew. She could already taste the precum coming out of his horse cock.

When he did finally cum in Jess's mouth, she was surprised at how much more he shot in her mouth. Jess gripped the base of his dick and started jerking it into her mouth so that she could swallow every last drop of his cum. She counted 12 to 14 ropes, thick and powerful streams of cum shooting out of his cock into the back of her throat.

Jess drank his semen greedily like it was the last Oreo shake on earth. "Hmm... Mmm... Mmm... Yeah... Oh Yeah."

When he stopped cumming in her mouth, she continued to suck his dick until he was hard again. Even though she really enjoyed him fucking her throat and really wanted him to cum in her mouth again, she already told them what was going to happen next.

Jess popped Josh's hard dick out of her mouth. Isabel was still wearing her yellow Playboy bunny suit and she was laying on her back so taking it off of her was not going to be a quick and easy task.

Like Jess, the bunny suit covered her ass. But all she had to do was move a flap of yellow fabric to the side and she could see Isabel's smooth glistening pussy staring back at her.

Jess held the fabric covering Isabel's crotch to the side and she guided Josh's dick into his wife's vagina with her hand. While John proceeded to hold Isabel's legs while he pounded her pussy Jess drove her fist into Isabel's ass, as well, practically trying to lick Isabel's clit. Josh's balls slapped with a muffled thud as he was fucking Jess in the ass making it hard to concentrate on anything.

"Oh god, oh fuck, oh fuck yeah, Josh, fuck my little ass, baby, cum in my ass," Jess begged.

Those words of encouragement, now that Jess no longer had a dick in her mouth, were all that Josh seemed to need because only a few ass-pounding thrusts later and Josh got a death grip on her ass cheeks as he grunted wildly.

Jess's moans grew increasingly louder, increasingly more sensual, "that's right baby, pound my fucking ass. Oh yeah, just like that, baby. Fuck me like you own me. You like fucking my tight little ass? Oh god, oh fuck, pound my fucking ass, yeah, I want to feel you cum in my ass. Oh shit, baby, you're going to make me cum again! Fuck!"

At the exact same moment Josh filled her ass full of cum, Jess had another orgasm.

After the rush of another anal orgasm passed, Jess looked down where only a few inches from her face, she saw Jon's gargantuan cock slaying his wife's tiny poor pussy. At the time, Josh was still pumping her ass, as she had instructed him to.

"Okay, Isabel, I love you, but you've got to take off the Bunny suit now."

After two orgasms Jess lost the fiery dominatrix-esque rage that filled her before, but she was still frustrated that this wasn't going exactly the way she wanted—mostly because Isabel was the only one still wearing clothes.

Jess flopped off of Isabel to the left side of the bed, and to her surprise, Josh flopped along with her. She had instructed him not to take his dick out of her asshole until she told him to, and to his credit, even laying on her side Josh never pulled out.

Now, as Jess lay on her tight left thigh, propped up by her elbow, Josh lay behind her, his chest pressed tightly to her back with one of his hands steadying her hips and one hand on her shoulder, so she didn't slide off the bed. Josh continued to pound her tight ass with his rock hard dick. Meanwhile, content with Jess no longer pulling back the fabric on Isabel's crotch, Jon was forced to pull out and help his wife out of her clothes.

To Jess's delight, she noticed that Isabel's tits and entire chest was still soaked with her cum and glistening in the pinky, purple, and blue color changing LED. Her yellow Bunny Suit appeared to change colors in the soft, shifting lights.

X-rated final in the same direction

Jess could feel Josh's cock harden inside of her once again, patiently awaiting her command to pull out. He continued thrusting in and out of her ass all the while maintaining a constant rhythm, until at last, it reached a point where she didn't want him to pull out. Jess wasn't sure if it was the drugs that were working, her feel this way, but She never wanted him to pull out. Jess dreaded the absence of it. She considered how incredibly uncomfortable She would be when it was gone, and how she could once again feel an orgasm coming over her from Josh alone. Trying her best to expedite her third anal orgasm, Jess started rubbing her clit in small, fast circles. "Don't stop, baby. I'm going to cum again."

"Again?" Josh sounded surprised, but he did not stop.

He obviously underestimated just how horny she was going into this foursome. When Jess looked up, she saw Isabel naked in front of her. The two girls were facing the same direction, Jon lay closely behind his wife, one hand wrapped around her breast, one hand wrapped around her butt cheek. Jon was fucking Isabel in the ass. And She appeared to be loving it even more that Jess. Isabel's eyes were rolling to the back of her head as she screamed like a woman possessed. Jess thought, "She didn't even know where she was." Then she joined in with Jess's voice, both women shouting bold commands at the men who were fucking them as if they were on a porno set. Jess and Isabel both screamed and moaned and touched themselves and touched each other.

"Oh my god, Jon, fuck my little ass. Yeah, you like that tiny asshole wrapped around your fat cock? Do you like fucking your wife's ass? Do you? Oh god, I love the way your dick feels in my ass, oh fuck yeah!"

Not to be out done, Jess also bellowed Moans of pleasure as she massaged her pussy aggressively.

"Don't Stop, Josh, keep fucking my ass until you fill it full of cum. I want to feel your hot cum in my ass as I cum at the same time. I'm going to squirt all over you!"

Based on the look on her face, Isabel and Jon beat Jess and Josh to the finish line. However, seeing the intense looks on their faces and primal screams directly in front of them helped

Josh explode again in Jess's ass. And as soon as she felt him cum inside her, that was enough for Jess to get off. The whole thing—all four of them having explosive orgasms—all happened within sixty seconds. It was only afterwards that Jess noticed her fears about having a foursome were realized. The two had broken off into two couples, just having sex in close proximity of one another. Just like Jess told Josh would happen.

"Okay, babe, you can pull out now." He did so gently.

Jess turned around on her side to give him a kiss of gratitude. "Thank you for cumming in my ass and for all of the orgasms, babe, but now I really want to watch you fuck Isabel... in her vagina," she felt like she had to add at the end.

Isabel and her husband were already in each others' arms and deep in a make out session. It looked like if Jess hadn't once again took control with her direction, Isabel and Jon would be having their own thing going and completely oblivious to the other couple in the room. Jess was starting to find foursomes more trouble than they were worth.

Jess cleared her throat. "Isabel? Is that okay with you?"

Isabel broke off the kiss with Jon and turned around to face Jess. A nervous look overtook how fucked up the Molly made her seem.

"Actually, there is this thing I want to try..."

She looked at Jon for approval. Smiling, he nodded, "Go ahead."

Isabel bit her lower lip. Her gaze fell on Josh.

"Do you think you could... could you, you know, fuck me... I mean, fuck my pussy while Jon fucks me in the ass?" Even after all of the drugs they did, this was the most nervous she had ever seen Isabel. She seemed really embarrassed to ask.

"You want us both to fuck you?" Josh looked at Jon, who was still smiling a lascivious smile. "Of course, Isabel. I'd love to." Josh didn't know what to say or how to properly accept her invitation. But Jess had a feeling that the logistics of it would fall on her. "That's okay," She thought, "I'm starting to like this control."

"That's awesome, Isabel. Good for you. You're so brave!" Jess didn't know what to say but wanted to offer words of encouragement so Isabel wouldn't seem so embarrassed for asking.

"If you like it, I might want to go next," She lied.

Jess had no intention of having two dicks in her at the same time. But her words made Isabel crack a smile.

"But I really want to watch this, so here is what we are going to do..."

As far as Jess was concerned there were two ways she could think of that would allow Isabel to get fucked in the pussy and ass at the same down time: Face down or face up.

Arguably the face down double penetration scenario is the simplest. Jess imagined that this would involve Josh laying flat on his back and Isabel laying horizontally on top of him with his dick in her pussy. Jess knew from experience how good Josh was from this position, how he could take control and drive her wild when she was on top without her very much effort on her part.

As Isabel lay flat with her tits pressed up against Josh's chest, Jon would take his wife from behind, while sitting upright on his haunches, being able to thrust his cock powerfully upward into her ass by bending from his thighs while sitting on his heels.

The only problem Jess had with this, was that Isabel would then be laying face down with her body pressed up flesh against Josh's. She knew that the one thing that turned Josh on above all else was a hot and passionate kiss, and although she had no problem with him fucking Isabel, she didn't want them kissing if she could avoid it.

And two, from that position, Jon would be obstructing her view and she wouldn't be able to watch Isabel getting fucked with two dicks in her at the same time. And Jess wanted to watch Isabel's double penetration up close—she had no idea if she would ever have the opportunity to see such a thing up close and personal again.

Although she had seen a few double penetration videos online out of sheer curiosity, the act did not look appetizing to her. The thought of getting fucked silly like that frightened her.

The thought of having both Josh and Jon's fully erect dicks— the biggest dicks she had ever laid her eyes on up close—inside her simultaneously was a terrifying prospect that gave her chills when she imagined what it might be like.

Jess wasn't sure if Isabel was brave and adventurous or crazy and reckless, but Jess had respect for the literal massive task before her. Or maybe she was just high and horny, like Jess.

The second position in which Jess envisioned Isabel getting double penetrated was slightly more complicated, and required a bit of balance and coordination. Although there were surely more ways to go about doing this, it was this second position that would allow Jess the best vantage point to the show.

Jess set to work instructing them, "Jon, lay down flat on your back here."

He looked at her like she was speaking Chinese. "What?"

Jess snapped her fingers at him and pointed to the center of the bed, between where she and Isabel were laying. "Lay!"

Jon gave Josh a look that said, "Is she fucking serious?" and Josh shrugged at him.

Not wanting to find out what would happen if he disobeyed her, Jon quickly complied, laying on his back in the center of the air mattress and erect cock was in the dead center, sticking up.

"Isabel," Jess called, and she immediately had her full, undivided attention. "I want you to sit right here on Jon's stomach. That's right, just like that. Now put your hands here on either side. Good. And just bend your feet under you with your legs spread open. Oh my God, that's perfect."

Jess had her face between Jon and Isabel's legs, making sure everything was to her liking.

Then Jon chuckled, "Jess, what are you, a porn director?"

"Tonight, I will be your orgy director. Failure to listen to me will result in punishment. I will also be your designated floater," Jess said in a commanding voice.

Jess pulled her hair back from out of her face and wrapped her lips around Jon's dick. She steadied it at the base with one hand and licked it as she slid her lips up and down Jon's fat cock, taking it into the back of her throat with ease.

"What if I want to be punished?" Jon chuckled.

Jess abruptly pulled his dick out of her mouth and flicked it with her finger. *Hard.*

Jon cringed back in pain.

"Then I'll make sure you get no lube. Don't piss the girl who has your cock in her mouth, dummy."

"Point taken. Ouch..." Jon whined.

"Isabel, honey, if you're ready for dick number one just lean back a bit and I'll help ease it in your butt."

Isabel did as she was told and leaned back on her hands. Jess could now see her entire pussy and ass.

"Um... Jess? I would like lube, please!" Isabel said hesitantly.

Evidently she did not want to piss Jess off either.

"Oh, honey, don't worry, I got you. Hold still." Instead of using lube, Jess worked off a bit of saliva in her mouth.

Again moving a fallen strand of hair out of the way, Jess leaned down so she could spread Isabel's butt cheeks and ran her tongue in circles all along the rim of her asshole.

"Ooh! That tickles!" Isabel giggled.

Being an agent of mischief, Jess starts gently flicking her tongue in and out of Isabel's ass in the most ticklish way possible. Her entire pussy began to quiver as Isabel laughed uncontrollably.

Jess grabbed her by the ass, holding her down as she proceeded to tickle Isabel all along her thighs, pussy, and ass until she was shaking, trying to break free from Jess's grip.

"Stop that! Jessss!" The more Isabel laughed, the more Jess wanted to hold her down and tickle her. I had no idea that you were so ticklish, Isabel."

"You don't know the half of it," commented Jon.

"Okay, okay, I'm done," Jess said as she released her hold on Isabel. She breathed a sigh of relief that her tickle torture was over. Of course, as soon as she let her guard down, Jess renewed her grip holding Isabel's ass down and flicked her tongue in her asshole a few more times. Isabel erupted in laughter once more.

"Stop! Stop!" she could barely manage to get the words out between fits of laughter.

"Oh my God, I could do this all day," Jess was really having fun teasing Isabel.

"Oh, I have," said Jon, "Her nipples are even ticklish."

"Jon! No! Don't tell them that!" Isabel gasped.

"Too late!" Jess immediately went to lick and tease Isabel's nipples with her tongue.

Because she was using her hands to support herself on the bed she could do nothing to cover up or protect herself. Jess only gave one of her nipples a gentle lick, teasing the tip of her tongue to the very tip of her nipple and Isabel erupted in another fit of laughter that was so violent she almost fell over.

"No More! No More! Mercy!" Tears were running down Isabel's face she was laughing so hard.

"Alright, Alright, I got sidetracked," Jess wanted to get Jon's dick in Isabel's ass while she was still laughing. So she quickly gave his dick one more quick visit to the back of her throat and then pointed the tip of Jon's hard, wet cock to Isabel's tightly shut asshole. And without her having to say anything, as soon as Jon felt the tip of his dick kiss Isabel's puckered ass he slowly thrusted the whole thing in at once. To Jess's surprise, Isabel's ass ate the entire shaft hungrily.

Jess had her face pressed just inches away from Isabel's ass. She had only seen anal sex this close up in porn videos and was excited to watch the real thing up close in front of her very eyes.

As soon as Jon shoved his horse dick up his wife's ass, she stopped laughing. With a gulp of air, her breath got caught in her throat. Her eyes went wider, her mouth opened and her lips formed an "O" but no words came out. Just hard, jagged breaths. As Jess watched Jon slide his dick effortlessly in and out of Isabel's ass, she was content, her saliva sufficed as lube. Jess was so mesmerized by the way her ass tightly conformed to every curve of Jon's dick that she forgot her duties as Orgy Director until Josh loudly cleared his throat behind her.

"Oh shit, babe. My bad. Here, put your dick in my mouth." She turned around and immediately grabbed her boyfriend's half-flaccid dick. After only a few seconds of deep throating Josh's cock, ("Mmm, yum, it tastes like my ass.") not only was it hard enough for its maiden voyage into Isabel's pussy, it was slick and lubricated with enough of Jess's saliva. After feeling his dick stiffen in her mouth, she was remiss that she had to stop and give it over to Isabel.

But these were the tough decisions and responsibilities of an orgy director and designated floater.

"Put your knees here, babe." By now Jon and Isabel had gotten into a groove and seemed to completely forget about Jess and Josh's presence. Isabel had suddenly found her voice.

"Oh, yeah, Jonny, oh, fuck me, yeah, that's good, right there is like that, ooh. Aw! Sorry, but Jon, you need to hold still for just one second. No, I said hold still. There. Good. Okay, Isabel, are you ready for dick number two?"

From her close up view, just inches away from Isabel's vagina, she heard her answer in a meek voice. "Yes."

"Ooh! Do you want it?" Jess teased.

Again, she heard a faint, "Yes."

Jess was now finding this very sexy. "How bad do you want it, Isabel?"

There was the briefest of pauses, and then, "I want it. I want your boyfriend's dick inside of me, Jess. Plee-hee-ease don't make me beg for it?" Isabel cried in a voice that was rife with lustful need.

Jess decided she would tease her no longer. She would give her what she desired. Jess pointed Josh's cock so that the tip of his dick just barely graced Isabel's small, wet pussy. Similar to Jon, as soon as Josh felt the tip of his cock kiss his vagina, he lifted his hips, gently thrusting his entire shaft into Isabel's little pussy.

"Oh, God, yes, that feels so good!" he moaned.

"Okay, boys!"

And with her blessing, Josh and Jon really started to lay into her. They couldn't seem to find a similar or consistent rhythm, which bothered Jess, but the look on Isabel's face told her that she clearly didn't mind. She was going absolutely crazy. Having two huge dicks inside of her at the same time seemed to drive her wild.

Her face was a flurry of different emotions and feelings, from looks of pain and anguish to looks of ecstasy and unadulterated bliss.

Isabel looked like she had found God. Or was possessed by the Devil himself.

Jess was beside herself, grinning, watching Isabel enjoy herself. "So, Isabel, how is it?"

She did not answer. She could not answer. She couldn't even form any words in that moment. Jess thought to herself, "So this is what it looks like to watch someone getting their brain sucked out."

Even though Jess wasn't involved in Isabel's double penetration fantasy, she did not feel left out. In fact, she was having the time of her life just watching, and cheering them on.

"Damn, you guys, that looks so fucking hot. Isabel, I wish you could see those two big dicks sliding in and out of your little ass and pussy. Fuck, watching this is getting me so wet... You know what? Fuck it."

Jess lay back on the side of the bed opposite Isabel, so that not only could she see Isabel clearly getting double fucked, Jess could also make eye contact with her. She spread her legs wide so Isabel could watch Jess watching her, rubbing her pussy and fingering her clit.

Jess started moaning lightly. "Ooh... Oh Yeah... Hmmm... Ahh... Yeah." They were barely whispers compared to the incoherent grunts and half-moans turned to screams of pleasure coming from Isabel.

"Fuck... Josh, did we bring any toys with us? Did you pack my Hitachi?" Jess was really starting to work herself up.

"Didn't think to bring it," Josh grunted as he continued to fuck Isabel aggressively. "Isabel, I'm going to cum soon. What do you want me to do?" He asked, like a gentleman.

"Cum-n-me," She managed in a single syllable.

"She's on birth control. I always cum in her pussy. Go ahead," Jon said without missing a beat. "But don't you blast your load inside my wife until she has a chance to cum first. Don't be a dick, Josh. This is a romantic experience."

Just then, Isabel starts screaming and grunting like she is trying to tell us something.

Isabel stuttered, "t-t-two."

"Two? Two what?" Josh asked.

"Yeah, babe, you still have two dicks inside ya," Jon clarified.

Isabel shook her head negative, then held up two fingers before she had to quickly return her hands to the bed to support her.

"She's saying that you can go ahead and cum inside of her whenever you want because she already had two orgasms," Jess yelled from the other side of the bed with both of her hands playing with her pussy in a frenzy.

Isabel starts nodding her head fervently.

"How did you know that, Jess?" Josh asked.

"Because I saw her have two orgasms! Geez, you bozos have your dicks eight inches inside her and you didn't even notice that? Christ, Jon, this is your wife!"

Jess could have sworn she saw Isabel laugh in between her torrent of moans.

"Race you to the finish line!" Jon yelled at Josh, and then the two guys started pumping and pounding their dicks into poor Isabel as quickly as possible.

It looked like she wanted to cry. Still, Jess felt delighted to check on her man in any competition.

"Go Josh! Go! You can do it! Fuck that pussy!"

Josh was the first one to cum inside of Isabel, with Jon cumming in her ass only 20 seconds or so afterward.

As soon as they were done, Isabel pushed them both off of her and flipped over to lay on the bed on her stomach, desperately trying to catch her breath. She looked so exasperated that Jess was no longer turned on.

Jess leapt to be at Isabel's side. She lay flat on her stomach, propped up by her boobs, next to Isabel.

"Isabel, honey, are you alright? Talk to me," Jess cooed sweetly.

"I'm... I'm fine," She said in a cheery tone that Jess suspected was forced.

"Are you hurt? You can tell me if you are. It's okay." Jess tried to sound as consoling as possible.

Isabel laughed. "No, really. I feel great. That was just very... Intense."

"Intense?" Jess smelled mischief to be had. "Are you ready to try it again?"

She laughed a tired laugh. "Jesus, No, no. It wasn't bad, Jess. Just not something I would do everyday."

Jess patted Isabel's butt, which was still surprisingly firm considering all it's been through today. "Okay, honey. Would you recommend it?"

"Everyone should try it at least once," she smirked, "but not for this girl." Isabel smiled with her teeth as she squeezed her eyes shut. She suddenly looked very tired.

"Well, if you want to rest, that's just fine, honey."

Jess was shaking Isabel's butt cheeks and watching them shake like a bowl full of jelly.

To her surprise, Isabel looked Jess in the eyes and said sleepily, "Okay, just for a bit."

Jess scrunched over and gave her a little kiss on the lips. "Alright, then. I'm going to suck your husband's dick while you're asleep, though, okay?" Jess said in the voice you would use on a child about to fall asleep.

"Okay, Jess." Isabel shut her eyes and yawned.

"I was going to have him titty-fuck me, too, Isabel."

Isabel spread her hands out under her head. "Uh-huh. He'd like that..." And then she was fast asleep.

"She always falls asleep after a really good orgasm," Jon explained. And Jess remembered last night how Isabel fell asleep almost immediately after Jess made her cum just by fingering her. "Now, what was this I hear about titty fucking?"

Jess sat up and turned her attention to the two naked men with massive erections sitting just on the other side of the bed. She looked at Jon and raised an eyebrow inquisitively. "Would you like that? I mean, your wife has, like, perfect tits. And I'm sure they were very expensive."

Jon suddenly looked very nervous and embarrassed. "Well, um, actually, See, the thing about that is..."

Jess extended her hands in a way that said, "Spit it out already!"

"One of the reasons I got Isabel her new boobs was because I've sort of got this... a kink."

"Do you have a fetish for titty fucking?" Jess in more of a curious way than an accusatory way.

The way that Jon avoided looking her in the eye told her everything. Jess was not trying to make him feel embarrassed. She tried to live her life in a non-judgemental way, but especially when it comes to other people's kinks and fetishes. As long as they were consensual and no one got hurt, Jess fully embraced them and didn't want to make anyone feel embarrassed.

Jess took Jon by the hand. "It's okay," She laid on her back, then adjusted her boobs to make sure they looked okay. "Jon, I want you to titty fuck me, and I want your dick in my mouth at the same time. Can you do that for me?"

He looked at her, first to see if she was making fun of him or not. When he saw that she was hot, he enthusiastically nodded his head. Jess smiled, happy to make a little pervert's dream come true.

Jess pushed her soft, supple, and naturally large breasts together tightly so that Jon could wedge his big dick in between them.

"Baby," Jess called to Josh who had disappeared from her line of vision.

"Yeah, Jess?" came his voice from somewhere in the tent. He was no longer on the bed.

"Baby, where are you?" Jess called again, this time a hint of fear in her voice.

Josh appeared next to her, naked, on the side of the bed. "I'm right here." He was holding something in his hand. "Here, I got you" He said, then opened a bottle of lube and squeezed it directly onto Jess's tits.

"Oh my God! That's cold!" Jess yelled.

Josh poured out a ton of lube onto Jess's chest.

"Thanks, bro," Jon said.

Josh gave him the strangest smile and said, "Enjoy."

Jess started rubbing in the cold, greasy lube all over her slippery, glistening tits.

"Baby, my pussy needs attention," Jess whined.

Half a second later, he felt her legs being spread apart. "Way ahead of you, love," Josh said, then Jess felt a hand covered in the same freezing cold lube slide across her vagina.

"Cold! Cold!" She cried.

"Stop whining," Josh said before he slid his entire hard cock into Jess's pussy and started fucking her with such force that it shook her entire body up and down the bed.

"Oh fuck yeah, Josh. Ahh. Hmmm. Oh, I want you to titty fuck me, Jon. I want your big cock in my mouth. Jon, I..."

Before she could get another word out, Jon's dick made its way between Jess's tightly pressed together tits and into her mouth.

As Josh worked up into a consistent, hard rhythm of thrusts between Jess's legs, Jon sat on her chest. As she squeezed her perfectly soft, supple breasts tightly together, she could feel Jon's thick cock sliding through them. He sat gently on top of her, she could feel his thighs clamping down around her ribs with excitement. Jon hunched forward and placed his hands behind Jess's head to support his body as he leaned over her face, watching his cock slide through her slippery tits.

As his dick pierced the fleshy folds of her tightly compacted big breasts, half of his dick appeared through the other side. As Jess held her boobs together as tightly as she could with all of her strength, she lifted her head up and opened her mouth wide so that the tip of Jon's cock would slide through Jess's tits and into her mouth.

His dick tasted strongly of lube, but Jess didn't care. She focused on the tactile sensation of his shaft quickly sliding in and out of her breasts and how the tip of his engorged cock still managed to fill up her entire mouth. After a few minutes of Jon titty-fucking her, all Jess wanted was to swallow his cum.

She wished he would hurry up already. Jess opened her mouth as wide as possible and extended her tongue as far as it would go.

She wrapped her lips around her teeth so that Jon's cock wouldn't accidentally ram into them and hurt himself. In Jess's experience, nothing took the wind out of a man's sail than rubbing his hard cock on a girl's teeth during a good, long blowjob. Jess wanted nothing more than to just grab a hold of Jon's dick and start deep-throating it until he came in her mouth, but Jon liked titty fucking Jess, so she afforded him this small concession.

After some time of this, Jess finally got her wish.

Jon started to make the loud, grunting noises characteristic of a man right before he is about to cum. While he was still thrusting away at the wedge she created between her breasts, but as soon as Jess tasted his pre-cum she immediately released her grip on her tits and they fell back into their regular position on her chest, tilting her head up as far as her neck would allow.

She took hold of his dick with both of her hands and started cranking it like a pepper mill. Jon graciously scooted up to the point where he was actually now sitting on her boobs, but at least now Jess had most of his sizable dick in her mouth by the time he started to cum.

Jess was happy she was able to wrap her lips around his cock; however, as she was swallowing his cum, she also swallowed quite a bit of lube. As unpleasant as it was to have to gulp down that much lube, it wasn't as bad as going down as it was coming out.

Drinking lube—even the ones that were safe to ingest, which this one was—almost always led to bouts of diarrhea. Fortunately, there were plenty of better alternatives that wouldn't wreck havoc on her bowels. Back at home, Jess and Josh most commonly used coconut oil because it was natural, safe, and delicious, not to mention just as good a lubricant as Astroglide, only better because it tastes like coconut.

Jess loved the act of swallowing a man's cum. She loved everything about it. It was her favorite part about sucking dick.

She loved the way that men reacted when she swallowed their cum.

She loved to feel it explode in the back of her throat.

She loved how warm it was.

She loved the sticky, slime texture.

She loved counting the number of times a man would cum in her mouth during an orgasm, or counting ropes, as she called it.

She loved the funny sounds men made.

She absolutely loved it when they told her how good she was at sucking dick because, like most young women, she prided herself on her unique dick sucking techniques.

She did not love the taste. Not at first. But considering that there were just so many things to love about swallowing a man's cum, the taste was something that she had come to love in the end. An acquired taste.

After she finished swallowing all of Jon's cum, she reluctantly took his dick out of her mouth. It was still covered in lube.

Jon sighed heavily before getting off of Jess's chest. Josh, meanwhile, had never stopped or slowed down fucking her. Jess was relieved that now it was just her and her boyfriend.

Seeing this, and realizing there was nothing left for him in the tent. His wife had passed out. He just came into Jess's mouth. He had his titty fucking fantasy fulfilled. Jon watched the intimate love making between Jess and Josh for a few seconds before deciding to take his leave.

"Whelp. I guess I'd better get sleeping beauty over here in bed."

"Okay," Josh said while maintaining eye contact with Jess.

"Uh-huh... Yeah," Jess breathed, though she wasn't exactly replying to Jon.

Jon cleared his throat, "Keep the pillows for now. We've got sleeping bags back in our tent."

Jon was eyeing Jess's breasts, still glistening from all the lube on them and how that she was no longer holding them, they were bouncing up and down as Josh continued to pound her pussy.

"Okay," Josh said dismissively. It was clear that he wanted Jon and Isabel gone, too. He wanted some private time alone to make love to his girlfriend.

"Alright, we're going to go now," He said.

This time, neither Josh nor Jess warranted him a response. Jon slid off the bed over to where Isabel lay fast asleep. He scooped his arms under her back and the crux of her knees, then lifted her out of bed with obvious effort.

"Uh, thank you for the lovely evening. We'll have to do it again some time." Jon was struggling under the weight of his wife. Jess thought this was preposterous, because Isabel couldn't have weighed more than 120 pounds. Maybe 140 if you include her breast implants.

Jess wanted to tell him that he better not drop his wife, but almost as soon as he had picked her up he was out of their tent. He was probably not very confident in his ability to carry her and wanted to lay her down as soon as possible.

Jess was happy he was gone.

"Alone at last," She said with a smile as she looked into Josh's eyes.

He had that very intense look on his face that he gets when he becomes overpowered with a desire to make love to his girlfriend.

"I love you, Jess," He continued with slow, rhythmic thrusts.

"Make love to me, darling," She said a moment before his lips touched hers in an intimate, passionate kiss that was very much unlike anything that had happened that night.

The two made love well into the night.

Jess never wanted it to end.

Chapter 17: The Final Day

Jess awoke much in the same way she did everyday: Naked, in Josh's arms, and both of them snuggled up close behind him.

It was the last day of the festival, and there was no music playing that morning. Or afternoon. Jess had no idea what time it was. And she didn't care.

She didn't want to get up. Because getting up would mean that they had to start packing up to leave the festival. And she had such a good time over the weekend, she never wanted to leave.

So as the sun continued to rise and the day grew hotter, Jess laid in bed with Josh's arms wrapped around her, nestled in the warmth and safety of his chest. She thought about everything that had happened since the day they arrived. She played back every moment in her head.

Seeing Jon's dick as they came in and the way Isabel freaked out that ticket booth guy for flashing him.

Her sexy rave outfit reveal with Ally.

Having a threesome with Ally.

Headbanging to all the awesome music.

Dancing with friends.

Watching Ally ride Josh's dick.

The way Josh punched out that one guy.

Having sex with Ally.

Booty shaking at the Shower Stage.

Hooking up with Crystal and Cheetch.

That threesome with Ally.

 Free Food.

 Free Clothes.

Get Slut.

Sex with Josh and Ally.

The Lake.

Sex with Isabel and Ally.

The romantic Ferris Wheel ride.

And that super hot threesome with Ally.

Ally.

Getting really high.

And Ally.

Jess realized that she started breathing quicker the more she replayed all of the weekend's memories.

But they were more than just memories to Jess. These were her private sex fantasies that actually came to fruition. Fantasies that she played out in her head hundreds of times and how they actually happened.

Her and Ally had been friends for a long time. Much longer than she had known Josh. But how she actually had her private fantasy fulfilled. It was something that she didn't tell anyone about—not her best friend and not her boyfriend. Still, having sex with both of them at the same time was now a memory that she would always cherish.

"Josh," She put her hand over his hand that cupped his breast and shook him.

"Josh," She wiggled her butt against his hips. "Baby, wake up. I want morning sex."

This at last stirred him awake. But just barely. He already had a boner that Jess could feel between her thighs. She scooted down a bit so she could rub her pussy along his morning wood. She was already soaked between her legs after playing back her sex fantasies come to life all morning. Jess grinded her butt into his hips.

"Wake up and fuck your girlfriend!" She commanded.

"Alright, babe, fine. Whatever you want..." With not much effort, he was able to feel his hips back and drive his hard cock up into her tight, wet hole.

"Ohh—that's more like it." She pulled on his arm that he had draped over her body. "Fuck me like you mean it."

Josh, without even opening his eyes, started jack-hammering her pussy while the two lay snuggled up in bed.

Jess shut her eyes tight and thought about all of the best parts of the music festival that weekend. She was thinking about Ally.

Just then the tent flap split open, flooding the dark room with afternoon light for just a moment before it shut. "Are you guys ready to—Whoops, Oh, never mind."

It was Ally, wearing a large white T-shirt that said "Electric Love Festival" on the front. Jess could easily see her nipples underneath. The shirt only came down to her uppermost thigh. If she raised her hands, the world would see her pussy.

Jess knew she only had half a second before she was gone and then this opportunity would be missed to her forever. "No, Ally, wait!"

She had her hand on the tent flap and was about to leave but froze where she stood and looked back, lips parted, her big, beautiful eyes staring back at her friend, her long, luxurious eyelashes. How Jess could get lost in those eyes. How she wanted to kiss those lips. The way the few rays of sun that looked into the tent hit her face, illuminating the profile of her face made her look like an angel.

Jess wanted to tell her she loved her. She wanted to tell her she wanted her. She wanted to tell her about all of the private little fantasies she has had about her friend over the many years they knew each other. But in that crucial moment when Ally looked back at her, she didn't know what to say.

"Stay with us," She said at last.

In a very uncharacteristic move, Josh stopped fucking his girlfriend out of respect for Ally's sudden presence. It was as if he could sense the mood between them. Although he stopped humping her he did not pull out.

"It looks like you guys are busy. I didn't mean to interrupt. Rick and I—" Ally had her hand on the tent flap, but she didn't leave.

"Not yet. Please, Ally. Join us," Jess begged.

She didn't move. She didn't say anything. And that drove Jess crazy.

"Please, Ally," She tried again. "Just come lay next to me for a little bit. I missed you."

A smile graced her gorgeous face and suddenly Jess felt her heart flutter. Ally slid up on the bed laying parallel next to Jess's naked body. Josh, meanwhile, didn't move or make a sound. For all Jess knew, he may have fallen back asleep again.

"I missed you, too," She smiled brightly at her friend. Suddenly, she had no idea what to say to her friend that she had known half her life.

"Have you always been so beautiful?" It was a cheesy thing to say, but Ally giggled and smiled all the same.

Fuck, Jess thought, *she is so fucking cute.*

She decided to just go for it. Jess wrapped her arm around Ally's back and pulled her into a kiss. Ally tilted her head and leaned into it. Jess closed her eyes and raised her tongue into Ally's mouth, licking her delicious lips. Jess moaned softly as she pulled Ally closer.

Those lips tasted even better than she remembered. Better than she had imagined. Jess drank her in. God, Ally just made her so horny. Without even realizing it, Jess was sliding herself up and down on Josh's dick as she kissed Ally with an increasing amount of lustful passion. Ally saw what she was doing and broke off the kiss.

"I'm sorry, Jess. It's just that I really like Rick and..." Ally started sliding off the bed.

Jess was worried she was about to lose her only opportunity.

"Where is Rick?" She asked with one hand outstretched at her friend as if she were trying to pull her back.

Ally hooked a thumb behind her back. "He's waiting for me out there. I told him I..."

"Invite him in," Jess said. It was not a question.

"Jess, I can't do that." Ally was still slinking closer to the tent exit.

Jess felt her window was closing.

"Why not? What better way for him to remember you forever than to invite him to a foursome with your best friend?" The look on Ally's face told Jess that she was giving it serious contemplation. "Plus, Ally... she had to say it. She was making her say it. "I want you. I want to be with you."

Jess felt her face go red.

"Jess, we already had our fun this weekend. You know I..."

"Please!" Jess said louder than she intended, then, softly, "please, Ally."

Her words were failing her. She felt them ball up in her throat. She couldn't get them out. Jess knew that her eyes began to water, the beginning of tears forming at the bottom of her eyes.

She took another breath, trying desperately to steady her voice, "please?"

If Ally said no, she didn't know what she would do if she ever faced her friend again.

For a painful moment that felt like an eternity of sorrow and forlornness to Jess, Ally just stared at her. Jess imagined how pathetic she must look. How gross and sad and weird Ally must think she was. How she must be regretting ever being friends with her all this time and how she wanted nothing more than to never see Jess again.

Jess did her best to fight back the sobs and choke back her tears, she did her best to appear normal to her friend until she was gone so she could at the very least save face.

Every second Ally stood at the exit to their tent was agony.

Jess tried to ask again, but her words were stuck in her throat. Instead, she closed her eyes and silently mouthed the word, "please."

And at last, Ally spoke, "Okay, Jess." Her honeyed voice, filling the tent like a bottle of Febreeze. "I'll do it for you, but only because I love you."

On her way out, Ally stuck the tip of her tongue between her teeth and gave Jess a private smile. A smile just for her. And at last, all was right in the world.

Jess was about to get what she wanted. But at what cost?

Chapter 15: New Beginnings

"Josh? Did you hear that?" Jess asked.

He wasn't talking. He wasn't moving. Jess hoped to God that he was breathing.

"What? I am awake," he snorted.

Then started moving his hips up and down, slowly and sleepily pushing his half-hard dick in and out between Jess's legs.

"Josh, just a heads up, Ally is on her way back with Rick. We're going to have another foursome."

"Uh-huh. Who's Rick?"

"That surfer-looking guy she met at the lake."

Josh yawned as he continued thrusting his dick into Ally, hardening it with each thrust. "Baby, I'm tired," he complained.

"Well, don't fall asleep again and just keep doing what you're doing right now. This feels nice," Jess whispered as she pushed her ass back into her boyfriend's hips.

He yawned again. "Okay, babe," He kissed her once on the back of her neck and kept on with the slow and steady thrusting grinding.

It was what Jess imagined having sex with a turtle was like. Other than that, he didn't move a muscle and was in the same spooning position that he was in all through the night. His chest pressed flat against her back.

They both lay on their sides with one arm underneath Jess's head, like a pillow, and the other one wrapped around her like a blanket, cupping her big hand cupping her big breast.

They fit together like a hand in a glove.

Jess liked to put her hand over the hand Josh had on her breast and squeezed it. Every time she gave the back of his hand a little squeeze, Josh always instinctively pulled her closer to him, whether he was awake or asleep—even if he was passed out, Josh's instinct was to pull her chest closer into his. It made Jess feel safer. It made Jess feel loved.

From outside the peaceful tent, Jess heard voices.

"I don't know. Are you sure it's okay?" Jess thought it was Rick's voice.

"I'm telling you, it'll be fun. Come on." That was unmistakably Ally's voice.

"But. I've never-"

He was cut short by Ally entering the tent, holding Rick's hand in tow. She just stood in the doorway of the tent with the flap held open, blinding light flooded the room.

"Close the door!" Jess yelled at him.

"Oh! Sorry." Rick stepped in and started zipping up the tent flap behind him. Jess wasn't sure if he just didn't understand what she meant or if he just wanted to avert his eyes anywhere other than the two naked bodies in front of him.

Jess saw Ally lean in close to Rick and whisper something in his ear that sounded like, "It's okay." Then, facing Jess and Josh on the bed, "Rick, you remember my friends Jess and Josh." She gestured to the bed.

Jess and Josh spoke at the same time.

"Hello."

"Hey Rick."

"Uhh. Hello. Again." He was shaking like a leaf.

"Don't be nervous," Ally whispered to him.

"It's nothing you haven't seen before, we were basically nude the first time we met you," Jess said, trying her best to make him feel at ease.

It did not seem to work. Rick erupted in nervous laughter.

"Join us on the bed, Rick. We don't bite," Josh made his best effort to sound as comforting as possible.

More nervous laughter from Rick. Clearly he had never been in a situation like this before.

"Okay," Ally whispered.

As she took Rick by the hand and walked him over to the bed, she had had enough of his nervous laughter as well. She quickly pulled the back of his head towards her. So she could have her lips on his. Jess watched excitedly.

Ally closed her eyes and moaned into Rick's mouth with passion. He kept his eyes open, looking down at her with appraisal the entire time. Once his gaze even darted in Jess's direction and then quickly back to Ally when he realized that was why Jess was watching him. Only a few seconds into their kiss, Ally pulled Rick's T-shirt off his perfectly lean body and tossed it to the ground.

Then her lips were on him again, her eyes closed in intimate intent as Ally fumbled with the button on his shorts. Rick rested both of his hands on the small of Jess's back over her oversized T-shirt and made no move to explore the rest of her body.

Jess started to wonder if the two had even had sex at all last night or if they were just playing cards.

Rick's shorts flopped to the floor. He was not wearing anything underneath and now stood before them just as naked as Jess and Josh. Even in the darkness of the tent, Jess got a good look at his package. Even flaccid he was hung.

Jess wondered, *if he doesn't have a small dick, then what on earth is he so nervous about?*

Then she remembered how both her and Josh made death threats against Rick when they first met. Could that also be why he seemed so passionless with Ally?

Ally dropped to her knees and took him in her mouth. Now that he could no longer hide behind Ally, Jess and Josh could get a good look at him.

The guy was scared out of his mind.

"What's wrong, Rick? Why won't you get hard?" Ally cried from her knees before putting his limp dick back in her mouth and going to work.

Jess tried to imagine what this poor guy must be going through. Getting dragged into a tent and having two strangers fucking on an air mattress just a few feet away from you, staring you down while getting your dick sucked. He was obviously feeling some sort of pressure. But Jess was tired of trying to make him feel comfortable. She would rather make mischief.

"Yeah, Rick, why won't you get hard?" Jess chimed in.

"What's wrong, Rick? Can't get hard?" Josh clearly knew how to play along as well.

At last, Ally stood up. He wasn't even halfway hard yet.

"Stop it! You guys are scaring him. See, Jess? This is why I didn't want to do this!" Ally cried.

Jess felt bad. "I'm sorry."

Ally looked angry but she ignored Jess all the same. She would not be defeated that easy. After all, she already had the guy naked in front of a bed.

After getting called out, Rick seemed to have found his balls. As soon as Ally stood up, he pulled her oversized T-shirt up and over her head. Ally had this look on her face that said, "Finally."

Now that they were all naked, Ally pulled Rick by the hand and fell backwards into bed right next to Jess. Rick took his spot on the opposite end, at the very edge of the air mattress.

Rick and Ally continued to make out on their side of the bed while Josh continued to fuck Jess over on their side. Ally's back was to Jess, and although that's not what she wanted, she used the opportunity to admire Ally's big firm boobs. She wanted to reach over and pinch it but she also didn't want Ally mad at her again.

After a bit more making out, Rick at last grabbed Ally by her arms and posted her to her back, kissing her as he held her down.

Jess looked down. Rick was hard at last. Not giving his erection the chance to fade away, he jumped up on his knees where he swiftly parted her legs as he nestled himself between them.

As soon as Rick was inside of Jess, he started pumping away at a pace that was more than twice as fast as that of Josh's. Jess's attention, however, was fixated on watching Ally's boobs bounce up and down.

As Rick laid into Ally, he was not aware that he was slowly moving her up the bed. If he continued at the pace and force he was using, Ally would fall off the edge of the bed in less than a minute. Jess waited until Ally noticed this before extending her hand out to her, trying to help steady her.

This was a little awkward at first, because Jess was laying on her back getting fucked and Ally was laying on her back getting fucked.

But the two girls were still side by side.

"Here, take my arm," Jess offered, as she wrapped both of her arms around Ally's back, pulling her towards Jess's hips.

Ally had to twist her torso to the side to meet Jess's awkward embrace, but at last Jess had Ally in her arms like she wanted, even if she was getting fucked so hard. She kept sliding upward.

At last, Ally tired of trying to remain in one place on the bed—her struggle was taking away from the pleasure of the act—and she signaled for Rick to move.

"Come over here," Ally tapped the empty spot on the bed behind her. "But don't pull out when you move."

She wasn't even done speaking before Rick pulled out, then laid down in the spot she indicated. Ally sighed in frustration.

"Oh, Sorry," Ricky apologized, then soon tried to guide his dick back inside Ally.

Ally sighed, "What's the matter?"

He seemed to be having trouble finding the right hole. While Rick was fumbling with his dick in his hand, Ally lifted up one leg and reached down between her legs to assist Rick in finding a home for his dick.

At last with his dick in Ally's pussy once more, he placed his hand on her hip and started thrusting upward with all his might.

Ally was making little grunts and moans of joyful pleasure, but Jess wasn't sure if they were entirely authentic or not.

Jess's plan was coming together, with both of the girl's men fucking them from behind, now there was nothing between Ally and Jess.

Maybe she did want them to be a thruple.

With Ally in her arms, Jess felt an overwhelming sense of calm and happiness. Jess quieted Ally's exaggerated moans by placing her mouth over Ally's.

As soon as their lips touched, as soon as Jess parted her lips in an intimate kiss that meant much more than friendship, she felt Ally melt into her arms.

All her muscles were relaxed at once. All of the tension went out of her body. After that happened, Ally gave herself over fully.

She started kissing Jess back—kissing her with meaning, with feeling, with love. This is what she wanted. This was the apex of the weekend.

This was her fantasies fulfilled.

Jess squeezed one of Ally's breasts in the palm of her hand, tweaking her nipple playfully as she folded her other hand around the back of her neck, both to prevent her from getting fucked off the bed and at the same time so Jess could pull her Ally closer to herself. Jess licked, sucked, bit, and kissed Ally's lips until they were puffy.

Listening to the horny little moans that Ally was making, feeling the vibrations of those sexy noises driven by lust and desire that turned Jess on the most.

Fuck, she felt good. But she didn't want to be the first out of the four to cum.

And then, as if reading her mind, Ally threw her head back and squeaked, "I'm going to cum!"

Jess pulled her head back towards Ally so both women sat touching their foreheads while laying on their sides getting fucked.

In a little voice meant only for Ally, Jess whispered, "Me too."

Jess put her lips on Ally once again so she could feel those sexy little vibrations that came from her feminine grunts and moans. She felt Ally's hot breath come in jagged puffs against her skin.

Holy fuck, that really turned Jess on.

"Cum with me," Jess whispered, dipping her face so that she could give Ally's nipple a little suck.

"I'm going to cum," Ally said again, this time quiet enough for only Jess to hear.

She could feel it. She was just on the cusp. It was tight there. Ally threw her head back again, "AHH! I'm coming! Oh God Yes!"

Watching Ally cum while she held her in her arms pushed Jess over the edge.

She wasn't thinking about Josh's dick in her when her knee-shaking orgasm hit. She was thinking about Ally's beautiful face. About Ally's beautiful body. And even as she was cumming, it was Ally's titties that she was sucking on.

And then she felt Josh cum inside of her, and the pleasure of that overwhelming feeling reminded her why she was with Josh and not Ally, and why being with Ally was, and always would be, a childish pipe dream.

But this moment was nice. Josh pulled out, and Rick pulled out, and then Jess and Ally were left alone on the bed, kissing, cuddling, and being themselves.

Jess heard Josh say, "Rick, grab your clothes, I need to talk to you outside for a second."

Rick got off the bed, but he was hesitant.

"But, couldn't I stay and watch?"

"No. Get your clothes. Get outside. Let them have their moment," Josh commanded.

Jess heard Rick fumbling around for his clothes on the ground. "And don't fucking look at my girlfriend!" Josh added, and it made Jess crack a smile.

The tent flap opened, closed, and they were gone.

Jess and Ally lay naked in each other's arms, their hands all over each other, making out on the bed. Both were too afraid to say anything, scared to address the elephant in the room—How would this change their friendship?

Jess delicately moved from Ally's luscious lips to her soft, supple nipples, from her nipples, running her mouth down, all along her flat stomach, until Jess ran her hands underneath Ally's thighs, lifting and spreading her legs.

"Jess, wait. What are we doing?" Ally said softly.

Jess had hoped she wouldn't ask that question. Why did she have to ask that question?

"I owe you an orgasm from the other night. I promised."

Ally laughed her angelic laugh, "We came at the same time!"

"But it was that dork Rick that made you cum, not me."

"Jess, of course it was you. It was your kiss, your moans, and god, the way you play with my nipples!" Ally's eyes rolled to the back of her head. "I'm pretty sure Rick came inside me, like, right away. After that, he wasn't even hard."

Her words made Jess's heart flutter. But she didn't want this to end just yet. "Okay, so how about I show you what else I can do."

"Jess, that's not what I mean." Jess sat up. Ally crossed her legs. "I mean I don't know, we've been friends since, like, always. And I don't know what I'd do in a world where you weren't my best friend."

Jess laid back down on her stomach next to Ally, kicking her legs up behind her in the air lazily.

"Ally, I feel the same way. What are you afraid of?"

Ally picked her finger on the blanket they laid on absently. It took her a few seconds to answer.

"I don't know... I guess I just don't want to be some bimbo you and Josh hook up with and then kick to the curb."

Jess put her hand on top of Ally's, patting her picking at the blanket.

"Is that really what you're worried about? Ally, we would never. I would never."

And then it hit her. Josh and Jess had already talked about this, and she knew exactly where he stood. Now there was no turning back. This was the only way.

"Ally, there is something I need to tell you. And it's not going to be easy."

"Oh no!" she cried with genuine despair. "That's never good!"

Uh oh, Jess thought. *So far, this is not going well.*

"Please just listen," Jess begged, and she could see the tension in Ally's face. Jess felt the same way.

"Ally, I love you. I've always loved you. I've always known that but I've only recently realized it because... Well, I've always kind of had these fantasies about you."

"Always? Like. Always always?"

Jess nodded. "That's why this weekend has been so magical, and, well... They say the festival ends when the music ends, but, Ally... I really love you, and I never want this to end."

Saying all of that felt like it was a huge weight lifted from Jess's shoulders. Not only that but after she got everything out in the open.

Ally was beaming at her. Seeing her smiling face was bliss. "I've always had these fantasies of things I'd like to do with you. Things I'd like to do to you. Ever since we met. Some of it, God, I could never say! But those fantasies came to life this weekend and, well, it was better than I could have ever imagined."

Jess's face lit up. "I never knew, but I'm so glad you feel the same way!"

"What about Josh?" Ally asked in a sad voice.

"Actually, Josh and I talked about, well not all of it, but he really likes you too, and we're on the same page about this."

"About what?"

Jess hesitated. She had no use for hesitation now. There was no turning back now.

"Ally, Josh and I really want you to be a couple with us."

"A couple of three?"

Jess nodded. "A Thruple."

Ally giggled. "And how would we do that?"

"Well, it would be just like this weekend. Only exclusively the three of us. So, on second thought, it wouldn't be anything at all like this weekend."

Both women shared a laugh. Jess wasn't sure when it happened but she noticed that she had her fingers laced together with Ally's hand.

"Josh and I are already totally in love with you. But to answer your question, I don't know what it will be like. I've never done anything like this before. But the three of us can find out together."

Jess closed her eyes and listened to Ally's heartbeat, then added, "Please tell me you'll do it. It would break my heart if you didn't."

There was a pregnant pause in which the two women lay there naked next to each other, searching each other's eyes, searching for something, searching for a sign.

Finally, Ally said, "You know what? Rick is kind of a dork, isn't he? Of course I'll be a thruple with you and Josh!"

"You will? Oh, Ally, I love you so much right now!"

With that, Jess jumped on Ally and started smothering her with kisses. The two women fell laughing onto the pile of pillows on the bed.

Ally threw a pillow at Jess because she was tickling her, then Jess got a pillow to defend herself, and a few moments later both girls were hurling pillows back and forth across the tent. When at last all of the pillows had been tossed from the bed and lay on the floor, Jess tackled Ally, who screamed as she pounced.

Jess sat on top of her with her legs on either side of her stomach, giggling as she pinned down her arms above her head. Jess stole a quick kiss on the lips.

"So, what else do I do that turns you on?" Jess asked, emboldened by Ally's answer.

Ally blushed. "Well, there is this little spot on my neck where, when you kiss me there, I go crazy." Ally tilted her head to one side, exposing her neck.

Jess started testing out spots on her neck with kiss after kiss.

"I'm going to find it!" Jess proclaimed.

Kiss.

"Here?"

"No!" Ally laughed.

Kiss.

"Here?"

"Jess!"

Kiss.

"Here?"

"Stop it!"

Kiss.

"Here?"

"Ooh shit! Oh God yes!"

"Really? I'll have to remember that. So, what else?"

"There is this one thing that only you do with my nipples. When you, like, push down on them really hard with the tip of your tongue, then you suck on them at the same time, then you, like, tickle my titty with your tongue. I don't know how else to describe it."

"Oh... You mean... Like this?"

With her hand still pinning down Ally's hands, Jess scooted down so she could get her mouth around Ally's nipples. Then she did the exact thing that Ally just described.

"Ye-eh-ess," Ally gave a throaty moan as she arched her back and crossed her legs together. It really did drive her wild.

Jess did the other nipple. It had a similar effect on Ally. She arched her back and squirmed under Jess's touch. Jess did it three more times in a row on the same nipple.

"Ahh! Fuck! Jess! Oh," She was breathing hard.

"Did I ever tell you how much your moans fucking turn me on," Jess cooed.

"Jess..." she said in a throaty whisper, when Jess looked at her.

Ally was biting her lower lip, giving her a look Jess did not need her to explain what that look meant: Bedroom eyes.

"Yeah," Jess laid her body on Ally, letting her hands go so she could cup her face as she closed her eyes and started making out right where they left off, only with renewed passion.

They were a couple now, or at least part of one.

While they were making out, Ally kept squeezing and playing with Jess's boobs. Jess knew how much she loved her boobs. It was then that Jess pulled back from their romantic embrace. She had to know.

"Tell me one of your fantasies, Right now!"

Ally blushed, but did not dismiss the question, while she was considering her answer. Jess started planting sucking little kisses all over Ally's chest.

"A well, a lot of them involve you and me in a sixty-nine."

Jess sat up with a gasp. "Oh my God, mine too!"

"You're just saying that to make me feel better."

Jess moved about an inch in front of Ally's face and brushed a strand of hair out of her face. "Oh, no I'm fucking hot. You have no idea how long I've been waiting for this."

She kissed Ally's lips then started to turn herself around into a sixty-nine position, but Ally caught her arm.

"Wait. Jess, I really want to do this with you, but not like this. I want it to be... Romantic."

"What's not romantic about this?" Jess waved an arm around the tent. It looked like a tornado came through a third world country.

"For one, the fact that you still have your boyfriend's cum still inside your snatch!"

"Oh... I guess you're right. But he's your boyfriend now, too."

"Really?" Ally seemed surprised by this.

"Yeah. That's how this works. But, listen, Ally, I love you so much, so if you're not ready for that yet, that's fine."

Ally sat upon the bed. "Aw, Jess, that's so sweet of you to say that. I really love you, too." Ally reached for the oversized Electric Love Festival T-shirt she was wearing and threw it over her head. "Maybe this is why none of my relationships have ever worked. Maybe the person I'm really supposed to be with has been with me all these years."

She leaned over and gave her a little kiss on the lips.

"You're making me horny just looking at you. Put some clothes on!" Ally was looking for Jess's clothes on the ground. She paused when she saw the Pink Playboy Bunny outfit.

"That's it? I'm disappointed we're not going to have sex!"

"We will. I promise. I just want it to be special. Didn't anyone ever tell you not to give it away on the first date?"

"Ally, you ALWAYS give it up on the first date."

"Exactly. And it never worked. So I'm trying something different."

Josh walked in the tent wearing jeans and a T-shirt. "Sorry to interrupt. They're making us take the tent and stuff down. We've got to go."

Jess bounced off the air mattress and went into a pack where she dug out a wrinkly blouse and yoga pants. She immediately started dressing.

"Josh, do you remember that talk we had about becoming a thruple with Ally?" She asked while threading her feet into her yoga pants.

"Yeah, how could I forget?"

"Well, she's down with it, too. So, it's official now!"

Jess threw the halter top on with no bra. It barely covered her massive tits.

"Yeah, I figured it would turn out something like that," Josh said cooly.

"You did? How did you know that? We didn't even know it ourselves!"

"The way you two look at each other? Christ, you've been in love all weekend!" Josh chucked to himself.

"You're not even surprised?" Ally asked.

"Not one bit, and I want you to know, Ally, that I have every bit as much love for you as Jess does," Josh said.

"Doubt it!" Jess yelled as she put her shoes on.

"Thank you, Josh. That means a lot. I'm really happy I can be a part of your lives," Allison said with a smile.

"I am too," Josh smirked. "Now can we please take this shit down? We are like the only camp left anywhere at the festival."

Jess suddenly looked up, as if she just remembered something important, "what happened to Rick?"

"Oh, I told him that Ally was trying to baby trap him and he booked it," Josh answered.

By the time they got everything packed away and loaded in the Jeep, it was nearly dusk. As they pulled out of the dirt and grass parking lot, the fire afterthoughts said one last goodbye to the festival.

"Wow, we really were the last ones to leave," Jess observed as they pulled out of the now empty lot.

"Who would have thought that a bunch of drug-addled ravers were all pro-active early bird types," Josh joked.

"Certainly not his drug-addled raver," Jon added.

"I had so much fun you guys. Thanks for bringing me. We should all go again next year." Isabel was so excited she was practically bouncing up and down on her seat.

"I had a lot of fun, too," Josh said. He stuck his head all the way past the window. "Thank you, Electric Love Festival for all the wonderful experiences. We are grateful to you!"

In the back seat, Jess and Ally sat next to each other holding hands. "Thank you for the lifetime of memories I'll never forget, Electric Love," Jess yelled.

"Thank you for helping me bring me closer to the ones I love. Best festival ever," Ally cheered.

"Bringing us closer to the ones we love, isn't that what the festival experience is all about?" Josh beamed. The festival had ended well for him.

"No," Jon butted in. "Festivals are about Drugs, Sex, and Music. Not always in that order."

"Well, then I guess I'm grateful for Drugs, Sex, and Music, too then," Josh added.

"We all are," Jess said as she leaned into Ally and snuck in a little kiss.

Ally giggled, "We all are," she repeated.

Other Books by Allison Eden

A Very Polyamory Series

www.ingramcontent.com/pod-product-compliance
Lightning Source LLC
Chambersburg PA
CBHW011925050726
47591CB00009B/2341